STORM SURGE

Nadine Laman

Arizona USA

Storm Surge

25th Anniversary Edition.

Cover Design by Nadine Laman
Cover Photo Seal Beach, California, USA by Nadine Laman

ISBN 978-1-947646-18-6

Published by Cactus Rain Publishing, San Tan Valley, Arizona, USA
Published December 5, 2024
Originally Printed in the United States of America

~ Dedication ~

To Charley Lawrence Laman
and our sons,
Sean Russell James Laman,
Maitiu Ioseph Lawrence Laman,
Tomas Andrew Lambert Laman

~~~

To my mentors:
Dr. Lois Johnson, Ilene Shrimplin Wood,
Jeannine Garsee, Janice Laman Zitek,
Judith McKee, and Ellen Lyon.

~~~

In affectionate memory of:
Julia Marquis, Governor Joan Finney,
Jean M. Flynn, G. Irene Unruh,
Irene Watson, and Karen Stewart.

~~~

A humble "thank you" to
Gladys Knight and Rhonda Holman,
two women who inspired me
and touched my heart and soul.

~~~

To Ann Zimmerman
for permission to use her lyrics.

~~~

To those who have profoundly come into my life,
you know who you are.

~~~

Other books by Nadine Laman

Kathryn's Beach
High Tide
The Trilogy

STORM SURGE

You are the person
you are
when you think no one is watching.

~ CHAPTER 1 ~

Anonymity

"How was your trip?" Karen asks of my month-long vacation, as she looks over the back of the sofa into the kitchen where the most wonderful smell of brewing coffee permeates the air.

"Great! Austria was great!" I turn to watch the final drip of coffee land into the pot.

"And Mr. Goldstein?" She inquires about my old friend, now living in Austria.

"Mr. Goldstein is absolutely wonderful!" I inhale the rich coffee-scented steam rising from the cups as I fill them. "He is—"

"Katey! Listen to this!" Karen interrupts.

Karen points the remote toward the television—rapidly increasing the volume.

Karen is the calmest "calm-under-fire" person I know. The sound of danger in her voice sets off alarms in me. My pulse races in response.

Bringing our coffee to the sofa, I hand Karen her cup and stand, inquisitively watching the screen for what piqued her attention. The image immediately catches my eye. My cup halts midway to my lips. My attention is glued to the special news report:

> ...just minutes ago at a scheduled press conference, Alistair McKenzie announced his retirement and that his granddaughter, Kathryn McKenzie, will assume control and management of his empire beginning immediately...

> No, we don't know anything about her. There wasn't a bio on her in the media packet...

The reporter's voice trails off in the distance of my mind while I study the old man leaving the press conference in the wheelchair. The camera perfectly captures my grandfather's compelling nature. He is in control and he knows it.

The reporters don't push, shove, or shout questions at him. No one dares show disrespect to the wealthiest man in California

—nor, tempt the scope of his anger. Even the cub reporters seem to know, if they are reckless, he will have them for lunch with a glance. It is no secret he is ruthless—and that is exactly how he wants it.

The station returns to the news studio where the anchorwoman reads a litany of the McKenzie holdings while each company logo appears on the inset in the corner of the screen. The list is impressive.

I had no idea the McKenzie family, my family, controlled so many companies.

My gaze remains fixed to the TV as I move to the edge of the sofa to join Karen. Still in a daze, I lean forward to set down my cup, nearly missing the coffee table.

Karen intervenes, guiding my hand to avoid the impending mishap.

"Beginning immediately?" I gasp, then breathe out the words stuck in my throat, releasing the others lodged behind them. "Life as I know it just ceased to exist." The whispering echo of my words haunt me with their truth.

Fiddling with the heart-shaped locket around my neck I seek strength from the people in the photos inside it. But my dead parents cannot rescue me from Alistair Winston McKenzie.

I feel the weight of great wealth laid upon my shoulders. Tears well in my eyes in response to what Grandfather has done to me. He should have been grooming me for this. The way he did this, my God, that was so cruel to announce it publicly before telling me.

Not once in the past four years has he hinted at his intentions to involve me in the family empire. I was perfectly happy thinking I had been disinherited by default, since he disinherited his son, my father, for marrying a Catholic.

The ringing phone jolts me back to the present. Pushing my hand against the sofa cushions, I fumble to get up.

Karen puts her hand on mine and applies slight pressure. "Don't answer that."

Her instincts are correct about the phone. The answering machine picks up the call, allowing us to listen while a reporter leaves a message requesting an interview with "Miss McKenzie."

I sigh in frustration. "I need to get an unlisted number first thing tomorrow."

The truth is, I don't want the spotlight. The thought of it makes me feel ill. I resent the intrusion into the privacy of my life. His world was never a world I wanted.

Karen moves to the answering machine that has suddenly been transformed from "secretary" to "shield" against the advancing army of reporters. She presses the record button and lowers her face toward the machine:

"Miss McKenzie is not accepting appointments for interviews at this time. A statement will be released at a later date. Thank you."

When Karen finishes recording, she smiles smugly and pushes the reset button. She takes the coffee cup from my hand before my lips can take a first sip of the steaming, life-sustaining liquid.

"What?" I hear her dump the coffee down the sink and set both cups in it.

"Get your purse and jacket. We're getting out of here." Karen proceeds to go through the apartment shutting off lights.

I grab my purse and Dodgers jacket. Karen takes the keys from my trembling hand and locks the dead bolt after us.

She keeps looking toward the street as we hurry down the stairs. We start for my car, but see a van from a local TV station rush into the driveway and stop abruptly in the fire lane of the parking lot.

Karen changes direction away from my car, pushing me around the corner of the building, toward the courtyard.

"This way. I parked on the side street."

We walk, slightly hurried, through the dimly lit courtyard toward the side entrance and her waiting car.

"Where are we going?"

"You're staying with me."

"But I need my car for work," I mumble in protest, looking back over my shoulder in the direction we had come.

My cell phone rings, startling me. My adrenalin spikes as I dig through my purse, fumbling to silence it before it calls attention to us.

We hear the thundering footsteps of someone running up the stairs. "Here it is! Over here," the voice shouts as pounding begins on a door: my door? We increase our stride and rush to the exterior of the complex.

When we reach the sidewalk, we slow to a hurried walk to be less obvious. Just as we are nearing Karen's car, someone hollers, "Do you know which apartment is Kathryn McKenzie's?"

"I don't live here, just visiting." Karen is deceptively truthful.

I keep my head down to avoid the streetlight, trying to act as composed as Karen. My heart is hammering in my chest. I feel dizzy from the adrenalin rush and steady myself against the car as I reach for the door handle and slide inside.

Karen clicks the door lock while shutting the door and sliding behind the steering wheel—all in one smooth move. I sink low in the seat, still trying to fasten my seat belt, as the car begins to move. A nervous laugh slips out as I continue to fidget with the seat belt latch. Karen is occupied with getting out of the parking space since the cars ahead and behind parked close, making it nearly impossible for her to maneuver away from the curb.

Another news van rushes past us and turns into the apartment complex across the street from mine. We giggle at the van driving intently—in the wrong direction. Misguided, but determined, they are driven to scoop their competitors for the first photos and interview with Miss McKenzie. If they only knew how close they were.

Around the corner, Karen slows to view the activity in front of my apartment. Two more news trucks have arrived. People are tramping the landscape with cavalier disregard for the other tenants and the property. Men carrying cameras, following reporters with trailing microphone cables, hurry to get the first words with the new "matriarch of money."

This whole thing is silly. I understand why Grandfather keeps them reined in. He masterfully manipulates them. Good for him.

But not so good for me. With the power of a few words, Grandfather turned our relaxing evening into chaos, and my life is permanently altered. It's his style to do this from time to time. He enjoys the attention he gets by keeping the media stirred up, to appear in the headlines with precise timing to accommodate his business agenda. What was it this time, a hostile takeover, a buyout? What?

Karen drives past the freeway entrance ramp. Instead, she pulls into a fast food drive-through and orders two coffees. When the drinks are in hand, she says, "To your new life, Kathryn McKenzie!"

Ordinarily, I might have laughed. Tonight is far from ordinary. She's right, it is a new life: full of protocol and spin doctors. I rise to the occasion and graciously accept the gesture. "And to old and dear friends."

Karen stays on the surface streets rather than the freeway. I need every extra minute the longer route affords. A new life has been set in motion for me—there will be no going back. I can no longer keep secret who I am. Whether I want it or not, my face will be as well known as his. The marker dye has been cast into the ocean. But the Coast Guard can't rescue me.

"He could have warned me. I need clothes for work tomorrow." I plead disconnected thoughts.

"Are you planning to work tomorrow?"

"Well—" I realize how ridiculous I sound. "I should at least go in and give notice, don't you think? It's the right thing to do. Isn't it?" I'm struggling to hold on to my life before every bit of it slips away.

"I should say goodbye to everyone at St. Mark's—and Shasta. I must talk to Shasta!"

Shasta may be in the fifth grade, but she is as definite about how life works as when she was a first grader. She still greets me at the door every morning, though now not so much, to make sure I am coming back, as it is our routine.

My mind is racing with memories. I long to get lost in them, to pretend the present doesn't exist, certainly not this present.

~~~

Karen is on point with the current situation.

"You can wear my robe while I wash what you have on."

"Mother Elizabeth doesn't allow jeans."

"I think she will make an exception this time."

Of course, Karen should understand her sister-turned-Franciscan-nun better than me.
~~~

My mind circles in amazed disbelief. Grandfather gave no indication of his plans, even as recently as last month when I visited him before my trip to Austria.

I was perfectly happy with things the way they are between us. Besides, I have my own money. I have worked for years, saved, and invested, except for the five years I lived in Nebraska and worked in a bar. I live within my means and have managed my money wisely. Even in Nebraska, my expenses were much less than my income. Plus, there is the trust my parents set up for me. Granted, none of this is like Grandfather's money, but certainly ample for me.

I don't want the McKenzie money, not one penny. I didn't expect anything from him, nothing monetary anyway. All I wanted was to get to know him. I know too well, there are no guarantees of the time we have to be together. His age and wheelchair remind me that we have lost too much time already.

"How could Grandfather do this to me?"

Ignoring my tone, Karen speaks to the issue, "Who else is he going to leave in charge?"

"In charge?"

"He isn't a young man—" Karen's voice trails off, then returns echoing my own thoughts, "You know your McKenzie cousins."

The recognition of the truth spoken aloud washes over me. Hurt enters my voice.

"Oh God! Is that why he found me? Was that the only reason that he wanted to connect with his long-lost granddaughter?"

When he arranged for us to meet, I thought he wanted to atone for the way he treated my parents, or maybe to make up for lost time with me, his first grandchild. Now, it seems it was all a business tactic, nothing personal. He wasn't looking for his lost granddaughter, only for a successor, his heir apparent. Hurt doesn't begin to describe my feelings. I feel used. Because he's family, it feels even worse. It's all that I can do not to scream or maybe simply cry, grieving the loss of my life.

The city lights blur past as Karen makes her way to her home in the foothills. I'm unable to take advantage of this last opportunity to be a commoner. Lights and confused thoughts, that's all there is; I have lost everything I had an hour ago.

Storm Surge

It's a relief to arrive at Karen's house, secure from the media. My mind is unfocused for a sustained conversation. We talk intermittently and drink coffee while my clothes launder. She was right about not waiting to pack a few things, even though it is inconvenient now. The media would have caught us if we had delayed even a moment longer.

She gives me a new toothbrush and toothpaste from the stockpile she keeps for when her daughters visit. Not having my own things only accents what has transpired this evening.

There is so much to think about. No doubt Grandfather expects me to move into Pacific Estate. I already spend a weekend a month at the mansion. But that isn't the same as being there full-time.

I certainly had not intended to "take on" my cousins who live with Grandfather. As a matter of fact, I have been careful not to play up the preferential treatment he gives me, or even acknowledge its existence.

Maybe it's because, out of the four grandchildren, I look the most like our grandmother. As a matter of fact, I look almost identical to the portrait of her hanging in the mansion's library.

I suppose it will be easier to learn the business if I lived with Grandfather for a few months. I hope this isn't his way to make me another possession, like my three cousins. I'd better keep a place of my own, so that he understands staying with him is temporary. Having my own apartment might be complicated, but it's worth having somewhere I can get away from the money-madness and go to the beach.

My thoughts are interrupted when Karen returns from the laundry room.

"Who called you?"

"What?"

"When we were leaving your apartment, didn't your cell phone ring?"

"I don't know. I shut it off so it wouldn't give us away."

She pauses, waiting for me to get the hint. When I don't seem to understand, she says, "Why don't you see who called?"

"Oh! Right. You don't think it was a reporter, do you?" I ask, half afraid to turn the phone on again. It is a relief to see the call is from my cousin Nick. I play back the message and roll my eyes, then grin at Karen. I play it again, this time with the speaker turned on.

"Katey, it's Nick. How 'bout a loan, Moneybags?"
Followed by a devilish laugh. "No really, I'm just checking
on you. If you need me, call. Love ya, Cuz."

"He's my cousin."

"Yes, I got that. Go ahead, call him back. I'll make sure your room is ready."

"Thanks. I'm fine. Really, I'm fine." I smile to make my point. We both know I'm not fine. I'm nowhere near fine.

It's good Karen was visiting when the announcement came on the TV. Imagine what would have happened if I hadn't known about it and reporters started banging on my door.

My cell phone rings. This time it is my cousin Ilene.

"Kate, I saw the news. Are you okay?"

"Yes, I'm at Karen's house for the night."

"You're welcome to stay with me, if you want."

"Thanks, I'm fine. Really," I lie.

"Did you know he was going to do that?"

"No, it was totally unexpected."

"Are you going to do it?"

"Do it?"

"You don't have to do what he says, you know."

"I haven't really had time to think about it yet."

Her point made, she changes the subject. "Aunt Grace is here. She says to make sure you are okay. She's heading home now, unless you want her to stop by tonight."

"No, I'm fine. Give her a hug for me. I'll call you in a few days —when I come up for air."

"I love you, Cuz. You know that."

"Yeah, I know. I love you too, Ilene."

My mother's family has gone into their rally-the-troops mode. God love them. I do need them. I can't think clearly. Never in my wildest dreams did I expect this from Grandfather McKenzie. I still can't believe it. This has to be a bad dream and I'll wake up any minute now.

I'm trying to be a good guest, but I'm squirrelly-restless.

Storm Surge

Karen seems to understand this is not the time to push me. She foregoes wearing her therapist's hat and gives me a break.

I go to bed. Just before I turn out the light, I think of my diary. The missing diary is just one more reminder of my abrupt, forced exile. Damn him.

Emotions and thoughts are bursting for expression, but I don't have the energy to speak them. My heart aches. I lie in the darkness thinking what I would write, if I had my diary.

I can only hope that life progresses at a sane pace, so that I can handle this gracefully.

~~~
~~~

~ CHAPTER 2 ~

The Morning After

Sleep is restless. I finally settle into REM sleep when Karen wakes me. She has breakfast ready, but I'm interested in the coffee she hands me.

"Good morning," I lie. I pretend to be a morning person because it fits into society's expectations better than being a night owl.

"Good morning, Kathryn. How are you?" She sounds honestly concerned.

"Better. I am better today," I lie some more. I will have to go to confession if I keep this up.

"What's the plan for today?" Karen asks, as she leans against the kitchen counter, sipping her coffee, watching me search for words.

Quickly, I collect the random thoughts I tossed and turned with during the night.

"I could," I take a careful sip of coffee to buy me another minute, "go to work. I need to tell Mother Elizabeth I'm resigning. And the clients, I want to tell them goodbye before I leave."

Karen nods affirmatively, but not necessarily inferring agreement.

"Have you called your grandfather?"

"No, I'm not at all happy with him at the moment. It's best I don't phone him. He hasn't called me either. He may think I'm still in Austria, for all I know."

We haven't watched the television again. Who knows what the reporters said when they found no one home last night.

"I need to arrange to move to the Estate. There's the press release," I continue, as my thoughts begin to find some semblance of order.

"Eventually, you're going to need to plan beyond the next few days, but you'll know the answers when you need them. This is a lot right now. Give yourself time. Be patient. You can do this, I know you can." Karen uses her seldom-used motherly tone.

"I hope you're right," I whisper, assuming she means this new duty, and manage to fake a reassuring smile.

We look at each other. It's awkward. Her eyes don't reveal her thoughts. I can only hope my eyes do likewise.

Karen picks up where I left off with the more immediate needs. "I'll drop you at work on my way to the office. Check the girls' bathroom for makeup, maybe there is something there you can use."

I check the bathroom and find a supply of unopened cosmetics. I settle for mascara and lip gloss. That should do.

~~~

The morning traffic is light. We find a media-swarm in a tight knot outside the front of St. Mark's convent when we arrive. Karen calls Mother Elizabeth.

"Okay, that works."

She drives past the mob and turns the corner. I think she is leaving until she drives through the alley. The garage door opens, and Karen pulls in next to one of the convent vans.

Mother Elizabeth is waiting with her hand poised at the door button on the wall. She doesn't speak. She simply puts the door down once we are parked. We follow her directly into the back door of her office.

Mother Elizabeth sits behind her desk, we sit in front of it. I'm waiting for her to say something, anything. I'm waiting for her to say I betrayed her by not telling her I was *that* McKenzie. I'm waiting for her to tell me that I could have trusted her with my real identity.

Alistair McKenzie is my grandfather, nothing more. The fact that he lives in a mansion overlooking the Pacific Ocean is no more out of the ordinary than people who live in convents and wear traditional habits.

It's a long silence. Sister Theresa brings a tray of cups and a pot of coffee. She sets down the tray, and grins a Cheshire cat grin at me when she hands me a cup. My love of coffee is world famous. Sister Theresa gives Karen a cup, but Mother Elizabeth waves off one for herself. Sister Theresa leaves the tray on Mother Elizabeth's desk and backs out of the office in the strangest fashion, even for her.
~~~

Mother Elizabeth's eyes are dancing, yet she's still not smiling. After all of this time, I should be able to read her, but the only thing I really know is that the nuns have heard the news that I am related to Alistair McKenzie.

Little Shasta appears at the door and invites herself into Mother's office. She announces my obvious indiscretions with her fists firmly on her waist.

"You came in the wrong door—AND, you didn't sign in!"

When she comes near, I push a curly wisp of blonde hair out of her eyes and ask, "Would you like to sign in for me?"

She still has her hands on her waist, sizing me up in a way that only an eleven-year-old can. To her, I am still plain old Kathryn. There seems to be no excuse for failing to follow the sign-in rule. It reassures me that being a McKenzie doesn't make any difference to her.

"Okay, this time."

"Thank you. Then, off to school. Sister will be looking for you."

Since she lived at Spirit of Hope for nearly two years, Shasta thinks she owns the place. She is the only non-resident student who freely comes and goes between the school and convent—as if anyone could stop her.

"Well, Kathryn?" Mother begins after Shasta leaves.

I wait for her to finish her sentence, but apparently she intends it as a prompt for me to begin. Begin what?

"Mother," I take a deep breath. This is awkward. "I don't know where to begin."

Karen comes to my rescue, intervening with her Sister-sister.

"Elizabeth, Kathryn feels she must resign her position. After the announcement last night, nothing is the same."

Nothing is the same, I repeat her words in my mind.

"I see."

Everything is in turmoil; perhaps Mother Elizabeth has decided it isn't worth discussing, since things will change from minute-to-minute until it reaches its equilibrium. Without a doubt, she is not silent because she doesn't have an opinion.

I clear my throat. "Thank you, Mother, for everything. Being here has been absolutely wonderful."

Words are inadequate to convey my appreciation that she hired me for this marvelous job. I'm willing to be totally exposed in the expression of my feeling of fondness for the experience, if I can find the right words.

How does one sum up the experiences of Monica, Race, Shasta, the nuns, driving lessons, Paul's taunting me from the pitcher's mound, secret passages, and seem-to-be miracles on St. Francis' feast?

"You're welcome, Kathryn. We have enjoyed having you," Mother answers with the standard remark, then corrects, "I have enjoyed having you with us." Her admission would have been awkward under normal circumstances, considering she is Mother Superior and all. But nothing is normal now.

My emotions are jumping around like the balls inside a bingo spinner.

"I, I should make the rounds and tell everyone 'goodbye'—not that leaving will be easy."

"Yes." Mother Elizabeth finally smiles.

She pours a cup of coffee. "I suppose we could disguise you two as Franciscans and send Sister Theresa out as a decoy."

A slow grin comes over both Karen and Mother Elizabeth when their eyes meet.

I feel on the outside of an inside joke between them. Her remark about a decoy nun surprises me. I've never heard her joke about anything religious. I meant it would be emotionally difficult to leave. Surely she knew what I meant. Perhaps it was too awkward, thus the joke.

"Let's have a going-away party for you. We'll invite all the past clients, too. Make an evening of it." She makes a note and circles it.

I don't mention it, but immediately think about how she can't invite Monica. Despite all the miracles that happen here, saving Monica was not one to be had.

I would rather tell everyone goodbye individually, but telling them as a group may have to suffice. I hear myself agreeing with Mother Elizabeth's suggestion. Thank God that she didn't call it a retirement party, that would have been too final, even if it is probably the truth.

"I'll have Sister Theresa set the date with you. For now, we should get you out of here—if we can."

Whether or not the reporters know what I look like, they know where I work. I don't know how they know. Maybe someone should tell them I don't work here, now that it's true. I don't like being held captive by their presence. Strangely, Mother Elizabeth's idea of a Franciscan disguise is revisited and begins to make sense.

"Come with me and we'll disguise both of you."

Oh lord! I wasn't sure her offer of disguise was serious, but I guess it is. Maybe she knows best. Surely, this isn't another of those glimpses of convent life meant as a recruitment tactic. Can I make all of this go away if I join the convent? If only things were that simple.

We follow Mother Elizabeth farther into the interior of the living quarters of the convent than I have been before. There is a distinct rustic feel to this area of the building. The doorways are smaller than the semi-public portion of the convent or the modern mid-century schools between the convent and parish church. The original building can't possibly meet code. Parts of it must be from the Franciscan padres who came with the conquistadores.

The hallway is narrower and darker. There is a communal dining room, a parlor for family visits, and another hall of tiny rooms each with a bed, chair, and desk. Mother Elizabeth calls the bedrooms "cells." Hers looks no different than the others, with the exception of a phone on her desk. This one room has been her home for thirty-five years, except her time as a novice. That concept seems inexplicably odd.

At the end of the hall is a dormitory with a few beds lined perpendicular to the wall. There are forty or so beds missing, probably commissioned to furnish Spirit of Hope's former homeless families.

I won't call it a homeless shelter because it is so much more than a homeless shelter. It is a home. It is what each of us should do to ease the pain of our fellow man.

Mother Elizabeth opens a built-in cabinet with habits hanging in the left portion. The right side has shelves with drawers. There are neatly folded veils and other habit parts on the shelves. Mother opens a drawer with Rosaries, Profession Crosses, and a smaller box with a half dozen gold wedding bands. None of them look new.

Mother Elizabeth and Karen select pieces of the habit, periodically holding them up to me for sizing. In a bit of a daze, I stand there and let them proceed.

It is interesting to see how the habit works. I hadn't really thought about it, but I notice they are each handsewn. The headpiece is a little odd. Maybe, my hair is too long to fit under it correctly.

It's fun to try to pull off an escape from the reporters. I think we should drive past the building in our costumes just to have one more look at them. I'd like to honk the horn, but that would be over the top, wouldn't it?

Mother Elizabeth turns to Karen for her turn to don a habit, but Karen waves her off.

"No thanks, Elizabeth. I am not the nun-type. I'll be fine as myself." She smiles, set in her decision.

No fair. "I'm not the 'nun-type' either." I'm only doing what Mother said to do. They don't listen that I'm not the nun-type.

Just as Karen clips a rosary to my belt, Sister Bridget comes in and interrupts in an un-nun-like panic.

"Mother, Sister Theresa needs help at the front door!"

I've never seen her like this. She didn't even acknowledge my costume, and there is nothing normal about me in a habit.

Mother Elizabeth turns for the door. Karen is at her heels. I hurry after them. I feel terrible about what Grandfather set in motion.

Change of plans. "I'll go talk with them," I interrupt, knowing full well this is my responsibility, whether I like it or not.

The fun of the idea of sneaking out the back door is gone. This isn't a childish game. We walk past the statues of saints in the alcoves with their hand-painted angelic faces, past the chapel where Mother Elizabeth and Sister genuflect on the run, while Karen and I only make a Sign of the Cross, and pass the reception area.

Mother Elizabeth is first to reach the door.

A wave of profound sadness rushes over me as I realize my time at St. Mark's is coming full circle from the first day when I walked through this door. I pull myself together mentally, not sure if it's the calm faces of the statutes, wearing the habit, or that I find the strength within me to go through that door and face the media. Maybe it is because Karen, Mother Elizabeth, and Sister Bridget are with me, like brown-robed reinforcements of Marines. I pause to straighten my veil and follow them outside.

The reporters become animated when the four of us arrive to join Sister Theresa. Several cameras flash in our faces. They don't know who we are, but they're afraid they might miss a photo op if they don't shoot us. They might think Karen is me since she's the one in civilian clothes. Microphones move back and forth in front of us like a snake's head zeroing in on a target.

I step one step forward of my friends. We stand silently, while the reporters shout questions with micro-tape recorders, cell phones, and real microphones thrust at us.

We wait silently for the reporters to settle down. One man, seemingly unaware of the protocol, pushes forward through the group and to the side to get closer to us. He's standing in the flower bed near the steps.

I look him straight in the eyes, then at his feet, then back to his eyes again.

He gets the message and steps back to the sidewalk.

Is this power because I am dressed as a nun, or is it because he thinks I am "Miss McKenzie," a female offshoot of the old man who keeps strict order at his press conferences?

"Ladies and gentlemen," I begin, "this place is people's home." There is an awkward look on their collective faces as they shuffle to attention. It is so quiet, one could hear a pin drop.

"I am Kathryn McKenzie. I will announce a press conference in a more appropriate location. Your press desks will be notified of the details."

Cameras flash. The microphones have moved slightly closer— almost in unison. Enjoying the power I hold over them, I add, "You have behaved badly today. There will be no more of this. My friends are off-limits. I expect each of you will apologize to Mother Elizabeth in writing." I gesture toward Mother.

I look intensely at each of them. They are wide-eyed silent.
"Is that clear?" I expect only one answer.

They nod understanding combined with murmured, "Yes. Yes, ma'am," and one, "Yes, Sister." Then, several others thinking that they should have said, "Yes, Sister," change their reply. It's all corny, but I might as well lay down the ground rules from the start. After all, I am Grandfather's heir.

For added flair, I raise my right hand, make the Sign of the Cross over the group, and dismiss them. Let them wonder whether I am a nun or not. Serves them right. A couple of them hasten to make the Sign of the Cross, just in case they should.

Won't that give Grandfather a jolt to see the newspapers' photos of me in a habit? It doesn't top what he did to me, but considering his feelings about Catholics, it is probably the wildest thing I can do.

Once we're inside the convent door, we burst into laughter.

"Katey, you are awful!" Sister Theresa reports.

"I know!" I say proudly, then laugh.

"You enjoyed that too much!" Karen says.

I continue laughing until I realize what I have done, and look cautiously at Mother Elizabeth to see if I am going directly to hell for mocking Religious Life. It wasn't my intention to be disrespectful. I was caught up in the moment. Maybe the blessing at the end was over the top, but I don't think the Pope is the only one allowed to do the Sign of the Cross over a group, is he?

Mother doesn't appear disturbed with the incident, nor is she overly amused. As I remember, she started this charade, then it took on a life of its own.

"You know, you have to become a nun after that, don't you?" Mother pauses, then loses her poker face and laughs.

With the reporters gone, I change back to civilian clothes. With the full veil on, they probably didn't get a good photo of my face. At the very least, I am a free person until they get the photos publicized.

"This is great fun, but I have to get to work." Karen brings us back to reality. She looks at Mother Elizabeth. "Call me if you need to, I should be in the office all day."

"Yes, me too." Mother Elizabeth smiles and departs.

~~~

Karen leaves her car keys with me. "Go, buy some clothes and whatever else you need. I'll call if I'll be later than 4:00. Call my cell phone if you need anything, that way you won't have to go through the switchboard."

I'm grateful that Karen is thinking of the details. God knows I can't focus right now.

Sister Theresa, obviously eager for a reason to drive, offers Karen a ride to work, which leaves me a few more minutes at St. Mark's.

Now that the commotion is over and Karen leaves, I turn and walk down the hallway to Mother Elizabeth's office for the last time, ever. I hope desperately that she is available. There are so many things I want to say to her, and this is my last chance to say them. I can't believe I will never practice social work again—especially, not at Spirit of Hope.

I knock gently on the open door. I feel as sad as when Maggie died. Maybe it's because my life is dying.

"Mother Elizabeth, may I come in?"

"Yes, Kathryn. Shut the door," she says, looking up from her work. Mother Elizabeth removes her half-glasses and squints a bit to adjust the focus of her eyes. It is an awkward silence. Even she seems to feel it and quickly offers me another cup of coffee.

Gratefully, I accept the warm cup into my hands. This is reminiscent of coffee with Maggie the day I returned from Nebraska after being "absent without leave" on a five-year, self-imposed exile.

Now, Mother Elizabeth and I are quietly having a cup of coffee before I go away again. Easily, I could cry without prompting. I suppose the only reason I don't cry is that I am numbed by the deep hurt of what Grandfather has done to my life—to me.

"Mother Elizabeth, I can't begin to tell you what Spirit of Hope has meant to me." I look into her beautiful, serene face as I speak, and feel the warmth of her spirit. "More than you know, you saved me by giving me this job. I have learned so much here. I have learned so much from you."
~~~

I stop speaking. The words are recalling moments of the past: Shasta and her secret passage; Monica preparing for her interview—wearing my scarf; playing baseball with the kids; Race's pronouncement of loyalty—unwavering loyalty—to Mother Elizabeth. I close my eyes and turn away, until she begins to speak.

"Kathryn, we needed you. You had the qualifications and the spirit I was looking for when I hired you. If you have ever thought that Karen pulled strings to get you hired, you were mistaken. We needed you and your social work skills, even more than I realized." Her voice gives way to a whisper.

Mother Elizabeth sips her coffee, then clears her throat. "Each person is a unique, irreplaceable representation of our Creator. We're each one ray of sunshine, one drop of rain, one song on the wind. All of us come together to make a symphony that brings joy to our Father."

She clasps her hands together on her desk, interlocking her fingers lightly, and leans forward ever so slightly. "Kathryn, you have been a gift, a gift sent by God. And now, He is sending you somewhere else."

She reaches for my hand curled around my coffee cup. I let go of the cup and respond to her reach. It is a little sad that we have never connected in this way before. I close my eyes to memorize this moment, knowing it will never come again. Tears well in my eyes.

Her hand is soft, yet strong. Holding hands lasts long enough that it might have been uncomfortable under any other circumstance. It wasn't an employer–employee exchange, it was a person-to-person moment. Maybe she is praying a blessing of some sort, but those are usually said aloud. At best, I can't describe this moment. It's awkward, but not.

~~~

After leaving Spirit of Hope, I head home to get my things. I know it is insane to go home, but it makes no sense to buy things I already have.

The sun flashes off something in a car parked directly across the street from my apartment complex. There is no traffic this time of day, so while stopped at the intersection, I watch the car
~~~

a moment. It looks like a person with binoculars trained at my front door and window.

It was naive to think I could slip in and out of my place without someone noticing. This new status is a bigger deal than I thought. After I drive past, I look back at him in the rearview mirror. It doesn't seem there was any sign of recognition; he is still watching my apartment, not for me to drive by him.

It is too bad they found my address, probably from the phone book. Or did Grandfather give it out for dramatic effect? No, it had to be the phone book. Right? Grandfather wouldn't test my stamina under fire like this, would he? Maybe someone on his staff sold the information. No, then everyone wouldn't have it, only the buyer. Nah. That wouldn't make sense. But how did they know about St. Mark's?

I don't know the answers.

Slowly getting wiser, I stop at an ATM to get cash. I am not going shopping with a credit card with my name on it. Without my photo published yet, I should be able to go shopping, as long as it isn't my usual stores where they know my name and might put two and two together.

The first purchase is a pair of sunglasses. Karen will need hers for driving. Mine are in my car. I understand why people hate the paparazzi and wear sunglasses, at least as a symbolic shield from the intrusions.

After the incident at St. Mark's, I am gun-shy and stay put at Karen's house for the next two days. It is relaxing to lounge beside the pool and read, or nap. My concentration is sporadic, but it isn't like I am studying for an exam. I don't have to be sharp. Tuesday I slept quite a bit. Today is better, just a few cat naps. I still haven't checked in with Grandfather. He hasn't called me either.

An early dinner is on the stove. Karen announces Sister Theresa has scheduled the party for this evening. Despite my best effort to be upbeat, I pick at my food listlessly. I had hoped for more time to prepare mentally and emotionally to say goodbye. I'd hoped to be more ready— to mysteriously rise to the McKenzie duty.

Karen keeps the dinner conversation simple.

I try to stay focused, but I stare across the table with little to say. Karen has kind eyes. That is all I can think of right now. I can't stay engaged in a conversation, but I look at her as if I am listening intently. I wouldn't have eaten at all, if I hadn't started feeling jittery from the coffee about midafternoon.

We store the leftovers and clear the dishes from the table. Karen leaves the television and radio off. It is a comfortable quiet, a soft quiet.

Our eyes meet briefly as we exchange food containers destined for the refrigerator.

"Well, we should get going," Karen says.

"Okay."

~~~

"Katey," she begins, as she moves her car into the traffic. "Let's talk while we can."

"All right."

"How are you doing with all of this?"

"I am still a little shaken, unsure of my instincts. All of this mania is leaving me unable to anticipate what will happen next."

"You don't have to concede to his announcement. He certainly didn't handle it well."

"I know, but if I don't do it now, it will be even more complicated later when he dies. I'll do it for my father."

"I think your grandfather sees in you the potential that the rest of us have seen all along. I know there have been hard times in the past, but you always rose to the occasion—and you will this time too."

I listen intently to every word. Karen doesn't seem to expect a response and I don't really know what to say. We both know I have to do this, at least for a while.

"I don't believe for one minute that he located you strictly for business purposes. I think he was reaching out to you because he knew his life wasn't complete without you in it. Finding you is as close as a man like Alistair McKenzie can come to admitting he was wrong about what he did to your parents. That admission, such as it is, doesn't come easy for him."

Karen is interrupted by the ringing of my cell phone. She nods for me to answer it.
~~~

"Kate, are you all right?" asks my aunt's gentle voice.

"Yes, Aunt Grace, I am fine."

"When you didn't answer your phone at home, I had to get your cell phone number from Ilene." She stops to take a breath. "Honey, I heard the news Sunday night. Is there anything I can do? Anything you need?" Her voice is maternal, as usual.

Aunt Grace is one of many of Mother's sisters who came to my aid when Mother became sick and later died from breast cancer. She was always my favorite aunt, and she lived up to every reason for that to be true.

"I'm sorry I didn't call. I left my apartment suddenly and just haven't caught my breath. I am staying with a friend. I'm okay."

"Does your friend work tomorrow? I don't want you spending the day alone. Spend it with me." She mothers me more than requests my presence.

"Yes, she does work. I'd like spending the day with you." We conclude with making plans for her to pick me up at Karen's house in the morning.

Karen resumes our conversation without missing a beat. "Katey, I think your grandfather sees what a capable woman you are, just like you saw the possibilities in Dana."

"Dana is a talented fashion designer. I had nothing to do with her success. Besides, it didn't hurt for Linda and Angela Whitmore to have her design their gowns. Once Angela wore one of Dana's gowns to the Academy Awards, everyone in Hollywood wanted her to design their gowns."

"True, but you did more than that. You helped her get off the street before you knew she was a fashion designer. You are the one who sent your friends to her for gowns. I think your grandfather can tell that you have the insight and intuition to make good business decisions for his companies."

There is nothing more to say. I appreciate the vote of confidence.

~~~
~~~

~ **CHAPTER 3** ~

Farewell

Sister Theresa orchestrated a nice party, especially on such short notice. I'm reflective. I memorize everyone's face and the feel of this place. I loved watching the disbelief in the eyes of the people as they came through the door the first time, then realize they are safe, warm, and fed. There is an honesty about them. I love them. And I love these nuns for opening their home to the homeless.

The farewell greetings are warm and heartfelt. Most hug me, even Race is tender as he bends down to my level and gently wraps his big arms around my shoulders. The clients give me a rosary as a going-away gift. Some of the children have drawn pictures for me. Sister Theresa pulls me aside and quietly gives me a key chain with Saint Christopher on it. I smile, thinking the Saint Christopher is a little late now that she has learned to drive. Her monthly stipend is ten dollars spending money, and it is touching she spent her money on me.

"Sister Theresa, it's perfect. Thank you." I hug her.

She responds with a tight embrace. Nearly too tight.

After the party, Karen and I help set the place right. Any excuse to stay longer is a good excuse. Finally, it's time to tell the nuns goodbye, one by one. It is even harder to do than I expected.

Mother Elizabeth's eyes water. She hands me a gift—a small statue of Saint Francis, complete with a gray seagull and tiny dried flower, which she attached to represent our time together in her garden. It is easy to see thought and time went into the gift.

"It's lovely, thank you. Thank you so much," I say as the tips of my fingers appreciate the coolness of the statue. My eyes burn. Dare I look up from the statue that is blurred by my tears?

"You're welcome, I just thought—" Her voice catches, causing me to look to her eyes.

"It's perfect," I whisper, feeling myself wanting to say, I love you, but I don't say anything more..

She draws me in for a lingering embrace. Her bulky habit becomes inconsequential. Mother whispers, "The will of God will never lead you where the grace of God cannot keep you."

The moment is powerful. Gone. But dwells inside of me.

~~~

Aunt Grace arrives early, but I'm up and dressed, thanks to Karen's early routine. We hug.

"It's good to see you. How are you?" she asks.

"Good to see you, too. I'm fine," I say, happy to have her company for the day.

The three of us have coffee together before Karen leaves for work. Aunt Grace keeps glancing at me with concerned eyes. She is eager to entertain me, but calm with concern for the impact Grandfather's announcement must have made.

She knows me as well as anyone. I have to make this be okay, so everyone stops worrying. Grandfather's deed shouldn't give him access to make the other side of my family and friends worry about me. I smile reassuringly at her and sip my coffee. I will make everything all right.

~~~

Aunt Grace and I walked on the beach often while my mother was dying, so it seems only natural for us to go there now. It is funny how people gravitate to the familiar for safety when things are haywire.

It is a beautiful day. The sky is clear blue with a slight breeze coming inland. We went to Santa Monica, rather than to my beach, Seal Beach. We stroll along the water's edge, pausing from time to time to inspect seashells left behind by the early morning's receding high tide. Aunt Grace finds a shell she likes, and gives it to me. It is a dainty thing, but obviously strong enough to ride the tide without being broken. I slide it in my pocket, happy to have it—mellow with the gesture of the gift, and its representation of strength and perseverance.

We walk to the end of the pier and lean on the railing in silence, watching the waves come and go, and the people on the beach. The kite vendor has done well this morning. Several kites are in the air, tugging in the breeze. There are a few surfers sitting astride their boards patiently waiting for a ride to shore.

Seagulls are squawking at the pier fishermen standing near us, casting lines over the rail. One young gull stands on top of a piling watching a boy bait his hook. Father and son are craning their necks back and forth, intent on the bait sliding on just right. The gull watches two miscasts, then he lunges for the third while it's mid-air, which is a deadly practice if he gets hooked.

The boy laughs and shouts excitedly as the gull swoops toward the water in pursuit of the bait. The young gull returns to the piling after failing, to wait for the next opportunity.

The father shoos the seagull and scolds him to search elsewhere for his breakfast. The bird moves away, then back when the boy is distracted from the bait bucket. The behavior seems rather analytical for a bird. I didn't know birds had abstract reasoning. Maybe he is only opportunistic. Clearly I am searching the day for signs of how to solve my "McKenzie problem." I'll take anything, a seagull or an angel.

Aunt Grace smiles at me, fondly. She always knows when to appear on my horizon. This time is no different.

"How long have you known your McKenzie grandfather?"

"He looked me up about four years ago," I say.

"He looked you up?" She tilts her head, surprise that I hadn't mentioned it showing on her face.

"Yes. It went all right though," I add.

My parents were successful architects. There was never any indication that we were the rich McKenzies. Aunt Grace seems to have known about him. I suppose Mom talked to her about the man she was marrying and his father's excommunication that occurred because of it.

"Is he kind to you?" Her voice betrays her concern.

"Yes. He's always been kind." I turn to face her squarely.

"Your mother wondered if this day would come, and if it did, how it would play out." She offers a weak smile. She and Mom were extremely close. I wonder if Aunt Grace felt a specific responsibility to look out for me after Mom died.

"Oh! I wonder, too." I try to make light of my situation, but feel the weight of it.

"Give it a try. You have other options, if it doesn't suit you," she says.

"I'll do my best," I promise, not quite realizing what she is trying to tell me.

She gently sweeps a strand of hair from my eyes. "Katey, your grandfather has a strong personality. Keep the integrity of who you are. You'll be fine." She smiles fondly, then looks back at the waves below. "You are a bright, talented, classy lady. I am confident you will do well." She looks at me. "You come from strong stock," she quotes her mother, my maternal grandmother.

"Yes, I do," I say, leaning on the railing next to her. Our family has been through a lot of ups and downs, and always landed on our feet. We stick together. That is the secret of our strength. No matter what, we stick together.

Slowly, I am developing a sense of perspective about my situation. After spending the day with Aunt Grace, I feel better knowing that no matter what happens with the McKenzie family, Mom's family and the beach will always be as they have been. And I find that very reassuring.

I ask to go by my apartment for a few things. When we pull into the parking lot, the man with the binoculars' car is still parked in the same place as yesterday, but I don't see him. It's obvious I can't return home until this media curiosity is replaced with a more interesting news cycle. I tell Aunt Grace that I've changed my mind. We go to Karen's house.

Staying with Karen is fun, but we both need to get back to our normal routine. For Karen, that is relatively easy. As for me, normal might never be used to describe my life again. I'll tell Karen when she gets home that it's time for me to go.

~~~

Karen is already home when we return. She looks to Aunt Grace for an indication of how the day went. After all we've been through, she could have simply asked me.

With an ally present, Karen corners me. "Have you called your grandfather?"

"No, I haven't. I'll arrange to stay with him for a while."

I'm careful not to mention the man outside my apartment to either of them. It will be good to let the media interest dissolve.
~~~

"You're taking this well." Karen is obviously more angry with Grandfather than I am at the moment.

The thought of staying at Pacific Estate is not appealing. Even in small doses, Brooke is obnoxious. Timmy follows her lead, but mostly he is a worthless playboy on the fast track to trouble. Danny is probably as trapped by Grandfather as I am. That summarizes my McKenzie cousins in a nutshell.

"No, not really. I'm angry, but the beach helped."

"You really don't *have* to do it." Aunt Grace solidifies her alliance with Karen.

I take a deep breath. "Don't worry. You taught me about family responsibility. The cousins are a mess. I've never met their parents. I'll do it until I come up with an alternative—hire someone, or something."

"Aren't you furious?" Karen is the psychologist again.

"I'm more than furious with him. The only way to win is to take control." The anger inside comes out in my tone, which is probably what she was after.

"It won't be easy," Aunt Grace says.

"You're going to have to set boundaries and not back down to him," Karen adds.

I don't feel that confident, but I nod and smile.

~~~

When I speak with Grandfather about staying with him, I put an emphasis on "short while," but there is no indication that he hears me.

Grandfather immediately says James will come and get me now. I ask to be picked up Saturday morning at the coffee shop down the street. Maybe it's selfish, but I want to spend one more day with Karen, and I don't want to risk the media coming to her house. Karen works a half day tomorrow. If I leave Saturday, we have tomorrow afternoon and evening together. Maybe we can get to the beach again before I leave.

I'm going to figure out a way to liberate my car, so I'm independently mobile again. The next thing on my agenda is to get a few clothes and my diary from my apartment.

"I should hire a look-alike and have her drive my car," I tell Karen. "With any luck, the media will follow her and I can get
~~~

some things from home." The idea is amusing, but I need to settle down and devise a real plan. We both know I'm not serious about hiring a double. She buys that some media may still be at my place, watching for me.

Staying with Grandfather for a month or two is fine. It isn't what I want to do long-term. Besides, the thought of living with my McKenzie cousins full-time makes me shudder.

Karen refills my cup with coffee. "You know, you might learn media management from your grandfather. He has it mastered. Be firm with him on everything else, that might be hard at first." She takes a long sip of her coffee—leaving her words hanging.

That sounds good, but how exactly do I set boundaries with Alistair McKenzie? "Any specific suggestions?"

"Take charge. Start with the media. Have James come here. Don't sneak away."

"What about you? What if the media follows James?"

She shrugs. "So what? They aren't interested in me. They won't hang around long." She rejects my concern. "I am sure James knows how to handle the media, don't worry about him either."

"That's probably true."

"Just be pleasant, not aloof, and go about your business. Don't give them control of the situation. Talk to them on your schedule and your terms. For now, just calmly get in the car, graciously."

"Charmingly unavailable?"

"Sure, why not?"

"If you are in the neighborhood, drop by," is all I manage to say, knowing the McKenzie mansion is not in anyone's neighborhood.

"I'll give you a couple of weeks. Get settled with your staff."

Staff? I hadn't thought about having staff of my own looking to me for direction.

Friday morning seems to last forever. Finally, Karen's home.

"It's nice to have someone here when I come home." Karen is happy to have a short day. Though, I never remember her working only a half day before. She drops her pager in the charger on the kitchen counter and looks toward the stove.

"Don't get used to having a personal chef."

Karen lifts the lid of the pot, releasing a burst of steam from the soup. "Mmm, smells good."

We lean against the counter, looking at each other across the kitchen like we will never see each other again.

"You know, we are still going to be friends," I say.

It is easy to imagine the future to be exactly the way we want it to be. It is just as easy to fear the worst. I promise myself to make the effort to sustain my friendship with Karen, despite the McKenzie empire obligations.

~~~

James knocks at Karen's door. I'm not ready to go. We haven't eaten. Karen entices James into having a cup of coffee, but he declines the offer of lunch.

I'm tempted to send him away. This isn't the time we agreed to meet. He's a day early. But it isn't James' fault Grandfather ignored my wishes, so there is no reason to take my frustration out on him.

My appetite is gone. Might as well pack. "Ha! I am a bag lady," I say softly to myself as I fold the navy sweatshirt Karen gave me and put it into the shopping bag with my other things. Karen is a real trouper, but her eyes don't lie very well. We say goodbye to the past we shared.

~~~

The limo pulls smoothly from the curb. Karen stands at the sidewalk waving goodbye. James drives, silently. I don't have anything to say, either. What's there to say when someone has such ultimate power to change the course of my life?

After a while, I say. "James, let's take PCH."

"Yes, Miss McKenzie."

James moves the limousine effortlessly through the traffic toward Pacific Coast Highway. The limo wasn't necessary. I'm sure that Grandfather is trying to give me first-class treatment. I suppose he doesn't understand that I didn't know about the family fortune, so I grew up valuing other things, such as people, not money. Or maybe he does understand and thought, rightly so, that I would decline the succession to the throne if I had advance warning.

The road veers back along the ocean. In some places the elevation is ten to fifteen feet above sea level. The limousine rounds a curve in the road and I see the familiar sight I have been waiting for—Father's Beach.

"James, stop here for a minute, please."

"Yes, Miss McKenzie."

~~~

I expect James to stay with the car, like drivers do in movies, but he follows a few steps behind me.

Turning to face him, I say, "James, you don't need to walk behind me. Come," I stretch out my hand, "and walk with me."

He hesitates a slight moment, nods to himself, and joins me. "Yes, ma'am."

He is barely old enough to be my father and he calls me "ma'am." I don't like it, but I understand it's his job, so I let it be. However, there is no need for this large Black man to follow behind me. He doesn't have to behave like a subservient staff member with me. "McKenzie" is my name, not who I am. I have no intention of treating James as poorly as Grandfather does. Although, I really don't think it is personal with Grandfather. He sees all of us, including me, in a diminished light compared to himself.

We walk from the parking lot to the beach through the tunnel under the highway. James looks at the rock formations in the shallows, the seabirds perched on them, and the rising rock walls surrounding us. The waves are calm and the water is a deep blue.

"Isn't it beautiful here, James?" I ask as if he's a dear old friend.

We are standing side by side, looking straight out to the distant horizon. My arms are comfortably folded across the front of me. James has his hands casually in his pockets. It is as if the universe is standing still and we have this corner of it to ourselves. The sounds of the waves, the slight breeze, the clear water—everything is perfect.

"My mother always called this place 'Father's Beach,'" I say aloud to my newest friend.

James stirs and looks around with more interest.
~~~

Storm Surge

It's not that I am disrespectful of Grandfather. I know we are going to be late arriving at the Estate, but I can't help taking these last few precious minutes, alive, free, and anonymous.

"James, I want to show you the next beach." I move to where the wall of rocks meets the water. I hold my hand parallel to my shoulder with the palm facing him, indicating for him to wait.

"When the wave goes out, follow me. Run. Run fast when I tell you."

Like waiting for a jump rope to swing out of the way, I gauge the motion of the waves. I wait for the biggest one in the series to pass, since it will recede the farthest and allow us more time to get around the rocks.

"Okay, get ready. Now! Go, now!" I run around the rocks through the temporary doorway the wave left behind when it went back to sea.

James clears the rocks just before the next wave comes in. We both turn to watch the passageway disappear underwater. The wave hits hard, then sprays into the air—majestically. James smiles a delighted smile, then we both laugh. His laugh is hearty and deep.

I show James the hidden entrance to the cave that leads to the next beach. He can touch the cave roof, if he stretches a bit. He is wearing dress shoes, so I advise caution on the wet sand and rock floor. I know we can only stay a short while because the tide is slowly coming in and will trap us here if we aren't alert, then we would have to mountain-goat our way back up to the road.

Besides, I remember that Grandfather is waiting for me. I just wanted one more visit to this place before I succumb to Grandfather's wishes, and I'm happy to have someone to share the experience.

~~~
~~~

Father's Beach

~ CHAPTER 4 ~

The Beginning of the End

On the way back to the car, we resume the roles defined by social obligation. Out of respect for James, I wait until he opens the limo door for me. We head north again. I no longer look at the ocean. This isn't the time to think about what's behind; what is ahead occupies my mind. I feel obligated to find out what is going on, not obligated to Grandfather, but to my father. The visit to Father's Beach was my way to confirm that I accept the proxy to stand in his place.

~~~

As we enter the gate of Pacific Estate, people scamper out the door and down the stairs. They look like actors hurrying for their mark before the curtain goes up.

By the time we reach the front of the mansion, everyone is standing properly—one person on each end of each step—like an honor guard. Stanley waits at the bottom of the stairs, ready to open the door and help me out of the limo with his white-gloved hand. I'm surprised there isn't a band—kidding.

I pause to acknowledge Stanley with a smile. "Thank you, Stanley."

I climb the steps beside him, acknowledging each person we meet with a nod and a smile. They are each dressed in costume-quality attire commensurate with their duties. Beginning today, I am the mistress of the manor—and that has changed everything.

Conner pushes Grandfather's wheelchair to the center of the porch. Grandfather sits there formally awaiting my ascent. It is as if this is an ancient, time-honored ceremony.

For an instant, I'm not sure if I should stoop and kiss him on the cheek, as I usually do when I arrive, or is something else the protocol?

I remind myself of Karen and Aunt Grace's advice: Be myself, or Grandfather truly owns me. I bend down and kiss his
~~~

cheek in front of his staff. He responds in his usual fashion by reaching for my upper arm to hold me in place slightly—just long enough to stretch the moment.

Conner looks uncomfortable in hospital whites. Usually, he wears Hawaiian shirts with his white slacks. As a matter of fact, except for Stanley, most of the staff are usually dressed less formally.

Grandfather and Conner lead into the mansion. The staff file in behind us like a wedding procession. Grandfather instructs Eleanor, the woman in charge of all the household staff, to take me to my room. She nods, turns abruptly, and exits.

Obviously, I am expected to follow her. I enter the foyer and begin to ascend the stairs behind her. The feel of the mahogany banister is luxurious beneath my hand. Looking up the stairs at the back of Eleanor advancing ahead of me, she strikes me as the "little general" around here. The place runs like clockwork. Everything is in its place—perfectly.

Eleanor rarely works weekends. The few occasions we've been here at the same time, she has been strictly business and we have never really conversed. Today is no different.

She reaches the landing, turns the corner and continues up the next flight of stairs. She walks steadily, paced, measured.

I follow silently, looking around at my surroundings. Every piece of furniture, portrait on the wall, vase—everything speaks of money—a great deal of old wealth.

I've never been on the second or third floors of the mansion. Grandfather's room is on the first floor due to his wheelchair. Conner has an adjoining room, so he can attend to him during the night. I have always slept in the main floor guest room overlooking the east gardens at the rear of the house.

Eleanor stops, opens a door, and waits for me to enter. "Miss McKenzie, this is your room." She opens the drapes, then turns to face me. "Stanley will bring up your luggage."

I stand in the center of the room, while she moves around settling the room for habitation. It is obviously someone else's room. There are personal items and photos on the dresser, reading books on the night stand, and stationery on the desk.

"Miss McKenzie. Miss McKenzie?"

"Oh. Yes, Eleanor."

"Will there be anything else?"

"No, no. Thank you. Thank you very much."

"Dinner is at seven," she says, looking me up and down. "Be sure to dress for dinner."

She leaves, shutting the door behind her.

"Dress for dinner?" I mumble to myself. My "luggage" consists of a pink shopping bag containing jeans, pajamas, and sweats. What I am wearing is as good as it gets—white slacks and a light sage-colored sweater. "This will have to do," I tell the mirror as I fuss with my hair.

With my dinner attire settled, I snoop. This is an older woman's room, I'd guess by the look of things. Inside the closet is a large, richly decorated dressing room. I pick up a pretty bottle from the table, remove the stopper, smell the sweet aroma of perfume, then return it to its place. My fingertips brush across the crisp lace on the dressing table.

The dressing room progresses into a wardrobe full of clothes, rich old lady clothes. Some are elegant evening wear, timeless classic lines and fabrics—satin, taffeta, brocade. My fingers move over the fabrics, imagining the woman who wore them. Obviously, this must have been Grandmother's room. Seeing her belongings makes me wish I had known her.

In the main room of the suite, I study the framed photographs on the desk and dresser. There is a photo of a middle-aged, regal woman. The resemblance with the woman in the painting downstairs confirms she is my grandmother. I lift the picture closer and tilt it to the light for more study. The woman seems familiar, but I decide that it is probably wishful thinking, and I return it to its spot on the dresser.

There's a photo of a young man and woman, and three young children. They must be the cousins who now live with our grandfather. I wonder how the cousins came to live here rather than with their parents? I study my McKenzie aunt in the same way I studied Grandmother's picture. She and I have a family resemblance.

There is a photo of my parents with me as a babe in arms. Only five years later, Father would be missing from our family photos. I wonder if she knew when her son died. I can't remember if I saw her at the funeral, there were so many people there. Surely she was there. It is curious that she has our photo.

It's also curious that Grandmother defied Grandfather and had a photo of her son, his Catholic wife, and the first grandchild, me. She must have been a headstrong woman to display a photo of the forbidden family. It looks like my parents made the effort to keep in touch with Grandmother. Good for them!

I love Grandfather, but he has a knack for destroying the people around him. I feel drained and frustrated. I back up, looking around the room, finally sitting on the bed. Good thing this is a temporary arrangement. As lovely as this is, my movie poster collection would be out of place here, just as I am out of place.

Grandmother's picture strengthens me with her look of security with herself. Maybe Grandfather will consider someone else for this "honor" and let me quietly slip away. I'm realistic enough to know that's unlikely.

At least this room has a view of the Pacific. It is interesting that Grandmother had her bedroom suite face west. I see a resemblance with my apartment across from the beach. I inhale the moment.

~~~

The dining room is dark. Apparently I misunderstood Eleanor. Just as the door closes behind me, the light switches on. Stepping back to investigate the unexpected activity, I hear the sound of talking and dishes being stacked. Opening the door slightly, I see the kitchen help in the butler's pantry. Maybe I have arrived early. I leave them to their duties.

I wait in the hallway, moving from one huge portrait to the next, examining the faces captured by the artists. Again, I study the one I most resemble.

"She is your grandmother," Grandfather says, as he approaches. "That was before we were married." He passes beside me. Conner wheels Grandfather directly into the dining room—promptly at seven-thirty.

I glance back one more time at the young, beautiful woman with chestnut-colored hair. I always wondered about the people
~~~

in the paintings—especially her. I assumed that she was Grandmother, and am glad for the confirmation.

Did Eleanor lie about dinner time? It is probably simply protocol that I wait on Grandfather, rather than risk him waiting on me. It's obvious Eleanor attends to every detail, anticipating every contingency. I bet she intends for me to know my place, and to have me get in it—quickly!

~~~

The wine glasses sparkle in the candlelight. The air is filled with the aroma of foods cooked to perfection. While Grandfather is settled at his place at the head of the table, I wait with my eyes closed, inhaling the warm bread and buttery spice smells of the Cornish hens, stuffing, snow peas, and all the rest.

Stanley seats me at Grandfather's left, which has always been my place when I visit. I glance at the other end of the table, the end where my McKenzie cousins sit, and am relieved there are no place settings. I'm not in the mood for Brooke's attitude after the week I have had.

Once the food is served, Grandfather says, "That will be all, Stanley." This is a bit unusual since the help always remains "at the ready" throughout the meal. After the door closes behind Stanley and his helpers, Grandfather pauses cutting his Cornish hen. "You haven't said 'thank you,' Kathryn."

"Thank you?" I repeat his words.

"Yes, for making you the most powerful woman in California." His tone seems to indicate that I have asked the obvious question.

"Grandfather, the only power I want—that I have ever wanted, is power over my own life. My apartment is like a crime scene—I can't get in." My voice is a soft, unemotional tone, though I would have rather screamed the words.

"Bring more rice." He looks at me and points to the side table with his fork. He is strictly business, but I can tell he is not pleased by my response.

"I'll send for your things tomorrow." He continues eating, undaunted.

"Grandfather, with all due respect, I would rather get my own things," I say firmly, but as pleasantly as possible.
~~~

"We will discuss it later, your food is getting cold."

Grandfather resumes cutting his meat. I wait for him to introduce the next topic of conversation, but he eats in silence. He doesn't seem the least disturbed by my remarks, but I feel bad—no doubt I have disappointed him.

I revisit the beginning of the conversation. "Grandfather, I do appreciate your confidence in me. It was so unexpected that I was caught off guard. I'm sorry I don't seem more appreciative."

"Pass the vegetables, Kathryn," he says as he looks up, again using his fork as a pointer.

I hand him the bowl of steamed snow peas. As he helps himself, he says, "That is how the world is, Kathryn. You are not going to be warned about the big things—only the insignificant things can be scheduled to your convenience."

So, this is my first lesson. He was certainly dramatic in the delivery of this tidbit of wisdom. I know he is old, maybe he doesn't feel like he has a lot of time for me to learn the workings of his empire. Maybe he doesn't feel he owes anyone a warning.

After a final drink of his wine, Grandfather tosses his napkin in his plate, then pushes his chair back from the table.

"Stanley," Grandfather calls toward the butler's pantry door.

Stanley appears immediately. "Yes, sir."

"I am ready for bed, call Conner."

Conner doesn't acknowledge my presence. He simply grips the handles of Grandfather's wheelchair and pushes him out of the room while Stanley holds the door open.

Just before reaching the hall, Grandfather looks back over his shoulder and says warmly, "Goodnight, Kathryn."

"Goodnight, Grandfather." I start to get up to go to him with a hug, but Conner wheels him away without waiting, though I know he saw me.

I examine how Grandfather easily keeps business and personal separate, and smoothly switches between the two.

I turn back to finish my dinner, but the kitchen crew is clearing the dishes from the table. Now what?

I hear Eleanor tell Stanley she is going to her room, and asks him to finish supervising the kitchen staff. Most of the lights are already off in the mansion. Grandfather usually stays up later than this when I come for visits. Often, we are the ones shutting off the lights after everyone, except Conner, is in bed.

Fingering my locket, I start up the ornate carved stairway, designed for grand entrances during past social gatherings.

Imagine this place in the forties. The McKenzie parties must have given the society column plenty of material. I imagine the young woman in the painting coming down the stairs to greet her guests. In the half-light, I can almost hear the music and see the expensive gowns. Now, the parties are quiet, and I feel the silence.

The staff quarters are located on the second floor. I don't know what else is there, but I don't snoop. I round the top of the stairs on the third floor and start for my room, but get drawn to the front windows to look toward the ocean. I throw open the drapery as Eleanor had in my room. The lawn is lit by the full moon. Farther away is the misty ocean. It seems surreal to be here—a little princess locked in the tower.

There is no possibility that I am going to bed by nine o'clock. In the medieval spirit of castles and princesses locked in towers, I explore my corner of the kingdom.

Past my room, I try the knob of the next door. It turns. I ease it open. It is dark inside the room compared to the moon-lit hallway. Rubbing my hand on the flocked wallpaper, I locate the light switch, go inside, shut the door, then turn on the light.

It's a bedroom, more masculine than mine. The furniture is heavy-looking even though it is draped with white sheets. The room is a mirror image of my room. When I open the closet door, there is a manly scent inside. More than half of the racks are empty. The remaining clothes are riding pants and boots, things Grandfather can't use now.

On a shelf is a silver chest that is monogrammed with Grandfather's initials. The chest is locked. I check under it and in several drawers for the key, but don't find it. There is drapery on the wall that is shared with my room. Behind the cloth is a door. Inside is a small, private sitting room and another door that opens into my room. Conjugal visits? How cute is that?

Back into the hall to the next room on my quest—the room across the hall from mine. It's locked. So are the next two down that side of the hall. Those three bedrooms must belong to my cousins—all of whom are apparently away from the estate tonight.

The fourth room on the other side of the stairs is unlocked. It is storage—a baby cradle, rocking horse, trunks, boxes, drafting table, and the like. Exploring this room is added to my mental "to-do" list for in the future.

Back across the hall to my side of the hall, there is a large parlor or sitting room. It's set up for entertaining a small informal group of household members—it's not designed to be seen by the public. Then, back toward the main stairs.

The stairs lead up to the next floor, but it is very dark up there. I haven't explored all I'd like for tonight, but the darkness above is unwelcoming. Besides, some exploring should be saved for the next boring evening.

In my room, I go through to the secluded parlor and lock the door to Grandfather's room. That allows me the use of both rooms with no unsecured entrances. Sitting in an overstuffed chair and putting my feet on the ottoman, I wish I had my diary and a cup of coffee.

As much as I would like to believe that I can return to my apartment in a few weeks, I am beginning to realize that isn't realistic. It's painfully obvious to me that I need to move into the mansion. It only makes sense. I need to be near Grandfather, not only for the little lessons he throws in my direction, but more importantly, to learn the art of managing the family businesses and make sure I'm not out of the loop —whatever the loop is.

The more time I spend with Grandfather, the more I can learn. With his health and age, time is a luxury I don't have. I do not like the idea, but feel more settled with the practical decision. My apartment can serve as a beach house for weekend retreats or when I need to stay in the city for business.

It's apparent this is to become my room. This whole arrangement is not going to be convenient, but I don't think convenience was a factor in Grandfather's decision to involve me in the empire.

Moving to the desk, I take a piece of stationery to make a list to organize my life again. I pause to touch the golden embossed letters, A-M-K, A. McKenzie. There's no name on the inside cover of the address book in the drawer, so I begin leafing through the pages. Under "Mc" is my parents' name and address. Birthdays have been added in the margin. Nothing in the drawer that reveals the meaning of "A."

Glancing at the photos on the dresser, I examine them again. Grandmother resembles Mother's "friend," Amelia. I tilt my head, remembering the times that Amelia came to our house for birthdays, holidays, and for no-particular-reason visits. Amelia came to see us often. The three of us would walk on the beach—me running ahead of them to collect shells, then run back to the women.

"Amelia, Mother's friend, was really my grandmother?" I whisper softly. I don't remember when she stopped visiting us—could it have been that she became ill and couldn't come again? It's funny how she came slumming in everyday clothes and an everyday car. I remember Amelia at Father's funeral now, but not at Mother's.

Tears fill my eyes and run down my face. I don't understand the secrecy about Grandmother's identity. There was no obvious point to sneaking around at our house. This makes no sense to me. I can only guess that it made sense to them. I try to remember every detail of Amelia's visits. She was very attentive and I loved her dearly. I'm glad for that.

I sit on the floor against the bed and lean forward to put my forehead down on my overlapping arms atop my bent knees. I'm tired of the deceit and frustrated with the games these people play with the lives around them, as if life is a plaything. How do I guard against Grandfather's knack for trumping my plans?

~~~

When I awaken the sun is nowhere in sight. Outside my window the moonlight is diminished and it's extremely dark in the predawn hours. Though it is early by anyone's standards, I am wide awake.

After a shower, I head for the kitchen in search of coffee.

Louise, Grandfather's cook, has always made it crystal clear the kitchen is her domain. No one is allowed to mess with her kitchen—that's final. She rarely works weekends. When I visited,
~~~

Grandfather and I made ourselves lunch—as long as Louise or Eleanor wasn't around to catch us. I don't think for one minute that Grandfather is afraid of Louise. But, if he was afraid of someone, it would probably be her. Ah Louise, her black curly hair cropped close to her head, and her bosom as large as her laugh.

My desire for coffee is strong enough to spur my courage to make a pot of the dark brew. "Ah, coffee!" I say, leaning back in the chair, glancing out the window beside the kitchen's prep table, watching the early rays of morning on the dewy garden. The beauty invites me outdoors.

I take a full cup of coffee and my Dodgers jacket to protect me from the chill. The gardens are absolutely beautiful. It's calming to walk through the expansive grounds, free again.

As I follow the paths around the gardens, I walk a little more confidently. Grandfather was correct, there aren't going to be warnings, dress rehearsals, or places to hide. I'm not so naive to think that I'll always and immediately wear this role expertly. I have to figure this out and make it work.

~~~

At thirty-four, I am too old to run from this. It's time to accept the responsibility that came with my birthright as heir apparent. And, I will do my best to hold on to those moments when it didn't matter what my name was.

The sun has cleared the horizon. It began as pastel colors in the distant sky, now it's halfway above the edge of the dark Earth. The bright morning colors contrast against the Earth until the light washes over everything.

The fragrance of the flowers is particularly rich with the morning dew. I take a deep breath of the sweet-smelling air. More than any other time, I think I can master this new world.

In the distance, a dark figure is slowly moving across the landscape. The figure is tall, with spindly appendages that angle toward its back. As it advances, I see a small person with a rake and hoe over his shoulder. Methodically, the figure moves closer.

We rendezvous in the rose garden.

"Good morning, miss," the figure says and half-bows quickly three times.
~~~

"Good morning, I'm Kathryn." I offer a handshake.

The little Chinese man removes his gardening gloves and shuffles the weight of his hoe and rake, bringing them down to lean against his body.

Extending his hand, "Juan, I am Juan." He smiles.

"Huang. Mr. Huang, it is nice to meet you." We shake hands. "The gardens are beautiful." I gesture at the rose garden, figuring he is responsible for the beauty.

"I am Juan, no mister, just Juan."

"Yes, Huang like the Yellow River—Huang He. Right?"

"No, no. Juan Garcia Li." He smiles, revealing a missing tooth from his upper jaw.

"Juan Garcia?" I ask, trying to force my mind to make the connection with the Mexican name and the little Chinese man.

He grins again. "My mother gave me American name."

The connection is not as clear to me as it seems to be to him. I nod in agreement, returning his smile.

He smiles again, then starts raking around the base of a rose bush.

By the time I am back to the mansion and open the door, Louise looks up. She can't be that bad, or she would be in prison, right?

"Good morning, Louise."

"Did you make this coffee, Kathryn?" she asks, looking into the cup in her hand.

"Yes, ma'am," I admit as confidently as possible, knowing the rumors of what happens when her territory is breached. It's Saturday, I didn't expect to see her.

"It's good. What's your secret?" she says nicely.

Is this a bonding moment? "I use two filters. I think it gives a less bitter taste," I answer, ready to tell her anything she wants to know to avoid confrontation.

"I'll have to try that. What do you want for breakfast?" She moves smoothly to the next topic.

"I'll take the breakfast special."

She eyes me for a moment, then smiles.

Grandfather is slow getting around this morning. He is usually up and about by the time I am. Maybe he doesn't see any need to rush around on Saturday morning. After all, I will be staying here for a while, why rush? However, that doesn't explain why Louise is here on a weekend day. Even though I am curious, I ask no questions.

~~~

Karen calls to touch base. My plan is to go home and get some of my things, including my car. She offers to give me a ride. James doesn't live at Pacific Estate, so I wouldn't think of calling him to come and drive me on his day off. There isn't anyone here who I feel comfortable to ask to drive me.

"That would be great, if you don't mind the drive," I say.

~~~

Back in my room at Grandmother's desk, I finish the list of things to pick up at home. In preparation for moving my things in, I look in the closet again. I have to show this closet to Karen. She's fashion conscious—she will get a kick out of this. Wonder why everything was left in its place after she died?

I check on Grandfather. He's back to his sweet, doting self. When I tell him Karen is picking me up to get my things, he genuinely seems interested in meeting my friend. He suggests I have the gate open, so she can get right to the house.

From the vantage of the higher elevation at the mansion, I see Karen pull through the gate toward the circular drive. She pulls ahead enough not to block the steps to the front door. I meet her at the bottom step, as Stanley always meets me.

"I see you are still alive," she says. She looks up at the mansion, taking in the full view, but says nothing about it.

"Yes, I am doing well." I reassure her. After all, everyone knows that dread is much worse than facing the things we fear.

~~~

Karen is an immediate hit with Grandfather. He likes people with grace and intelligence. After years of working in the political arena, she can work any room with ease.

While I watch Grandfather and Karen interact, I realize she is just as curious about my mysterious grandfather as he is about my friends. The difference is she is more relaxed. He seems to be desperately making an effort to make a winning impression on her. More than any other time since I met him, he
~~~

seems to realize that he knows little about me and the people in my life. It's as if it hadn't occurred to him before now that I lived in a world outside of his domain.

I tell him we are going to have a girls-only day and hang out, moving some of my things.

"You ladies will have to move Grandmother's things."

"Is there anywhere in particular you want them moved?" I ask, careful about disturbing the shrine that has been carefully maintained.

"No, she doesn't need them—do what you want to with them," he answers pragmatically.

It surprises me a little that Grandfather gave us carte blanche. It appears there was simply no particular reason to move her things, so no one did.

Karen's reaction walking up the stairs is like mine was. "Oh, this is a step back in time!" she says with wonderment.

"Yes, it is like walking into a movie; imagine the music."

"What is on this floor?" She looks around as we hit the landing of the second floor.

"Live-in staff. I don't know if there is anything else."

She looks down the hall as we round the steps to ascend to the next level. We see no one.

On the third floor she looks around. "What a marvelous wall of windows," she comments on the windows that look out upon the ocean. She moves closer for a bird's-eye view of the dark blue Pacific.

"Yes, it is beautiful. You can see for miles from here."

We turn away, toward my room. She follows slowly, continuing to absorb the ambiance of the place. Her curiosity gets the best of her.

"What else is up here?"

"I'm not sure. I think these three rooms" pointing across the hall belong to my cousins. That room was Grandfather's when he was able to take the stairs, and at the end of the hall is storage there and a sitting room across from it."

Karen tilts her head to look up the stairs to the next floor.

"What's up there?" she asks, moving toward the flight of stairs to the floor above.

"I don't know. Let's look." We pause, exchange glances, then nod in agreement.

Karen takes the lead. We move up the stairs quickly and quietly. It is dark and the air is stuffy as we reach the landing.

"Feel along the wall for a light switch."

Karen checks the wall to our right. I go to the left. In the dim light I get a sense there is a hallway running perpendicular to the stairs. There should be a light switch somewhere near the stairs—it only makes sense. Karen misses the corner of the hallway and works herself along the wall parallel to the stairs until she is opposite the landing.

Suddenly, sunlight floods the area. She found the window directly above the window on my floor and opened the drapery. Dust floats in the air on the beams of sunlight. There are two sets of French doors facing the stairs, opposite the window.

"Well, now we can find the light switch!" I tease about her ingenuity.

Once we have the light on, we open the French doors. The light from the windows and the hall shines through the opening. It doesn't shed light to the back of the room, but it is enough for us to see into the first few yards.

We look at each other in astonishment and slowly walk into the semi-dark room together. Around the perimeter of the room are tables with chairs turned upside down on them.

"Lights, Katey. Let's find the lights!"

"I'm on it. Is this what I think it is?" I ask excitedly as I walk across the room in search of the light panel.

"It's a ballroom," she half-whispers with excitement. "Katey, it's a ballroom!"

This is well worth all of the frustration of last week. "It's like an old black-and-white movie!" I echo her excitement.

I love the romance of the old movies and the lifestyle that went with them. It's as if we walked back in time and all of my little-girl dreams are reality.

Karen finds the light switch. A massive chandelier in the center of the room comes to life. I'm frozen in awe of my surroundings. This place is absolutely amazing. My eyes drink in every inch. The deep mint-green walls are stenciled with gold designs that were typical in the 1940s. The lower portion of the wall is painted burgundy. Despite the years of dust on it, the wooden floor feels smooth as glass under my feet.

I turn to look at Karen. She is dancing across the floor—she and her imaginary prince charming. I had forgotten that she loves to dance. What a magical place this is! Her face looks serene in a way that I have never seen before.

Breathless, Karen dances toward me. "I love your new house!" she laughs and dances away.

"I'll get this place cleaned up. Then, we'll have a party!" I encourage her excitement, as well as my own.

"Great! Come on—let's get you moved in, so we can get started."

~~~

"This isn't quite as grand as the ballroom, but look at this closet," I say as I open the doors to Grandmother's closet. We enter and finger all of the garments on the racks. "Isn't this something?" I remark, brushing my hand across the rack of ball gowns.

"Look at this one." Karen pulls out one of Grandmother's gowns and holds it up against her body.

"You look loverly, my dear."

"Thank you, Miss McKenzie."

We both laugh. Karen takes one last look at the dress and starts to return it to its place. "Let's move all of these to that rack. There, that should be enough space for my clothes until I have time to sort through these." I start to move the clothes.

"You're right, we have to get moving, but I will help you sort through these—how about next weekend?"

"Sounds great. Let's make a day of it. Champagne brunch on the patio—the whole deal! Shall I see if Dana wants to join the party?" My mind is racing with ideas.

"Oooh, she would love this! Yes, invite her!"

We relocate the clothes, tell Grandfather "Goodbye," and head south. Regardless of where the conversation veers, Karen always comes back to the ballroom.

What a discovery. How could I have visited Grandfather so many times and never learned about the ballroom? Granted, I
~~~

slept in the first floor guest room, and never snooped around the mansion before now. It seems that it might have been mentioned by someone in a passing comment or something.

~~~
~~~

~ CHAPTER 5 ~

Home, Sweet Home

We pass a man reading a newspaper in a car parked across from my apartment. It doesn't look like the same car, but the man looks like the guy with the binoculars. My anxiety rises.

Lots of people come to the beach to read. If they aren't on the beach with a paperback, they are usually on a bench under a tree on the green near the pier. I suppose there is no hard, fast rule he can't read in his car. I'm being paranoid.

When we drive into the parking lot, a sigh of relief slips loose. No reporters are in sight. It's good to be home. It may not have a ballroom, but it does have a beach.

I don't know what I expect to find when I open my door, but I open it slower than usual and look carefully inside. Once we're inside, I quickly lock the door. Everything is just as we left it. It takes a minute for the unfounded, spooked feeling to pass.

We pack the clothes on my list, while a pot of coffee brews. Until Grandmother's things are sorted, there isn't room for all of my clothes. I leave things here for when I need a weekend at the beach.

I slip my diary into my purse, look around, and move the last suitcase near the door. "Well, I think that's about it."

We have time for a walk on the beach. The man in the car is just that, a man in a car reading a newspaper. He doesn't appear to take notice of us crossing the street to the beach.

This time of year it's anyone's guess what the weather will be, but today is a nice spring afternoon. Low tide was a couple of hours ago. There is a slight breeze. A jacket might be nice, but not absolutely necessary.

"This beach has shared many life experiences with us," Karen says.

"Yes, it has witnessed the best and worst times of our lives."

"Have you ever heard from Joseph?" she asks, knowing he is mentioned somewhere in my previous answer.

"No. No, I haven't heard from him since he returned to Ireland— other than the roses on Thanksgiving every year, since—" I still don't mention Maggie's death out loud very easily. "Why do you ask?"

"He wrote and—"

I interrupt. "Joseph wrote? He never wrote to me, even when he should have written to save me the trip to Ireland. Maybe he's heard that I'm *that* McKenzie."

"I'll give you that one. Do you want to know the rest?"

"Sorry, I guess he is still a sore spot. But no, I really don't want to know the rest. Sorry." I soften my tone.

She studies me a moment. "No. I am the one who should apologize. I'm sorry. I shouldn't have mentioned him." She looks at me a bit more intensely than I like.

The seagull sounds come into my awareness, waking me from thoughts of my former lover. "I forgive you," I whisper. "Want to get a drink at Ruby's on the pier?" I deliberately move the conversation in a different direction.

Karen looks like she is going to say something more, but seems to think better of it. I don't press her. I will trust her judgment to leave it unsaid.

After a lengthy pause, I suggest, "Let's call Dana and invite her to join us Saturday and go through Grandmother's closet. We can play 'dress-up' all afternoon."

Dress-up? That's out of character. I was a serious child. I never, ever played dress-up, except to be a nun. When Father was killed, I went from shy to serious at the ripe old age of six.

"Dana would love it," she says.

"Can you imagine her eyes when she sees the vintage gowns?"

"Maybe she can alter some of them to fit you."

"Hmm, I hadn't thought of that, but it would be fun to wear one of Grandmother's dresses."

"This has been a good day. I still can't believe that ballroom," Karen signals she is ready to leave.

I pick up the tab.

"No, I'll get this. I missed your birthday while you were in Vienna." She smiles with a I-bet-you-thought-I-forgot look.

"All right, thank you."

As we walk back down the pier toward my apartment she asks, "Are you heading north now?"

"I think I will stay here tonight. I can go to Mass without making an issue of it with Grandfather."

"He knows you are Catholic. He must know you attend Mass." There is her logic again.

"I want to go to my parish this time."

~~~

After Karen leaves, I brew a pot of coffee, and put on music. The rich musical scores from my collection of movie music plays in the background of my thoughts. I look around the room at my movie posters, studying them, memorizing them. They are as different as night and day from Grandfather's expensive art and commissioned portraits. We really do come from two different worlds.

The whole idea of being an heiress is an uneasy fit. But when I consider his alternatives in the family, I understand his choice. In my heart, I know it had to fall to me. Brooke is a selfish, spoiled brat. Tim is a worthless, wild drunk. Danny doesn't have the self-confidence to take on something like this. With his stammering, he would be eaten alive by the media, like he is by his brother and sister.

I'm the heir apparent, the eldest heir of my generation. I am the only one who bears the family name, my cousins' last name is Anderson.

Sigh. He didn't choose me; destiny chose me. As ridiculous as it sounds, I have to do this. The dye has been cast on the water. All of this is just a chess game. What's your next move, Katey? Swim for shore?

~~~

That's it. I'm out of here. I grab my keys and walk the six blocks to my parish church. With a profound sense of clarity, I know exactly what to do: Get a fresh start. It is time to say goodbye to the past and look to the future.

I bless myself with the Holy Water from the font just inside the door. The church is empty; it's a typical Saturday afternoon. There are a few votive lights burning by Our Lady's statue. The afternoon sun is bathing the walls with yellow-and-rose-colored light from the stained glass windows.

I walk down the center aisle, genuflect, and select a seat. I slip into the pew, bend to lower the kneeler, and slide to my knees.

"In the name of the Father, Son, and Holy Spirit," I whisper, as I make the Sign of the Cross and look into the face of the sculpture on the cross above the altar. I close my eyes and pour out my heart.

I'm ready now. The door to the confessional shuts. The light switches off when my weight settles on the kneeler. The window's door slides open in the wall in front of me. He is silent, but I know he is there because of the smell of his aftershave. Old Spice? Perhaps.

"Bless me, Father, for I have sinned. It has been awhile since my last confession." I speak into the dark, through the black screen between us.

"Proceed," says the pragmatic male voice from the other side of the darkened screen.

I thought I was ready, but the words stick in my throat. I clear my throat and try again. "Father, I—I love a married man." I bow my head in shame even though no one sees me. Why has it taken me so long to admit that I still feel love for Joseph?

"Are you having an affair?"

"No, Father."

"Are you interfering in his marriage in any way?"

"I don't think so."

"Is he in love with you?"

"No, Father, I don't believe that he is—maybe he never was." It is painful to admit, but it's true. I tell Father everything; I admit it all.

"Have you considered there is a difference between loving someone and being in love with them?" He talks me through the confusion of the remnants of feelings for Joseph.

I listen beyond the soothing sound of his voice, to the wisdom of his words. His counsel comforts my hurting spirit and untangles my confused emotions.

"Is there anything else?" Father asks in the darkness.

Storm Surge

"There is one other thing, a duty that I must do. The person who gave me the task had no other choice, but still, I am angry with him because of it. I am selfishly thinking of myself and my feelings, rather than my duty."

Again, Father counsels.

When I finish saying the Act of Contrition and receiving absolution, Father says, "Katey, go and sin no more."

I take a quick breath at the loss of anonymity. Even in the dark, I cannot hide.

After finishing my penance, I stay in the church a long while. The quiet feels good after all of the noise in my thoughts lately. People begin to file into the church for Mass. We stand for the processional song.

~~~

The silent apartment is satisfyingly peaceful. I am glad to be home alone and have the outside world come to a halt for one evening.

~~~

Early Sunday morning, the hungry sandpipers search for breakfast while chasing the waves. The seagulls are noisily flocking on the deserted beach. Even though I haven't seen Livingston for a couple of years, I still watch for him when a flock of seagulls gather. Livingston isn't here. I suspect he is dead, but what a spirit for life he once had.

The morning slips away. Before I know it, it's time to return to the mansion. Tomorrow I start my new job. I'll put my things away and relax one more night. I might even get to bed early. My plan is to hit the floor running in the morning. I take a deep breath. I can do this.

~~~

Louise has breakfast ready when I come inside from my morning garden-walk. I am not anxious about the unknown expectations of the day. The McKenzie companies have been around for a long time. I am sure things are in place to run smoothly, and I can ease into my new duties.

After breakfast, Grandfather and I visit in the library while we wait for his secretary to arrive. She walks into the library exactly at 8:59 a.m. sharp, duty ready.
~~~

"Kathryn, I would like you to meet Mrs. Bailey.

"Mrs. Bailey, I'd like you to meet my granddaughter, Kathryn McKenzie. Get her settled."

He hasn't allowed the usual pause for the exchange of pleasantries between us.

"Yes, Mr. McKenzie." Mrs. Bailey excuses herself, turning to leave without looking in my direction or saying a word directly to me. Grandfather nods for me to follow her. She walks into a room down the hall that is obviously her office.

"These files are the companies you'll visit." She points with her ballpoint pen to a stack of files on a side table. She sits behind her desk and begins working as if I am not in the room.

When I turn away from her to see where Mrs. Bailey pointed, I mouth the word, "Visit?" The stack of files is actually two stacks of thick manila files, the shorter one hidden by the taller stack in front.

"Your schedule is in the top file," she adds.

There doesn't seem to be anywhere in this room for me to look through the files. Just as I am about to ask where I work, she looks up. "Are you still here?"

"No, ma'am!" I answer, stack all the files together, and leave with the combined stack bulging in my arms.

Clearly she enjoyed the fact that she has tossed her new boss out of her office. It seems to me that she runs her schedule with only a token gesture to Grandfather that he is in charge.

I wish I had thought to ask Grandfather where my office is. Unfortunately, there is only one solution. I return to the library with the unpleasant duty of admitting that I don't know where to go. Grandfather looks up when I enter, then goes back to reading his newspaper.

"Grandfather, where should I work?"

"Use my office. It's through that door." He nods toward the door. "Here's the key." He shifts in his wheelchair, struggles to reach into his sweater pocket and produces a key chain with a gold McKenzie medallion bobble.

"Thank you," I give him a kiss on the cheek and take the key chain. I collect the files from the nearby table.

"You'll do fine."

"Thanks," I say over my shoulder, hoping he is right.

The office is masculine, with large, heavy, dark furniture. I put the files on the empty desktop and pull the chair over from the work table since there isn't a desk chair—obviously because he is in a wheelchair. The straight-back chair isn't the right height for working comfortably at the desk, but it will do until I have a space of my own. In the event that Mrs. Bailey comes in unexpectedly, I want to be sitting behind the desk —not at the work table.

The stack of files is mountainous. I let out a deep sigh while unlocking the desk to locate a pen and a pad for taking notes.

Opening the top manila file, I am amazed to see Mrs. Bailey has scheduled me to start by traveling to two cities this week, Chicago and Memphis, and three cities next week, Hoboken, St. Paul, and Tulsa. The pen drops from my hand. The real surprise is that I am to be on Grandfather's private jet at 4:00 p.m. this afternoon!

I need coffee—lots of coffee! Louise reads minds. I smell a pot of coffee brewing long before I enter the kitchen.

Settling in with my coffee, I tackle the files again. They range in thickness from one to two inches. I flip through the next file in the stack. It contains business reports. Determined, I sort through the stack of files to locate the companies I'm scheduled to visit this week and next. The files are neither in alphabetical or geographic order, making it more difficult to locate the ones I need. The annual reports are bound, but not with the files. Is Mrs. Bailey a bit passive-aggressive?

The rest of the files get squeezed into the file cabinet for later review. I lock the cabinet and take the key. I haven't owned a briefcase for ten years. Borrowing the briefcase from the closet, I shove the files into it to take with me.

I come out of the office and lock the door behind me. I leave my annoyance inside the office. It's typical to be out of step with things in a new job. It will get better, it always does. I have to get my head clear. I have to quit burning daylight and take control of this situation.

Grandfather is in the library reading. He waves off my offer to return the office key and agrees to the use of his briefcase.

"I'll be gone the rest of the week, so I need to pack and go by my apartment to pick up a few things."

Without knowing exactly what to expect when I get to the companies, I will have to pack a wider variety of clothes than I brought to the mansion. Memphis can be cool, even in April. And most certainly, Chicago can be unexpectedly cold well into late spring.

"Have James take you, then you won't have to park at the airport."

"Thank you."

~~~

James waits patiently while I pack a few cool weather clothes. Since I haven't been on the jet, I don't know what to expect, so I fill a thermos of coffee to take with me.

James delivers me to the airport, gets my luggage and me to the jet. He tells me he will send the helicopter for me Friday night, but I decline. "I'll take a cab to my apartment and ride to the mansion with Karen on Saturday."

~~~

There is a staff of three on the plane: pilot, co-pilot, and one crew person. Not only is the McKenzie logo on the side of the plane, it's on the back of the seats, cups, and everything imaginable. It's clearly a reminder of my duty—and wealth.

Once we are airborne, I settle back and continue studying the files. The itinerary for my trip is thin. It lists where I am to be and when, but not who to meet, or what I am to do once I get there.

By the state of the company files it's apparent Mrs. Bailey went to a great deal of trouble to give me files of disorganized non-information. It looks like the pages have been deliberately disordered. I had been mistaken to assume the volume of paper was equal to the amount of information contained on them.

At least I have my laptop. When I purchased it, I was thinking only of using it on the beach. In my wildest dreams, I would have never thought I would need it in a private jet to research Alistair McKenzie's companies. The internet yields useful information, though nothing confidential. Mrs. Bailey has tripped me up this time, but she won't have power over me in the future.

Storm Surge

For the duration of the flight, I study the information from the internet and anything I can glean from the paper files. My eyes are tired, but I am better informed.

We land at Chicago's Midway Airport on the downtown side of Lake Michigan. The crew has better information than I do. We take a cab to the hotel. The flight crew has a McKenzie credit card to take care of our rooms. I put my expenses on my personal credit card, and will get reimbursed later. Mrs. Bailey "forgot" a company credit card for me.

A fax of my schedule is waiting at the concierge's desk when I check in. I don't have a meeting today after all. My meeting is at 10:00 a.m. tomorrow. Mrs. Bailey's behavior is definitely passive-aggressive. Now that I realize what she is doing, I'll just stay on top of the crucial matters. I'll get control of my schedule. I won't play her game, and I won't deliberately engage her.

After getting dressed for bed, I pull out a new diary to match my new job. I refer to my diaries "Maggie," after my best friend. It helps me to feel like I am talking things over with her by doing it this way. I could tell her anything, not that I always did—but I could have. I'll stick with what works. There will be plenty of other changes for now.

Maggie, Amid the confusion that is churning in me comes the realization that this isn't any more difficult than many other things I have done. I can do this. I would have thought by now there wasn't much that could cause me to question my ability or stamina, but this perpendicular change has done just that. Maybe if I had more desire for wealth, I would gulp in this experience. I don't want to become as harsh as Grandfather is with everyone, everyone except me. Who would guess that self-confidence is so pliable? I simply have to find the delicate balance in this and make it me, rather than make me fit it.

~~~

It's a short cab ride to the company office. They're all dusted and polished to make a good first impression. I hadn't thought about it before, but it makes sense to curry my favor. At my age, they could be stuck with me for a long time.

The meeting begins promptly, the presentation folders are well prepared and impressive. From the jet, I'd checked the stock prices for the last eighteen months. It feels like a good investment. I'm expected
~~~

to speak. Without experience in manufacturing, I speak of the future and the integrity of the McKenzie name brand—the usual pep talk melded with kudos for a job well done. They're polite, apparently genuinely so. I'm on the low end of a huge learning curve.

The crew and I catch a Cubs game, then head for Memphis where Southern hospitality comes with an easy smile. There are two McKenzie companies in Memphis, one bio-tech and the other manufacturing of technology components. Both tap into the presence of the artesian well water. The white-lab-coat-wearing scientists from the bio-tech company, younger than I'd expect, insist on Friday night out at Hollywood Disco. How retro!

Finally, it's time for the flight home. It would have been nice to know beforehand that I was scheduled to go dancing in Memphis. Oh, well. I have a new dress out of the deal. Overall, things went well. I collected information that will be useful in the future, both from my observations of the physical management of the plants and from the board of directors' meetings.

This blind date won't be repeated next week. I'll spend Sunday researching next week's companies. Mrs. Bailey won't get the best of me again.

~~~

It was great to sleep in my own bed the little bit that was left of last night. I take my coffee to the beach until Karen and Dana arrive for the trip to the mansion.

It's cool at the beach this morning. The sunrise is bright. The birds are busy competing with each other for breakfast tidbits in the morning surf. The steaming coffee tastes absolutely wonderful.

Karen and Dana arrive around 9:30 a.m. We sit on the patio while I give them the gifts I purchased on the trip. I didn't have time to shop for anything in Memphis, but I did get to the Navy Pier shops in Chicago. They both loved their silk scarves, red for Dana, and blue paisley for Karen.

I bought each of the household staff something small with "Navy Pier" written on it. I'll hand them out on Monday before I fly out for my next whirlwind week. For Grandfather, I bought a cashmere winter scarf to keep his neck warm when I wheel him around the garden.

~~~

Karen tells Dana about the mansion. They tease me that they knew me when I was a mere mortal. Very funny. I listen to Karen describe the ballroom.

Dana looks at me, astonished. "Maybe I need to find a gentleman friend and get married again, so I can dance in your ballroom."

"You are welcome to dance in the ballroom anytime, with anyone, and without something as drastic as marriage."

Married again? I repeat to myself. I didn't know Dana was married. It stands to reason, I guess. She is a beautiful, talented, intelligent woman. Her time as a bag lady, when I met her, was only a short down-on-her-luck time.

Recessions are hard on fashion designers. The fickle fashion trends here in L.A. make fashion design a volatile business. Hollywood keeps the fashion machine changing faster than the industry can keep up. But she isn't down on her luck any longer.

~~~

The drive to the mansion helps me make the transition between my two worlds. The sound of my friends laughing and talking lulls me into a satisfying calmness.

The closer we get to the mansion, the more excited Karen gets. She can hardly wait to show Dana the ballroom. I hadn't known Dana likes ballroom dancing too. Those two women are a mess, for sure!

Grandfather is gracious to my guests. He says it's nice to have young people visit. He is so cute. I'm thirty-four. Karen is about fifteen years older. I'm not sure how old Dana is. She looked older when she was a bag lady than she looks now.

The odd thing about his comment is my cousins have lived here for years. Did their friends not visit?

In anticipation of our arrival, Grandfather asked Louise to come in on Saturday and prepare lunch for us on the patio. I wonder what she thinks of working all of these Saturdays, now that I'm around. I'm sure the pay is comparable, so she won't fuss enough to go elsewhere.

I wheel him outside. He fits right in and jokes about living in the city when there is all of this space here. Maybe if Karen could stay in the ballroom, she would take him up on the offer—though they were just joking around. I can't imagine how Karen and Dana are able to wait through lunch before running up the stairs to dance in the ballroom. Somehow they do wait—not rushing Grandfather's hospitality. The idea of my friends at ease at the mansion pleases me.

As soon as Grandfather leaves for his afternoon rest, Karen is ready for the stairs. She has to see Dana's face when the ballroom lights come on. It might have been more of a surprise if Karen hadn't told Dana about it in the first place. Karen is so funny. Miss Calm, Cool, and Collected can't keep secrets very secret. Karen takes the lead up the stairs, hardly giving Dana a chance to look around as we ascend.

At the fourth-floor landing Karen grabs Dana's hand, instructs her to shut her eyes, and leads her to the French doors. I move into position
~~~

on the other side of Dana. Karen and I swing open the ballroom doors. They wait at the threshold while I turn on the main chandelier and leave the sconces around the room turned off. Karen instructs Dana to wait to open her eyes until I rejoin them.

"Now, open your eyes!" Karen lets out an excited giggle.

Dana opens her eyes mysteriously. Her gaze goes to the chandelier in the center of the ballroom.

Her mouth drops open, "Oooh, my God! Oh, MY God! How beautiful! Oh, MY GOD! Katey! Is all of this yours?"

Her eyes scan the room, taking in every detail. Her hand is on her breast as if she is certain her heart will jump out of her chest. Pointing excitedly, Dana utters "Look!" and "Oh, my God," in amazement. "Look, at the wall. Look at the place for a band. Look—"

We exchange imaginings of the parties that must have been held here. "One of the three of us has to get married and have the wedding dance here," Dana says.

"One wedding? Make that three weddings!" Karen says.

They both look at me and grin.

"We could have a dance without a wedding!" I say.

In reality, Karen is the only one dating at the moment. She and Keith are more likely to marry before Dana or me; definitely not me.

Finally Karen says, "Okay, let's see this closet of yours," ending all talk of marriages. Thank God.

We start with the gowns. Karen holds one up to me. It is a dark, royal purple. Both Karen and Dana think it is a good color for me. Dana says it needs a little altering to fit perfectly.

"Let's start a dry cleaning pile here," I say, laying the gown on the bed.

Dana holds up a red taffeta gown in front of me. "No, I think this one would look good on you, Dana," I say, taking the gown from her hand and turning it toward her. I know red is her favorite color.

Dana's expression shows she is thinking about the offer. I turn her toward the mirror. She takes the gown and holds it against her body. It is the perfect red for her ebony skin.

Karen agrees and we convince Dana to accept the gift.

"Now, Karen, you need to pick out a dress," I say.

"Take that one and try it." Dana points at a dress.

"Turquoise? Really?" Karen asks.

I have never seen Karen wear turquoise, but I think Dana is correct. It's the gown she first noticed last week when we were in the closet. The turquoise does look good next to her skin when Karen holds it up.

"Who wants the white sequined one?" I ask.

Storm Surge

They hesitate.

"White looks horrible on me—someone speak up," I say.

So go the rest of the gowns. Next, we go through the rest of the clothes.

The shoes are to die for, but none fit us. The vintage ones would have been fun to wear with the vintage outfits, but we put them in a box to give to the nuns at St. Mark's for the homeless women. Won't they be stepping out in style! That should be good for their self-esteem, wearing Mrs. McKenzie's expensive shoes. Or maybe a benefit auction? I'll let Mother Elizabeth decide that question.

The afternoon drifts away. Karen and Dana decline a dinner invitation and leave. Karen takes the gowns we have selected to keep, to drop them at the cleaners. She will have them delivered to Dana, who has measured both of us in every possible way one can be measured —no wonder her gowns fit perfectly and are so popular.

~~~

Grandfather went to his room early again tonight. The cousins are still away. I don't know where they are or when they will return.

Frankly, I am relieved that they aren't here, and it would be fine with me if they didn't return for a few weeks, enough time for me to get settled before dealing with Brooke's sarcasm.

The live-in staff are in their rooms or out for the evening—I don't know which. As best as I can tell, I have the house to myself, if you can call this a house. Might as well start working on next week's files since there isn't really anything else to do after I finish putting away my things.

By the time I finish unpacking, I rethink my earlier decision to work awhile. I'm too tired to work. In addition to setting boundaries with the staff, I need to set them for myself. I'll work tomorrow, but not tonight. It is too bad I can't go to the beach for a walk. A walk in Juan's garden with a fresh cup of coffee will have to do.

The roses are beautiful in the moonlight. Juan really has a way with them. I am not sure what all of the other flowers are. I recognize some of them. There are blue campanula, my mother's favorite. How funny. The man who kept my mother out of his life has her favorite flower in his garden. We are all connected to one another, more than we know.

There is a brisk breeze coming off of the ocean from below the cliffs on the other side of the highway. I snap my Dodgers jacket closed and wrap my fingers around my hot cup to warm my hands.

I love Grandfather dearly, but I don't want to become like him. I don't want to become cruel with a stony heart just because I have power and wealth. It will take constant vigilance to make sure I don't slip down that road—down Grandfather's road.
~~~

~~~

Morning comes too early. I follow my emerging routine: a cup of coffee and a walk in the garden before breakfast. It is still cool out, but the rising sun is promising a warm spring day. If I am going to maintain my identity, then I can't alter my religious practices just because Grandfather has no use for "heathen" Catholics. He has never said anything to me about religion, and I don't plan to wave my faith in his face, but I am going to Mass in town this morning.

When I return, Grandfather is reading the Sunday paper in the library.

"Good morning, Grandfather," I say, as I move behind him and reach around the side of his wheelchair to give him a kiss on the cheek and a hug around the neck.

"Good morning, Kathryn." He lays the paper in his lap. "How was your week?"

"It was good. Hectic. I learned a lot, though." I still haven't figured out if Mrs. Bailey's sabotage was part of his lessons or if he even knows what she is really like. I don't mention her influence in my experience. Most certainly, I am not going to whine about her treatment of me, but I am going to figure out if Grandfather had a role in this.

"What do you have planned for today, Kathryn?"

"I am reviewing the files of the companies I am visiting this week."

"Sometimes you have to put in the hours on weekends. I can't tell you it will ever get easier."

Maybe so, but this job does not warrant my weekend attention in the way that emergency child abuse investigations did. Grandfather probably won't understand, and I don't care to attempt to explain it.

"Do you mind if I work in here with you?"

"No, work where you like." He appears uninterested and goes back to reading his paper.

"I'm going to get a cup of coffee, do you want one?"

"No, thank you." He doesn't look away from his paper, as if I am a pesky intrusion. His loss.

After a couple of hours reading the files, I can't focus any longer. I lay down my pen and rub my eyes. This is tedious work. I need to think a minute.

Grandfather likes trial by fire. Is that what Mrs. Bailey's game is? Is she acting on his instructions to test me or my stamina, or is she just an old witch? Is he aware of what is going on? I have no idea, and this guessing game is pointless. It takes too much energy to be reactive. I need to stay sharp and be proactive.

"Grandfather, I need your help."
~~~

He lays down his paper, his eyes twinkle. "I wondered when you would ask." He wheels himself to the table. "Let me see what you have there."

Sheesh, why didn't I think of this before? I tell him what I've done and where I've been, my flight schedule for this week, which companies I am visiting, and which files I have studied thus far.

"Who set this up?" He sounds annoyed.

"I thought you did."

"No, this is an inefficient use of your time. You can tour the facilities later." He controls his anger quite well. He clears his throat. "Get your tablet, take notes."

I feel relieved to have his help. I'm thankful I spoke up rather than operate on assumptions of his involvement in Mrs. Bailey's mischief— an assumption that was 100 percent wrong.

"These are our manufacturing holdings..." He lists the companies from memory. "These are banking and finance..."

For nearly an hour he lists categories and the companies within each category. I start to take a drink of my coffee, but my cup is empty. He notices the depleted coffee and suggests we take a break.

When we come back to work, our break is definitely over. Grandfather turns to me squarely.

"Tomorrow, tell Mrs. Bailey to cancel all of your appointments until further notice, and to give you a list of all companies who are bidding government contracts this quarter, and all companies who currently have government contracts. And tell her to have them on your desk by noon. When she gives the lists to you, tell her you want this year's budget and current stock prices for the public companies. And, Kathryn, never let an employee run your agenda again—make it perfectly clear you are in charge."

I don't want to miss a word. I stop taking notes and listen intensely, studying his face, while he gives me a well-deserved management lesson. When he stops, I take a quick drink of coffee.

"Tell her to have the budgets by two o'clock. When she brings them, tell her that you want a list of the CEOs as well as the members of the board of directors for each company in these files by noon on Tuesday." He smiles. "Let her know who is in charge." He winks.

"Thank you for your help," I say tenderly.

"Don't wait so long to ask next time," he grumps the words. This man has a reputation for ruthlessness, and it is well deserved, but he isn't comfortable when I get sappy-sentimental with him. He has no idea of the depth of my appreciation.

~~~
~~~

CHAPTER 6

Moving Up to the Major Leagues

As usual, I follow my morning routine in the gardens, complete with a cup of coffee and my Dodgers jacket. When I come into the house, Mrs. Bailey is in the kitchen with Louise, Eleanor, and James. Usually, I'm getting dressed by now and miss the meeting in the kitchen, but today I arrive during their morning briefing.

The conversation stops abruptly when I enter. That can mean only one of two things: either they were talking about me or they were saying something they didn't want me to hear. I feel their eyes follow me across the room for a refill of coffee.

As I walk up the back stairs, the servant's stairs, I hear them resume the conversation. If they were talking about me, I'm not going to assume that it was bad.

Once the day officially begins, I approach Mrs. Bailey pleasantly, but firmly (if not confidently), with the directives Grandfather outlined yesterday. I had rehearsed with my notes before facing her, and execute the directives flawlessly.

Mrs. Bailey is not receptive to my requests. She doesn't say anything directly to me, but if looks could kill—I'd be dead. I know change is difficult at her age. I leave her to slam her file cabinet drawers in private. She'd better enjoy it, she isn't always going to get this luxury.

This only serves to further accent the contrast with this place and Spirit of Hope. Sister Theresa would never treat Mother Elizabeth the way Mrs. Bailey treats me.

~~~

A quick call to Mother Elizabeth is the perfect remedy for my homesickness. It hasn't been that long, but I am suffering from withdrawal symptoms, separation anxiety. It seems much longer; maybe, a lifetime.

Mother Elizabeth doesn't hide her delight in hearing from me. I'm shamelessly pleased to feel loved. I think about the antics with the Spirit of Hope kids on the playground and anything that
~~~

has to do with little Shasta; the client's triumphs, large and small; and the nuns—they were much different from how I viewed them as a child in school. What an enjoyable place to work, a perfect example for me to follow.

Now I can return to reviewing the information I collected from Grandfather's mentoring yesterday. My eyes are tired from the excessive reading lately. I guess I'll have to bite the bullet and get an eye exam for reading glasses. I make the call. The receptionist has a cancellation for tomorrow morning, so I take it. The sooner I get glasses, the better.

~~~

Mrs. Bailey delivers the first set of reports an hour earlier than the deadline. I praise her, then request the next items on the list. She is almost timid, like she doesn't seem sure how to take this upheaval in her domain, but she probably will be way ahead of me again before long. Although, she might feel the familiarity of Grandfather in the background coaching me.

By midafternoon, I conclude that reading reports is terribly boring, not to mention my brain has turned to mush. I'm well aware that at seventy-four, Grandfather has me beat, but I'll get up to speed as soon as I get my glasses. Just watch me.

~~~

While it is unlikely that one week of intense reading caused enough eyestrain to require reading glasses, it brought it to my attention. Now, I will be able to look over my glasses at people, like Mother Elizabeth does with her half-glasses, but my glasses will be cooler than hers.

After my eye appointment, I stop by Mr. Bradford's office. Obviously, I run to him because he is a connection, albeit a loose one, to my parents. Perhaps a third-party opinion to this situation is a good idea.

"I heard the announcement. How's that working out?"

"Truthfully, I don't know. I feel like a rookie."

"Are you the CEO of any of the companies?" He asks a point I haven't considered.

"Oh I hope not!" I gasp. "I'm in over my head as it is. I need help sorting out all of these companies. I can't even begin to formulate the legal questions that are sure to come. My schedule is out of control. I inherited the secretary from hell!" I blurt out an immense amount of frustration.

"Kathryn, I don't have the time to help you with a project like this," he says bluntly.

And truly, I have known all along that Mr. Bradford is swamped with his work and continues to manage my trust accounts only because of a long-ago friendship with my parents. Still, I am disappointed.

"I need someone I can trust."

"There is a young lawyer who works for me part-time. I'd highly recommend him."

I study Mr. Bradford for a moment. "You really trust him, don't you?"

He nods, "Yes, I think he has promise, quite sharp."

"Then, that's good enough for me," I agree, sure that Mr. Bradford would never steer me wrong.

The lawyer is Sam Jackson. I remember the name from when I was looking for Judge Jones' law clerk on the quest to find his daughter. Mr. Bradford calls Sam and passes the phone to me after a brief conversation.

It sounds like Sam is interested in talking about working for me. We arrange for a meeting at the mansion tomorrow morning. Apparently, he doesn't have much of a practice or he wouldn't have the time to do the things I outlined, especially on such short notice.

After the phone call, I get advice on the fee to expect from Sam. Until I feel it is a good working situation, I'll give Mr. Jackson one project at his hourly rate, which is considerably less than Mr. Bradford's rate. If it works out for both of us, I will offer him a permanent retainer.

~~~

It is midafternoon, so I spend the night at my apartment again. I talk Karen into coming over for dinner, Chinese takeout, but late, to accommodate her schedule. I have plenty of time for a stop by St. Marks on the way home, and still have a solitary walk on the beach before Karen arrives.

I am reminded of the first time I stood at St. Mark's door. This time, I walk in rather than knock. When Sister Theresa sees
~~~

me, she rushes to give me a quick hug, which is quite different from our first meeting.

It is painfully obvious, I have moved to visitor status now. I am treated to warm cookies fresh from the oven with my coffee. I feel a tearful fondness toward these people, but I don't cry.

Soon the nuns prepare for Evening Prayers, leaving me alone. Mother Elizabeth comes from her meeting. She invites me to Evening Prayers. This time isn't as awkward as the first time. I enjoy the singing and the prayers. Mother and I visit for a short while before she leaves for mealtime. I've waved off the invitation, but imagine it to be much like it was for Whoopi Goldberg in *Sister Act*.

At least it was a momentary diversion. Evening Prayers gave me a curiously delightful mood to take to the beach. Little does Mother Elizabeth know—or maybe she does know—I needed this today.

~~~

The man in his car reading his newspaper is here again. He is almost a regular now. Wonder what his story is? He looks up as I cross the street, so I wave, "Hello."

He nods and almost smiles. His presence is certainly curious.

The water is rough. The spring storm off the coast of Baja California is violently churning north, which is unusual. It is easy for me to identify with the ocean's restlessness. The two weeks since Grandfather made his announcement have been a churning mass of emotions for me.

Nearly everyone is off the beach. As I walk to the estuary with the sound of the sisters' voices playing through my mind, it isn't long before my steps are into the rhythm of the waves. The breakers are running high up the beach. The heavily misted air feels good on my face. The wind tugs on my jacket. In the strangest way it is almost as if the beach has missed me as much as I've missed her.

~~~

Since it is Karen's turn to bring the food, I have lingered on the beach long enough to walk off my uncertainty. The days of walking the beach with Mr. Goldstein are in my thoughts as I walk home. I miss walking with him. I miss our conversations and his counsel. But he is happy in Austria, and I have made peace with his relocation.

Karen arrives as I cross the street back to my apartment. We walk together from the parking lot. The aroma from the packages make me hungry. The wind has turned colder and it's good to get back inside. I start the coffee and get out the dishes while Karen unpacks the wire-handled cartons.

"I didn't get a chance to ask, how did last week go?"

"I was completely out of my element. It would have been easier if Grandfather's secretary had been helpful. It might be a little strong, but the word 'sabotage' comes to mind." I smile, but there isn't anything humorous about Mrs. Bailey.

Karen squints. "Okay, what did she do?"

"It wasn't so much what she did, as what she didn't do. I had enough information to barely get by, but getting by isn't enough in my position." I attempt to explain the problem, but now it sounds a little lame saying it out loud.

"You want someone who plays on your team. None of the passive-aggressive nonsense, right?"

"Yes! Exactly. I want useful information and I don't want to wonder what has been withheld. I don't have time for power games."

"I have just the person you are looking for—Zoe."

"Zoe?"

"Yes, Zoe. She is my right arm."

"Then, why don't you keep her?"

"She is perfect—young, energetic, takes direction well, smart."

"Karen," I stop her glowing endorsement. "Why aren't you keeping her?"

"I'm not letting her go. She's the best secretary I've ever had, but she is looking for another job. Our reports are too graphic. She can't take typing them." Karen stops for a bite of her food. "She can type like the wind." She takes another bite. "I lean against her desk and dictate letters. In a day she can crank out a week's worth of correspondence."

Karen looks squarely at me, "Katey, you won't be sorry if you hire her."

There seems to be a pattern in Karen's unofficial job placement service. Karen must have talked to Mother Elizabeth, despite what Mother said. Nonetheless, I'm sure that Mother Elizabeth made the final decision.

I agree with Karen's assessment. "Have her call me, if she's interested."

"There is one catch. Her anniversary is a month away. If she stays until then, she will accrue another week of vacation."

"Okay. I can live with that."

~~~

I deliberately get up early to have a sunrise walk on the beach before I head to the mansion. The storm is gone. There are glimpses of daylight peeking through the clearing cloud cover. The tide has crested and is beginning to move out to some other beach.

I hardly notice the trip back to the mansion. I am looking forward to meeting with Mr. Jackson. Maybe we can figure out a way to help me "step up to the plate." My mind is busy defining exactly what I need him to do. What task would be the best test of his skills and our ability to work together?

~~~

The scene at the mansion is just as though I never left. God bless Louise, she keeps fresh coffee brewing all day long.

Grandfather is reading by the window in the library. I didn't know Grandfather McKenzie when I was young, but my other grandfather would sit in his big burgundy chair by his window and read the Sunday comics aloud, complete with different voices for each character. He was a man who made each of his twenty-seven grandchildren feel special.

On the other hand, Grandfather McKenzie has only four grand-children and has known me for less than five years—by his own choice. And where are his other grandchildren? I have been here two weeks and no one has mentioned them.

Mrs. Bailey announces, "There is a Mr. Jackson here to see you."

"Thank you, Mrs. Bailey."

"You know, he doesn't have an appointment," she quips.

He does have an appointment, but I don't bother to tell her.

Nadine Laman

"Hello, Mr. Jackson. Let's go in my office."

"Thank you, Miss McKenzie."

"Tell me a little about yourself, Mr. Jackson."

"I have an MBA in addition to my JD." He smiles. We both know he has this job pegged.

I like his succinct answer. He's right. An MBA is more useful to me at the moment than his law degree. Still, it's good to have an in-house lawyer. Maybe Grandfather has a firm of lawyers. I don't know. I do know that I want one of my own on *my* team.

I hire him on the spot. Negotiating the terms is quick. I give him the stack of files Mrs. Bailey gave me. Just to find out how he thinks, I don't give him specific directions—only that we will meet tomorrow afternoon to discuss his impressions.

With Mr. Jackson using the office, I go to check my messages. Mrs. Bailey is on the phone. There is a pink envelope with my name on it in her trash basket. She eyes me when I lift the envelope out of the trash. There is a wadded piece of pink paper under the envelope. I deliberately straighten the paper on the corner of her desk. Mrs. Bailey stops talking and the phone drops from her mouth.

I read the note as I walk out of the room.

Dear Katey:

    I don't know if you remember me. You traded airline tickets with me, so I could stay longer in Ireland.

    I had a wonderful time, but I didn't know how to reach you to tell you, "thank you" for your kindness until I saw your name in the newspaper.

    Enclosed is a photo of us in Ireland, along with a small token of my appreciation.

            Sincerely ~

            Gwen

Yes, I remember Gwen, the ultimate tourist. I double-check the envelope—no photo. Wonder what else she sent? I can't believe Mrs. Bailey opened my personal mail. I'll put a stop to this. Homicide comes to mind.

When I reenter her office, Mrs. Bailey is off the phone. She jumps into action shuffling the papers on her desk. Oh, really? Nervous? Who would have guessed?

"Mrs. Bailey, where are the things that came with this letter?" I ask as calmly as if I was asking for the phone book.

She fusses with the papers on her desk, then reaches in the bottom drawer and hands me a photo, a business card, and a beautiful silk scarf.

"Mrs. Bailey, starting now, I will open all of the mail: personal, and otherwise." I look her in the eye. "Understand?"

"Yes, Miss McKenzie," she says with a tone that poorly hides the indignation in her voice.

I hang the scarf around my neck and put the photo and business card along with the note inside the envelope. Ah, coffee.

While I am pouring a cup of brew, my cell phone rings.

"Katey, are you sitting down?"

"No, not really. What's up, Karen?"

"Keith just brought me a copy of one of the tabloids from the grocery checkout counter. I think you need to see this!"

"Why do I need to see it?" I never read that stuff.

"Your picture is on the cover: 'NUN has alien baby' is the headline!"

"What! You're kidding. This is a joke, isn't it?"

"No, really. Go get a copy. The picture of you isn't all that bad." Clearly at my expense, she laughs devilishly.

Oh, great! She has to be kidding. "Okay, I'll get a copy. I need a break anyway."

~~~
~~~

CHAPTER 7

Aliens and Yachts—I Need More Coffee!

The lady in front of me in the checkout line picks up a supermarket rag. I peer over her shoulder at the front page. It is definitely a photo of me in the habit. The woman says, "Kathryn McKenzie probably isn't having an affair with an extraterrestrial."

The other people in line laugh. The conversation becomes a group project.

Another lady says, "I have no sympathy for that spoiled little rich girl."

My cheeks suddenly feel hot.

The checker notices the resemblance between the photo and me. Of course, I deny everything. "Do I look like a nun?" I ask and top it off with cheesy smile.

"You could be the model they used for the picture."

I soften my tone. "Thanks, but I'm not a model." I laugh again and pick up a couple of packs of gum. I've seen what I came to see, no need to purchase the paper. They will have to do without my money.

~~~

Mrs. Bailey flags me down as I come in the kitchen door. Looks like the whole staff has been watching for me to return. She has an urgent phone message. I really hope this isn't about the photo.

No, it's an international number. "Please, make the call. I'll take it in the office." I grab a cup of coffee to take with me.

Within minutes, she comes into the office and shuts the door behind her. Her face is pale. She discovered something more than my latest encounter with extraterrestrials.

"Frank, the McKenzie media manager, says that he found a Mediterranean newspaper headline that reads: 'Kathryn Headed for Disaster!'"

First, I didn't know there was a McKenzie media manager. Secondly, this seems a bit over the top about extraterrestrials.
~~~

"I'm afraid I don't understand." Acting like Mother Elizabeth, I look over my glasses to encourage her to elaborate.

Reading from her notes she says, with desperation in her voice, "The newspaper reported—on a path to destruction."

"Mrs. Bailey, I'm not following you." I try my best not to dismiss this entire conversation as ridiculous and give her one more chance to make her point.

"Brooke and Tim are on the yacht. The article is about their behaviors on the *Kathryn!*" There is heightened panic in her voice the minute she mentions Brooke and Tim.

"There is a boat named *Kathryn* and the cousins are on it?" The picture is beginning to emerge. "This is probably something you should tell Grandfather."

"No, ma'am," she says emphatically. "I'm not telling Mr. McKenzie about this! And, it isn't a 'boat,' it's a 268-foot yacht off the west coast of Africa!"

She is in a full-bloom panic, wanting me to fix it, and fix it fast before Grandfather finds out about it.

"Okay, I will take care of it. Thank you." I come to her side, gently take the note from her hand, and open the office door for her exit. I thought about touching her shoulder as I showed her out, to comfort or calm her. I refrained, deciding that it was too soon to soften after setting boundaries.

I don't blame her for not wanting to tell Grandfather. No sane person would want to tell him. Damn, those cousins. What have they gotten themselves into now? What about Danny? Is he with them?

This sounds like a good job for Mr. Jackson's counsel. I open the door and walk into the library as if I am passing through. Grandfather has his wheelchair moved closer to the window.

Mr. Jackson doesn't look up from his work. I had hoped to catch his eye and motion for him to join me.

"I'm going for coffee, do you need a break?"

He mumbles a distracted, "No thanks," and scribbles a note.

Damn! Changing course slightly, I pass close to his table and tap it quietly. "Sure?"

He looks up, then lays down his pen.

I give a "look," hoping he gets that I want him to follow me.

He hesitates enough that I'm sure I am going to have to be more verbal. Damn! We need a code word for the times I don't want to say much in front of Grandfather.

Mr. Jackson finally gets the hint and gets up. "Yeah, I think I do need a break." He stretches as he says it. Not an award-winning performance, but he joins me.

We step into the hallway where I tell him what I know. I give him Frank's phone number and ask him to figure out what is going on. I'd like to make a suggestion about the solution, maybe excommunication? After he gets back to me, I'll decide whether or what to tell Grandfather.

Mrs. Bailey is watching from her desk. She motions us to the door when I notice her. She whispers, "You can use this phone."

She drives me nuts, but she seems so vulnerable at this moment that I smile at her. "Come take a break with me, Mrs. Bailey. Let's let the gentleman have the room to himself."

She practically leaps up and is gone, beating me to the kitchen in record time.

Aliens and yachts—just what I need.

It isn't exactly the sinking of the *Titanic*, but I have no desire to go down with the ship or, ah, the yacht. A yacht? For God's sake, what are we doing with a yacht?

This sounds like a typical Brooke escapade. She is about thirty-two; it's time she grows up. I don't even know what to do with Tim. I think he has a bigger problem than his drinking. Again, where is Daniel?

Mrs. Bailey pulls up a chair at the kitchen table where the staff holds court. She and Eleanor exchange looks. Louise looks up from her food prep work and joins the two at the table.

I pour a cup of coffee and join the staff. Another round of wordless glances ensues. My engagement efforts are met with one word terminal answers.

I'm about to pour my second cup when Mr. Jackson comes into the kitchen.

"Coffee?" I hoist the pot in his direction.

He's getting wise that the question is more than about coffee. "Yes, thanks."

"Let's take our coffee outside."

He nods.

Once the door is closed and we have cleared the patio, a good bit away from the house, I ask, "What do we have going on?"

"The yacht's home port is on the French Riviera. The captain filed that they'd be out for a couple of months with no specific destination. They've been out for three weeks, wreaking havoc everywhere they go, especially in the Mediterranean port cities."

"Havoc? Do I want to know the details?"

"No, ma'am. You don't want the details," he says. "Remember the Reagan years?"

"No."

He grins, "Deny-ability!"

"They partied around the Med until they were run off by one government after another. Now, an island government is threatening to seize the yacht." He turns his tablet around, so I can read his notes, and points to their location.

"Okay. Do I have the authority to intervene, or do I have to take this to Grandfather?"

"I want to call Mr. Bradford. I think if you can handle it, you should. It is a real mess. Mr. McKenzie won't be happy."

"And, neither am I. Go ahead; call Mr. Bradford. I'll call—who is it that I need to speak with on the island?" I look at his notes again and pull out my cell phone.

"Hello, this is Miss Kathryn McKenzie. I understand we have a common problem with the McKenzie yacht. Yes, I'll wait." I sip my coffee, poised for a response from someone in charge on the other end of the phone.

Mr. Jackson finishes his call to Mr. Bradford and writes a note on his tablet, then turns it my direction so I can read it right-side up.

I set my coffee on the sundial and write back, "the McKenzie family—not the business?"

He whispers, "No, YOU, Kathryn McKenzie—NOT the family, and not McKenzie Enterprises!"

Our eyes meet. I stare at him in amazement. It's my boat? That certainly simplifies things. I can do what I want and don't have to ask Grandfather's permission.

"Please hold for the Prince," a voice says on my phone.

"Your Highness, I'm Kathryn McKenzie. Thank you for speaking with me. How can I help with this problem my cousins are causing?"

The voice on the phone is very polite and formal. A soft and gentle voice, but sure of itself.

"I see. Very well. I am sure the captain and crew had no culpability in the matter. I will guarantee the payment of fines for the captain and crew, if you will let them take the boat back to its home port. As for the others on board, they are yours. They can answer to your laws, then find their own way home." Let's just say, I'm steamed. They better take the slow route home.

"Yes, I understand. Yes, your Navy has my permission to board the boat, um, the vessel. We have been unable to reach the captain, could you have him contact me as soon as your people are on board? I'll be at this number until I hear from you." I conclude the conversation by giving him my cell phone number. I don't want these calls going through Mrs. Bailey. He was very polite, but we both know he didn't need my permission to do anything.

Mr. Jackson looks at me, wanting information, but he doesn't ask for it. I have something more important to do than have a discussion with him. I turn toward the house in search of Mrs. Bailey. She's still in the kitchen with the breakfast meeting group. She makes clear her loyalties to Brooke. I know she has no loyalty to me, not even now.

I interrupt quietly. "Brooke and Tim have gotten into trouble. I want no one, absolutely no one, to mention it to Grandfather. Keep the televisions off the news stations. Mrs. Bailey, check the morning paper before you give it to him tomorrow, and bring Conner up to speed."

They stare at me as if they are about to fall asleep from boredom.

"The paper isn't my job," Mrs. Bailey informs me.

"It is now. Mr. McKenzie is to know nothing about this. Nothing, *THAT* is your job. Protect Mr. McKenzie." I correct her publically because she questioned me publically. I make eye contact with each of them. Mr. Jackson is somewhere behind me me. But I don't look to him on this matter. They are my staff, whether they like it or not.

I hear a weak, "Yes, ma'am," just as I walk out.

I go to Mrs. Bailey's office and look through the file cabinets for anything about this yacht. Her files are nicely organized, but I don't find anything. I'll have to get the info from Mr. Bradford. I head to my office, where Mr. Jackson is scribbling quick notes on a legal pad.

"Mr. Jackson, how about another walk in the garden?" I ask, expecting he understands now this isn't really a question requiring an answer.

He takes the hint. "Please, call me Sam. I'll pass on the coffee this time, but the walk sounds good."

I pick up my cell phone and take it with me. I have lots of questions for Sam.

"How bad is my liability, Sam?" How did the boat get put in my name? How long have I owned it? What's Brooke and Tim doing partying around the Mediterranean with a boatload of— who are those people?

"You have the liability of owning the yacht, but I think we can prove you didn't give them permission to use it or had any knowledge of ownership." He checks his notes. "They were on board before the announcement. As your trustee, Mr. Bradford should have been notified, but wasn't. I think Mr. McKenzie is clever enough to claim deniability. I think we're all okay on this"... his voice trails off.

It is obvious the lawyer wheels are turning in his head, but he doesn't elaborate.

"I see." I look up at him. He's going to be worth every penny.

The phone rings, startling me by vibrating in my hand. "Hello, this is Kathryn McKenzie."

I can hear someone speaking French.

"Parlez-vous anglais?" I ask the voice on the phone. Apparently not. I turn to Sam, "Sam, do you speak French?"

"I am rusty, but I'll give it a try." He takes the phone.

"Ask if any of the crew speaks English," I suggest.

He is right. His French is rudimentary—about as good as my Spanish. We're doomed if none of the crew speaks English.

"The navigator speaks some English," Sam says as he hands me the phone.

"This is Kathryn McKenzie. Hello? Yes." A pause. "I am Kathryn McKenzie. No, I am her granddaughter. Yes, I own the ship. You have been boarded by the local authorities? Navy? All right. Cooperate with them. Right. Yes. Please, tell the captain I have arranged for his and the crew's release." I hear muffled French as he speaks to someone there. "Take the boat back to its berth. Notify me when you arrive." More muffled speaking as he translates my words to the captain. "Thank you, and tell the captain, 'Thank you' for me."

Turning to Sam, "I want Brooke, Tim, and their friends to find their own way home. If they have a McKenzie Enterprise credit card, I want it canceled immediately. And, anything in my name, cancel it. I am not condoning their behavior, and I am not bailing them out of this mess." My tone is more revealing than I'd like, but this really takes the cake.

Sam nods understanding.

"Do we know where Danny is?" I move to the next item on my mental list.

"No, I haven't found anything on him yet." He surprises me that he was one step ahead of me.

~~~

When we return to the house, I fill my coffee cup and go check for messages. Mrs. Bailey doesn't see me at first. She's on the phone.

"Brooke, dear. We'll get you out of this." Mrs. Bailey looks uneasy when she sees me. I reach for the phone. She hesitantly gives it to me.

"Brooke, this is Kathryn. No, no, I am not going to bail you out of jail. Go ahead, ask Grandfather if you want. No, I'm sending the ship home." She hangs up on me after describing me with a string of hyphenated "colorful adjectives."

There is no point in telling Mrs. Bailey not to accept calls from Brooke or Tim. I can tell by the tone she is fond of her. I might be out of a job when Grandfather finds what I have done, but I am going to do what I think is right. Besides, I wouldn't mind being fired. I bet Mother Elizabeth will hire me.
~~~

Storm Surge

Sam is talking to the island authorities again. When he ends the conversation, I tell him, "We'll pay the crew severance pay when they get the ship back to port, no doubt they put up with plenty. Make arrangements to sell the yacht to pay the fines and the crew. Don't spend a dime on Brooke, Tim, or their friends."

"They found drugs on board. Brooke and Tim are facing up to fifteen years in prison."

"Oh crap! Any chance they were in international waters?"

"I'll find someone who can talk with the captain."

"Let Brooke and Tim stay in jail until we sort this out. At least we'll know where they are."

"Tim has already assaulted one of the officers."

"Oh, great! Do you want to work tomorrow?"

Sam nods.

"Would you take my cell phone home with you tonight? Just add it to your bill."

I haven't had much time to spend with Grandfather. I ask him about getting two cell phones for work; one for Mr. Jackson, and the other for me. I'll keep my personal phone for personal calls.

Grandfather says to call the finance office and arrange for a credit card, cell phones, a voucher to reimburse my travel expenses from last week, and some petty cash.

I ask Sam to pick up the phones on his way to work in the morning. I'll get reimbursed later. So far, this new job is costing me nothing but headaches and money. Damn, speaking of headaches. I need to take something for my headache.

Before bed, I write in my diary to help clear my mind and organize my thoughts. The only good thing about Maggie's death is she isn't here to torment me about my current circumstance. She would have enjoyed teasing me about owning a yacht.

Maggie, I'm exhausted. I feel the sobering effect of responsibility descending upon me. I must find the strength to hold on to who I am, and to wear the title, "Kathryn the Great." There are so many things I need to set straight. Where do I begin?

~~~

When I come from my morning walk, Conner is wheeling Grandfather to the dining room for breakfast. He invites me to
~~~

join him and I accept. After we're settled and the food has been served, I turn to say, "Good morning, Grandfather," but he speaks over me.

"Brooke and Tim are on their way home."

Well, what can I say? He knows, but how much does he know? Who told him? Did he bail them out? I just look at him and smile sweetly. I am keeping my mouth shut.

He eyes my Dodgers jacket hanging on the back of my chair. He takes another bite of scrambled eggs, then wipes his mouth with his linen napkin.

"Baseball fan?"

"Yes, the Dodgers are playing Friday night, do you want to go with me?"

"No, I'm an Angels fan." He resumes eating.

That explains why everyone stopped talking when I came in the room wearing a Dodgers jacket. It's humorous how the staff worry about my jacket. I don't think Grandfather is going to fire me for not being an Angels fan, but the Brooke and Tim issue might just do the trick. Shall I pack?

"I'm giving you James as your driver."

I know he means he is assigning James to drive for me, but I don't like his choice of words. He makes it sound like he owns James. Maybe I am just being sensitive because James is Black. Would I find his words as offensive if James was White? I think it over. Yeah, I would find it offensive, but I don't think he understands the implications, or maybe he simply thinks he is superior to all of us.

"Where's Danny?" I ask, risking a mention of the yacht.

"He is visiting his parents at that damn commune they live in. His mother had surgery, and he is helping with her care." He says it as if I knew about the "damn" commune.

~~~

Waiting for my turn at the coffee pot, I think about Danny with his parents while his mother has surgery and the other two off raising hell halfway around the world. The surgery must have been serious for Danny to be gone so long. I wonder if they need anything—any help from us? I wonder if I should offer, or wait it out and see what comes.
~~~

Sam comes in, picks up a cup, and gets in line behind me. I fill his cup while I have the pot in my hand, then introduce him to the breakfast crowd. He smiles at James.

"Hello, son," James says to Sam.

"Son? Why didn't you tell me James is your father?" I ask Sam, amazed by this well-kept secret.

"James? His name is Garrett." He seems surprised.

"Garrett?"

"Mr. McKenzie liked to say, 'Home, James,' and it stuck. My name is Garrett. I'm named after Garrett Morgan, the Black man who invented traffic signals in 1923."

I thought about who invented traffic lights. I wonder if there is a familial relationship, but I don't ask.

"Then, I will call you 'Garrett' and so will everyone else." Then I look at the breakfast-board-meeting group.

"Me, too," says Louise, followed with a stout laugh.

"Anyone else have an alias?"

"Honey, you wouldn't want to call me my other name." Louise grins widely.

Okay, I'll bite, "Louise, what is your other name?"

"Honey Bum, my Edgar calls me, Honey Bum." Louise laughs. "He's a Black Brit, you know."

Well no, I didn't know she was married to a Brit. I smile while the others laugh at my expense. No, I am not touching that one. She has a very ornery side to her. Besides, Sam and I need to get to work and discuss the yacht incident.

~~~

Sam had received a call in the middle of the night. Brooke's friend's parents sprang for everyone's bail and purchased their airline tickets. At least, Grandfather didn't bail them out. That is certainly interesting.

"The yacht is in your name, because it was purchased with your money."

"My money? Are you sure?" I don't understand how a yacht was purchased with my money. I have a headache. Literally, I have a headache. It has to be stress or the new glasses.

"It's complicated. Let me get a report written with the details for you."
~~~

~~~

Sam goes to work. I talk to Eleanor about an office for Sam. I know I can do what I want, but I think for now it is a good strategy to let her keep her place as the Mistress of the Manor.

Eleanor shows me three rooms, each perfect for offices, two on the second floor and one on the main floor. I select the main floor office for Sam because we are going to be running back and forth from each other's office until we get things figured out and settled down. Maybe eventually Sam will work downtown and not have to make the daily commute to the mansion. Maybe someday I can do the same and move back to my beach.

Sam tells me he has an idea. His plan involves hiring a computer whiz. A "geek named Chico" to get all of the McKenzie Enterprises information on a database and organized in a usable format for me—not at all like the files Mrs. Bailey set up. I agree about Mrs. Bailey's files, but Chico?

Let's review this: There is a Chinese gardener named Juan Garcia Li, because his non-English speaking, emigrant parents wanted their son to have an American name; a driver not named James; and I am not even going to ask about Honey Bum! Chico? This place is like a very bad, B-rated movie. And Mrs. Bailey is the innocent-seeming star.

~~~

Brooke and Tim are on their way home. I have another headache. Nothing over the counter seems to work on my head. How long did they say it would take to adjust to these glasses?

"Miss McKenzie, the press is ready in the library," Mrs. Bailey announces.

"What! Who scheduled that?"

"Frank. He thought you should answer questions about the yacht." She doesn't seem to think that anything is wrong with Frank's action.

Grandfather is nowhere in sight. I catch Sam's eye as he is coming out of the office and tilt my head for him to follow me.

~~~

This place is out of control. I straighten my skirt, button my jacket, and take a deep breath before entering the library— confidently, with a camera-ready smile.
~~~

I quickly move near the podium that has been set up. Sam takes up a position at the back of the room, directly in front of me. Good move, Sam! Cameras begin to flash in my eyes.

"Ladies and Gentlemen. As you know by now, I am Kathryn McKenzie. First, let me clear up the rumors. I have never had an alien boyfriend!"

Subdued laughter comes from a few of the reporters who get what I'm talking about.

"I have begun to tour the McKenzie holdings. In the coming weeks, I will continue to familiarize myself with the family business." I continue with the usual stuff about McKenzie Enterprises and feel pretty good about what I've pulled together off the top of my head.

One reporter takes advantage of the pause in my statement. "Is it true you own a 200-foot yacht, Miss McKenzie?"

I look at Sam who shakes his head negatively.

"No, it is not true. That is all for today. Thank you for coming."

I conclude my first press conference and manage to elude a barrage of questions about the yacht incident.

Apparently, not all of the reporters understand that we are done here. They remain in their seats. I don't want to get caught with questions about Brooke and Tim, and the yacht.

Sam comes to the front of the room and says, "Thank you for coming. Mrs. Bailey will show you out." He puts his hand on my elbow and escorts me out of the library.

Mrs. Bailey is standing outside the room. "They're all yours, Mrs. Bailey. Show them out, but don't answer any questions," Sam says.

She squints at him a moment with a defiant look in her eyes, then she goes into the library.

"Thanks for rescuing me," I whisper to Sam as we walk down the hall toward the kitchen—the opposite direction the reporters will be going.

"You're welcome. Coffee?"

"Yes, please."

I take a sip of the fresh brew while he fills his cup. Then I move slightly toward the back door. He gets the message and follows. It is risky to go outside while reporters are on the grounds, but I don't plan to venture off the patio.

He follows me out the door and stands beside me. We look straight ahead and talk, like we are in a spy movie and are pretending we don't know each other.

"Why did you tell me to answer 'no' to that reporter?"

"Two things: One is he had the length incorrect. You have never owned a 200-foot yacht." He grins at the technicality. "And, second, I have the yacht sold—so you don't own a yacht."

"You *are* clever," I compliment his legal mind. "You sold the boat. Good. Now what?"

"I might have been able to get another half million, but I didn't think you wanted to delay the deal, did you?"

I shake my head in agreement with his decision. "Do we know what the damage is for this joyride? Will the yacht price cover the crew and damage expenses?"

"I think there will be some money left over. Most of the offended countries were happy to settle for a promise the yacht gets sold. It was the prince you spoke with who wanted to purchase the boat. The Paris office is making arrangements for the money transfer. Everything will be ready by the time they reach port." His tone reassures me.

It amuses me that I have him calling it a boat too. "The prince could have impounded the boat, but it's nice that he bought it."

Sam raises his eyebrows and tilts his head like he is confirming that I'm right about his ability to impound the boat.

"Good. Now, how do I fire Frank? I am not happy. I don't want any more unauthorized press conferences." Maybe firing Frank will put Mrs. Bailey on notice.

"I'll find out if he works for the family or the Enterprise. He may not be an employee—we might be contracting with an agency."

I notice he said, "We," which means he is bonding with his new client—me.

"Get control of him. You can always fire him later," he says.

"You have a point. The person who really needs to go is Mrs. Bailey. She isn't making the transition. I don't have time to wait for her."

"Yes, she's going to cost you, if you keep her."

"There is someone who can start next month."

"That is a good idea; build your own staff," he says.

"Sam, would you consider working for me—exclusively?"

"What! Close my booming practice?" He feigns shock, then laughs.

"I know it will be a sacrifice, but let me know as soon as you decide."

I turn away enough so he doesn't see me smile. He seems to take everything in stride. I like that about him. I need someone who can keep pace with me. He has already saved me money for the daily cost of owning a yacht. If Frank hadn't tattled on Brooke and Tim, I don't know when I would have found out about the yacht. Maybe Frank can be salvaged.

"What did you decide about Chico?"

"Write up what he'll cost me and how much I can save by hiring him." Then, I think a minute. "I would like to meet with him and see his résumé. You're all the reference he needs."

"I'll tell him. When do you want to see him?"

"Let's look at my calendar." I turn back to the house.

Mrs. Bailey hesitantly gives me my appointment calendar. It's comical and a little sad to see her struggling to hand it over. We select a time on Monday. She stresses when I write on "her" appointment book. She reminds me of a mother cat who has to wash her kittens every time someone touches them. It's really not my intention to cause her anxiety.

I motion for Sam to follow me up the stairs to the second floor. I show him both of the offices Eleanor showed me earlier.

"We'll put Chico up here—at least in the beginning. I need a price list of the hardware and software he will need, and—" Sam's wide smile interrupts my words.

"Thank you, Miss McKenzie."

"Look, Sam, as long as you advise me well, your opinion will carry a lot of weight with me. Understand?"

"Yes, ma'am. I understand perfectly."

"All right then, let's get back to work."

When he leaves the room, I pop a couple of pills to dull my headache. What a day. Is it noon yet?

This has been a lovely twenty-four hours. As a matter of fact, this has been a lovely week, and it's only Thursday. To top everything, Booke and Tim will be home for dinner tonight.

~~~

There is a commotion in the foyer. I had gone upstairs to get something for my headache, giving me a vantage point from the landing for the cousins' return.

Tim was flippant at first and laughed off the whole ordeal with the yacht, planting a kiss on Eleanor when she came to investigate the noise as they arrived home.

Brooke came with an attitude of vengeance. She rightly accused me of helping remove her from the yacht. She stopped short when she said I acted like I owned the ship, and Stanley—who had joined the group —gives her a silencing look from the doorway.

Did Brooke know who owned the yacht? Or is she just lashing out at me, the newest addition to the family? Did she go quiet only because no one wants Grandfather to hear her?

From my vantage point, I have assessed Brooke's mood. I brace for more of the same, and descend the stairs into the midst of the group. Surprisingly, Brooke quietly says hello as she passes me to acquire the stairs.

It's not that I think Grandfather needs my company, but I decide to come to dinner with him rather than make a quick sandwich and head for bed early.

The mood at the table is thicker than the gravy. The conversation is primarily brazenly formed, halted retorts. They are cruelly frank with each other. I observe their interaction in amazement. They aren't enjoying the meal or each other's presence. Grandfather remains silent, but not sullen.

~~~

I excuse myself as soon as I finish eating and go to my room. I'm tired. This allows them to have a private conversation, not that any of them worry about privacy.

It isn't nice of me, but I'm glad when I hear Brooke and Tim come upstairs, then leave again. I hope they can stay out of trouble, but they need to blow off some steam before they come home. They are disruptive to the household.

With my last cup of coffee for the day, I sit back in the chair and pick up a book from the stack of three books on the side table. Robert Frost. I am not a fan of his poetry. The only poem of his I like is *The Road Not Taken*.

I flip through the book to confirm I don't like his work. An envelope addressed to me falls out of the book. Addressed to me? I put the book down and open the envelope. Inside is a note that is handwritten. It's very curious that a note would be written to me years ago, and hidden in such a place as Robert Frost's collective works.

> A M K
>
> Dear Katey:
> It was a privilege to get to know you when you were young. You are everything I hoped my namesake would be. I am confident you are worthy of the duties that will befall you. I send you all of my love.
> Your grandmother,
> Amelia Kathryn McKenzie

"Amelia KATHRYN McKenzie?"

Oh, I forgot that the last initial goes in the middle of monograms. Wrongly, I thought the "K" was the "Kenzie" part of McKenzie.

"Then the yacht is named after Grandmother," I whisper in amazement. I rub my finger across the embossed monogram, thinking of the woman who wrote the note.

It's time to talk with Mr. Bradford again. He has a wealth of information that is pertinent to my life, but makes me stumble across it before he divulges anything. He gives the least required information. It's time for him to come clean with everything he knows about me, my parents, and the McKenzie family.

I need to know everything he knows about the McKenzie machine. Surprise jewelry is one thing, but if I'm going to manage my family's assets, I need to know everything. I have neither the patience nor the time to eke out information in bits and pieces. This is the big league. I am writing the play book, and it's my "at bat." No yachts or press conferences without my approval.

God help us all, if this household is any indication of the status of things in the company. Grandfather must have let things run on autopilot as he aged. Everything is a mess.

There are so many elements to develop among the staff: loyalty, efficiency, teamwork... I will cut some players, and draft replacements. This is spring training.

Most important, I need to prioritize how we review this enterprise. An independent analysis of every company in the McKenzie Enterprise is warranted. It all seems overwhelming, unless I look at the trees more than the forest for a while. There is so much to do, just thinking about it gives me a headache.

Tomorrow night the Dodgers have a home game. After I meet with Mr. Bradford, I'll stay at the beach and take in the game—maybe I will spend the entire weekend at the beach. The game is the perfect excuse to spend time with someone from the other side of my family—the sane side.

~~~

I beat Mr. Li to the garden again. I like smelling each variety of roses in the rose garden. It is peaceful out here. No one interrupts me during my walks.

Sam has Chico waiting when I come to work. Chico is a bright kid. I can tell by his bright eyes and easy smile. As Sam said, Chico's résumé is impressive. Chico indicates he is ready to begin work today. I wonder what Sam told him?

Chico's first task is to make a list of the equipment he must have, and a wish list of what else he would like to have—then he can leave for the day. He pulls both lists out of his laptop case.

Okay, I'm impressed.

Sam smiles with delight.

"Mr. Jackson will coordinate your duties, but you answer to me. Any problem with that?"
~~~

"No, ma'am. No problem." He grins excitedly, followed by a pleasant shiver of energy running the length of his slim body.

I nod approval to Sam and he takes Chico to see his office.

Sam returns and asks to meet with me. He has decided to be in-house counsel. He accepts the salary I offer him, and negotiates for insurance coverage. I tell him to make an appointment for himself and Chico with the human resources director at the home office in L.A.

A courier arrives. Mrs. Bailey hands me an envelope from the pouch. It is our paychecks. I completely forgot about being paid. When I get out of her view, I peek into the envelope to see what my value translates to in dollars and cents. I nearly fall through the floor, even though there is no basement below. Fifty thousand dollars for two weeks' work! This is insane! I need a cup of coffee.

When I return to the office, Sam says he has the information I requested on Mrs. Bailey.

"That was quick!" I had forgotten I'd asked for it, and I'm not sure I was dead serious at the time. Besides, we've decided she is leaving.

"Not really. I asked my dad." He smiles. "He said that Mrs. Bailey's husband was injured in a mining accident. Your grandmother had bought the mine days before. The day after the accident, she sold the mine. She paid all of Mr. Bailey's medical bills. He died six months later. His wife had no marketable skills and four children to feed, so Mrs. McKenzie hired his widow, put the kids through college, helped out where she saw a need."

"I see." That's more insight into Grandmother than into Mrs. Bailey.

"Now you know what I know." He grins again.

"Thank you." She isn't making the transition, not only to me, but to the technology that I'm going to bring. The issue is whether I structure her job to fit her abilities and ignore her opinion of me. I think it is better to offer early retirement. If she has to work with me, she may become accustomed to me or she may end her career miserably. Considering how close she and Brooke are, it is unlikely she will ever accept me. I'll stick with the Zoe plan.

Nadine Laman

Before I leave for L.A., I write in my diary.

~~~

The cousins went out last night and aren't home yet. Guess we'll miss each other until next week. Too bad.

I need to get moving to be on time for my appointment with Mr. Bradford. My car is waiting, as usual, in the front of the house. Since there are plenty of clothes at my apartment, I don't have to pack to spend the night at home—my real home.

I toss Grandfather's briefcase on the floor behind the driver's seat, and begin to pull around the circle and down the drive. I slide on my sunglasses and lay my reading glasses on the dashboard. It's a beautiful day for a drive, but I am busy thinking about my appointment and formulating last-minute questions for Mr. Bradford. I want to guarantee I actually get information from him this time.

Suddenly, something hard smacks into the windshield.

"What the hell?"

In a moment another hole blasts through the glass and my reading glasses fly to the floor. In that split second everything seems in slow motion, and I see a hole rip into the headrest of the passenger seat. At the same time—I don't know how that is possible—but at the same time I see the hole in the windshield is a bullet hole.

Immediately, I dive down in the passenger seat. When I duck, my foot comes off the clutch causing the engine to lurch and die. My mind begins to move in normal speed. I realize someone is shooting at me. But why? Why would anyone do that?

~~~

CHAPTER 8

The Bevy

Another rifle retort sounds, but it doesn't hit the windshield. There is a thud, but I don't know where it hit this time. Another shot fires, and seems to miss my car entirely. Everything is a blur. I'm scared out of my wits: too scared to think or cry.

My cell phone begins ringing. I struggle to fish the phone from my pocket, while still lying low across the car seats. The shifter knob finds a soft spot above my hip and digs into my side. I wrench with the unexpected pain.

"Hello?" My voice is shaky. I clear my throat. "Yes, I'm all right." A big fat lie. "What's going on?" I ask, pretending to be calm as possible. Am I convincing? I don't know.

"There is someone behind the front gate with a rifle, firing at you." Sam's voice is rapid, hushed, distressed. His breath is hurried, not at all reassuring.

"Why would someone do that? Are they trying to kill me?" I beg for a reasonable answer, one I can comprehend.

"I don't know. Stay put. I've called the police." There is a long pause. "And, Kathryn," he says kindly, "I'll stay on the phone with you until this is over."

"Thank you. I'm all right, Sam. You don't have to stay on the phone. Keep everyone away from the windows. Check on Grandfather. I am worried about where the shot went that didn't hit my car. Make sure he is away from the front windows. Sam, please." I don't try to hide my concern for the final mark of the missing bullet.

Two more shots hit the windshield. The last one shatters the glass, spewing glass bits on me. I cover my mouth to muffle a scream, and quickly turn my head down into the seat cushion to keep the glass off of my face and away from my eyes.

Sirens come out of the distance. It seems like hours. Finally, someone opens the passenger door and reaches in to touch my hand that is contorted to shield my head from the glass. I hear soft voices, Garrett, then Sam, then Stanley, who turns toward the group of worried household staff congregated on the front stairs, and he reports that I am alive.

When I sit up, glass falls inside the back of my blouse.

Paramedics are beside the open door. I tell them I am fine and I can get out of the car from the driver's side. They insist on the passenger side because it's facing away from the gate, but I point to the gearshift obstructing my movement in their direction and they finally get the picture.

Garrett stands guard as close as he can without being shooed out of the way.

"Garrett, have Eleanor come to the car," I request, then smile reassuringly.

Eleanor arrives almost instantly. I ask her to go to the driver's door. Garrett is at her side and opens the door. This time the paramedics have to stand back.

I reach my left hand in his direction. "Just steady me, let me pull myself up." As I inch myself out of the car, the glass finds the small of my back, pricking my flesh. I stop dead. My eyes close and my back arches with the pain.

Garrett freezes.

Catching my breath, I begin to inch again. There is no avoiding the glass, all I can do is to continue to steadily pull myself toward Garrett. Eleanor reaches for my right hand before my feet hit the ground.

I lean in close to Eleanor as I stand. She steps back a half step, then forward again when she understands I want to whisper to her.

"I have glass inside my blouse. Pull the back of my blouse out of my waistband so the glass will fall out rather than lodge and cut me with every move."

She is gentle, and even picks a few dime-size pieces of glass from my hair to protect against them falling in my face and eyes.

"Be careful, don't cut yourself," I warn.

She whispers, as she leans close, "Your grandfather is terribly worried. Wave to him."

"Thanks. I will. Would you get me a robe? I need to get out of these clothes—they're full of glass."

Eleanor moves toward the house, stops to say something to Grandfather, pats his shoulder, and disappears through the door.

The paramedics want me to sit on the back of their truck. I decline because of the glass, some now inside my waistband. I can't sit down for fear of driving glass into my skin. There are a few scratches on my hands and a small one on the back of my neck—all from the glass that fell on me. Otherwise, I am fine—and I tell them so.

They insist on irrigating my hands, inspecting them now that the blood is washed away, and dressing the wound on my neck. They would have had my blouse off in front of all my staff, if I hadn't protested.

~~~

Everyone is talking at me at the same time. The sheriff wants my car for evidence, which is fine with me since it has to be towed anyway to get the windshield replaced, and to repair the radiator where one of the "missing" bullets landed. I ask for my purse and briefcase. For a minute I think he's going to claim that it's evidence. I'm ready to inform him otherwise. He sends someone to get my stuff. Smart man. Today is not the day to argue with me.

The sheriff says they caught the shooter. The man just stood there looking confused when the officers drove up with sirens blaring. No one seems to know why he was shooting at me, or if he was specifically aiming for me—though it does look like I was the target.

For a brief moment I think about Brooke. She is probably furious with me, but I don't think even she would hire someone to shoot me. Besides, I believe some part of her enjoys having me here to fling her anger toward.

The officers take statements from Mrs. Bailey, Mr. Li who was working in the front garden, Grandfather, and Sam—everyone else saw nothing—the witnesses only saw the man from a distance after the shooting began. Mr. Li had seen movement by the gate, but dropped to the ground like a rock when the first shot was fired. He had grown up in a rough neighborhood in San Francisco and knew quite well the meaning of the sound he heard.
~~~

Sam promises that I will give a statement later, after I remove the glass from my clothes and hair.

Garrett comes around the corner with the golf cart to give me a ride to the back so I don't have to take the steps and dig the glass in farther with each step. He eases me on the back where I stand, holding tight. I see Grandfather looking out of the window and wave to let him know that I'm fine. Garrett drives slowly, but each bump feels like a boulder-laden trail.

My knuckles are white. My breath is caught in my ribs. The thought of stepping down horrifies me. I whisper to undo my slacks fastener. Garrett hesitates. Eleanor is at his side, so she does the duty. The glass slips, but the pressure driving them into my skin is released enough that I move my hand to Garrett's, ease to the ground, and inch to the patio door.

Louise spreads plastic trash bags on the laundry room floor, hands me the robe Eleanor brought, and tells me to undress. I stand for a moment, alone. I take a deep breath, hesitant to move and give liberty to the glass' torture.

Alone, tears pour down my face as I ease off my clothes. I feel dizzy, probably more from emotional shock than from the minor injures. I don't dare sit. I'd rather be anywhere but here, and have any name but McKenzie.

When I have the robe on, Eleanor is followed by Louise who has a damp cloth and tells me to wipe the bottom of my feet to make sure that there aren't glass slivers on them before I put on my slippers. Eleanor offers her hand to steady me as I balance to follow Louise's directive. Mrs. Bailey joins Louise and Eleanor —making the bevy of household women complete.

Eleanor put Mrs. Bailey in charge of shooing the men from the kitchen before Louise will let me out of the laundry room, even though I have on a robe. Nothing like a good shooting spree to bring all of us together. Despite my tongue-in-cheek thoughts, I am glad for their company. I feel shaky, but try to appear as calm as possible.

Louise sends Eleanor upstairs for my shampoo and cream rinse. In the meantime, she carefully inspects my wounds in the event the paramedics didn't do a thorough job. When she finishes with my hands, she gives me a cup of coffee.

Storm Surge

My hand shakes, requiring both hands to hold the cup. She carefully cups her hands around mine so I can take a sip. Aaah. I admit, the coffee tastes marvelous. Louise is a saint.

Outside, there is the sound of a helicopter overhead. Stanley reports through the door that the helicopter belongs to a news station. Mrs. Bailey pulls down the shades and turns on the kitchen television. We watch a live bird's-eye picture of the activity in our front yard. It is eerie to see that what happened is real.

Eleanor returns breathless—apparently, she did not take the stairs in her usual measured fashion. Louise places a large pot in the sink and instructs me to put my head down over it. She pours diluted cream rinse over my hair and turns the water spray as low as possible and still be able to spray. Her theory is the cream rinse will make the glass slide out of my hair. She repeats the process three times, being very careful not to squirt water in my face or down the back of my neck where the bandage is. I limply comply with her instructions while I wait for the caffeine to enter my system.

Louise isn't satisfied that all the glass has been removed. She asks Eleanor to get her cream rinse, since mine is depleted.

"Wait, wait. This is good enough. I'll take a shower."

As Louise drapes a towel over my hair I add, "Thank you, thank you all for your help. I really appreciate it."

I start to leave without letting on how frightened I am.

Eleanor insists on helping me up the stairs, though she doesn't know where to safely touch me. She carefully removes the bandages since the bleeding has stopped and they are going to get wet in the shower anyway. Then she waits in my room, feeling, no doubt, that being on the main floor is too far away if I need assistance. I'm secretly relieved she stays nearby.

~~~

The warm water feels good on my increasingly tensing back muscles. I know it's just nerves. I put shampoo in my hands and make a rich lather that I dab on my shoulders, hoping that the foam washes down and takes away any remaining glass particles on my back. The shampoo stings in the cuts on my hands and back. Slowly, carefully, I begin to wash my body. The
~~~

stream of water runs through my hair until I am convinced that there are no pieces of glass missed by Louise's cream rinse treatment. Then, I dab shampoo lather on my hair.

All of the emotions of being shot at well up inside of me. With crossed arms I hold my sides as I begin to cry nearly hysterically —gasping—while the water pours over me. I bend over as if I have stomach cramps. The last three weeks have been a nightmare. My left hand comes up to my forehead to cover my eyes—I bow my head crying, sobbing, lost. It's as if I will never stop pouring out the sadness, fear, and frustration that is inside of me.

Over the sound of the water, I hear knocking on the door. I try to regain my composure. The door opens slightly and Eleanor is standing in the door, looking awkwardly away from me in the shower.

"Kathryn? Kathryn?"

I take a sobbing breath, "Yes, I'm all right."

"The sheriff's ready for your statement," she says gently.

"I'll be down in a minute."

What can I tell him that someone else hasn't? I consider pulling on sweats and leaving my hair damp, but I pull it together enough to put on slacks and a blouse, fix my hair and makeup.

My position requires a public presence, regardless of my personal situation. I'll entertain my fear and frailty later.

It's too early to know anything concrete about the shooter. So far they haven't found a connection with him and McKenzie Enterprises, or any discernable connection to me. I don't remember him from any of my old cases. One of the officers calls Karen to run the name through her department's database, since she would have cases that didn't go to court that the law enforcement computer wouldn't have. When they finish, Karen asks to speak with me.

"What's going on?"

"I'll have to get back to you, okay?" I hope she catches the implication that our conversation isn't private.

"Katey?" she asks, insistently. Then, she relinquishes, "All right, call me. Please, call me back."

"Yes, I'll call, I promise."

The sheriff has an impatient tone. "Miss McKenzie, can we finish this?"

"Yes, of course. Honestly, I can't think of anything that connects this man to me." I'm not going to implicate my cousins without facts. If there is evidence of Brooke's involvement, they will have to find it on their own.

"Miss McKenzie, if you are holding back any information—" His threat is interrupted by another officer who tells him they have located the shooter's wife.

He just as much called me a liar to my face, the jerk, but I smile the McKenzie gracious-dame smile.

He looks back at me with an untrusting glance, hesitates, then follows the other officer out of the room. He turns back at the door and gives me a look to indicate that he isn't finished with me yet—and wants me to know it.

"We'll post an officer outside," is all he says before he is gone.

~~~

As soon as he leaves the property, I call the posted officer inside. "I am going to let the staff leave early. Would you drive down to the gate and make sure it is clear? I'm sure that it is—but just as a precaution."

"Yes, I will. Have the last one out to flash their headlights at me."

"Thank you. Oh, my cousins might be back tonight. I don't know for sure. I'll see if someone can give you identifying information." They've been gone since after dinner last night.

"I'll take care of it, Miss McKenzie." He puts on his hat as he opens the door, stops and turns back. "And, ignore Schmidty. He's harmless."

Until we find out why that guy was shooting at me, we don't know if there are other shooters out there, somewhere, or who the target is for certain—though it seems to be me. The rule will be "caution" until we know more.

"Mrs. Bailey, please tell everyone to put their work away and go home immediately. Do you know if Brooke, or Tim, or Dan are coming back tonight? The officer should be told how to identify them. Oh, find Sam, I need to speak with him."
~~~

It occurs to me that I haven't talked to Grandfather since the shooting. After checking the library for him, I go to his bedroom door and knock softly. Conner comes to the door ready to "shush" the person knocking on the door until he sees it is me. He opens the door wider and whispers for me to come in.

"How is he?" I whisper, looking at the frail old man lying on the bed with a blanket tucked over his shoulders. He looks small and defenseless lying there.

"He is terribly shaken," he whispers back.

"You two are making enough noise to wake the—" he stops before saying the word "dead."

I smile a reassurance to Conner.

"Hello, Grandfather," I move to his side. "It's Kathryn."

"I know who you are! I'm not senile, you know."

He doesn't fool me for one minute. He can be as grumpy as he wants, but I know he was shaken by the shooting. We all were scared—and still are.

"I just wanted to let you know I am all right. I'm sending the staff home early. I'll be back after I'm sure everyone has left," I excuse myself and nod at Conner with a smile on my way out.

Sam and Mr. Li are in the kitchen with the breakfast board: Mrs. Bailey, Garrett, Stanley, Eleanor, and Louise.

"Everyone needs to go home. Call Monday before you come in and we'll see where we are with things."

I turn to Mrs. Bailey. "Have you reached the cousins?"

I just guessed that she called them. It stands to reason that she would at least call Brooke. It's Friday night, maybe they won't come home until midafternoon tomorrow.

Mrs. Bailey doesn't answer me, so I continue. "When you drive out, give the officers at the gate the information about the cousins, so they can identify them and let them in."

I hope Mrs. Bailey gets the hint that the cousins shouldn't come home tonight and passes the message on to them.

Louise protests leaving early because she has dinner to prepare.

"No, go. We can manage."

Eleanor agrees with me that we can handle dinner. And we can, but Louise gives instructions to Eleanor anyway.

I ask Sam to bring up the rear of the caravan and flash his lights at the officer to indicate he is the last to leave.

Unexpectedly, Brooke and Tim make their usual dramatic entrance. Tim grabs for Eleanor. She jumps back, so he misses.

We are all still jumpy. Clearly, Eleanor didn't care for the familiarity from a boy young enough to be her son, but she says nothing about it. The cousins seem unaware of the shooting, at least they don't mention it. They are aware something is up and ask suspiciously about the cop outside.

Mrs. Bailey moves near Brooke in a protective manner.

Perhaps she, like I, had a fleeting thought that Brooke might be somehow involved in the shooting.

Brooke and Tim disappear up the stairs, Mrs. Bailey leaves with the other staff. Stanley, Eleanor, and I are left. It's an awkward silence.

Someone has to move. I go to the kitchen and the waiting coffee. The others follow me to the table.

After a cup of coffee, Eleanor gets up and looks in the refrigerator. Stanley moves to the patio door and locks it, then to the back door to lock it. Lastly, he heads for the front door.

I slip away to call Karen and tell her the latest activity at the mansion before she hears it on the news, but I'm too late. Karen wants to come. I convince her we are fine and not to make the trip. She offers to bring Keith for added protection.

It's not safe for anyone to come right now. We need answers, such as, was it a lone shooter or are there others to take his place? And motive, what was the motive?

"Check with me tomorrow. Tonight I need to be available for Grandfather."

She says she understands, then falls silent. I wonder if she is worried she will lose me, like she lost Maggie. She rarely mentions it, but I know Maggie's death was hard on her.

"Karen, you won't lose me, I promise."

She gasps. "Katey, don't say that!" Her voice trembles.

It's obvious that she needs to see me to know that I am fine. She won't say it, but I know it's true.

"I'll send the helicopter for you and Keith at one o'clock tomorrow. You won't have to drive. Besides, it's fun to fly in it."

"We would love it. I'll tell Keith." She sounds relieved.

We make the arrangements for tomorrow and say goodnight. I call and tell the pilot tomorrow's flight schedule.

When I return to the kitchen, Conner is telling Eleanor that he and Grandfather will eat in the bedroom suite tonight. Eleanor hesitates when I offer to help prepare their dinner. I haven't always had a private chef—I can cook.

Her silence speaks volumes, so I don't comment further. All right then, I'll find something else to do.

~~~

The sheriff's Blazer is at the gate.

I walk out on the front steps. It isn't that I want to die, but I am not going to be a captive of fear.

The Blazer begins to back around and turn toward the front of the house. I stand and watch it approach.

The officer who climbs out of the vehicle looks as if he is considering scolding me for being on the porch. I beat him to the punch.

"Can I offer you coffee or dinner—or both?"

He is distracted from his duty long enough to smile. "No, ma'am," he answers immediately.

"Did you bring dinner with you? We're a long way from town." I watch the other officer scanning the fence line and the gate with binoculars.

The first officer returns to the vehicle, says something to the officer behind the wheel, and brings a thermos with him.

They will eat in shifts, for now he takes the coffee. Stanley and Eleanor observe my conversation with the officer. They seem more settled now that they know another shift of officers will come tonight.

Conner comes and makes a sandwich for himself. He says Grandfather isn't hungry and is going to bed. I tell him to come get me if Grandfather wakes up, and he agrees to do so.

There is a short clip about the incident on the six o'clock news. They don't know anything, but the overhead view of the house and grounds flash on the screen. They show a file photo of Grandfather and one of me taken at the press conference in the library. Both are pretty decent pictures.
~~~

Stanley and Eleanor aren't used to having a McKenzie spend off-duty time with them. I go upstairs and get one of Grandmother's three books from my room—not Robert Frost. The choices are Marco Polo's *Travels*, or *American Women of the Twentieth Century*. I'll take the women over Frost or Marco.

On the way down the stairs, I consider whether to remain in the kitchen or go to the library to read. I want to be a presence of strength for the staff, but I don't want to intrude on their space when they should be off-duty.

To the library it is. They can find me if they need me. There are more comfortable chairs in there anyway. I pull up an ottoman and put my feet up, carefully.

The book is laid out with a chapter for each woman, and is about an event in their life that is the most memorable to them, not necessarily the famous event. They are social reformers, political activists, scientific pioneers, aviators and astronauts, Nobel Prize winners, philanthropists, and female greats in male-dominated fields—even the Unsinkable Molly Brown, someone I have always admired.

Reaching for my glasses and not having them reminds me again of being shot at—the very thing I am trying to escape. I don't know how long I will be able to read without them, but select Eleanor Roosevelt's chapter. She writes about her work with the United Nations on the U.N. Children's Bill of Rights. One quote catches my attention: "*I think somehow, we learn who we really are and then live with that decision.*"

I skim through the book, reading bits and pieces of several stories. The women rarely write about the thing that made them famous. Their opinion of what was important differed from history's public opinion. My eyes are tired.

I know why Grandmother kept this book in her room. It inspires greatness. In comparison to these women, I have had a fairly easy life. The book will be an excellent training manual.

The officers take turns coming inside for dinner. I join them in the kitchen while they eat. There is no threatening activity on the grounds. The report is that the shooter laid down in his cell and went to sleep after he was processed into the system. When they woke him, he seemed to have no memory of the incident, then went back to sleep. His wife had no answers to why he was shooting at me. She didn't even know he had purchased a rifle.

After all of us have eaten, I help clean the kitchen. When Eleanor and I finish putting away the food, I say with a smile, "I guess I will read a little longer." My eyes should be rested now, besides, I crave the inspiration I found in Grandmother's book. I'm not ready to sleep.

"Miss McKenzie, sleep in the guest room or with us on the second floor." Eleanor and Stanley have separate quarters— both on the second floor. She is a widow. I don't know Stanley's story.

Did she notice that I was crying in the shower?

She seems a little less detached from me than she has in the past. I consider her suggestion, but finally decide to stay in my own room. Other than my furious cousins, the third floor is safe.

"I am fine, thank you. Do you think we should give the officers a key to the front door, or maybe have the night shift stay inside?" I ask both Eleanor and Stanley. I want them to have a voice in the decision so they feel a sense of control.

"I can take a nap, then stay up," Stanley offers.

"You probably don't have to do that, but I'll leave the decision to you." He knows his duties better than I.

At about ten o'clock, Eleanor comes to the library. I close my book when she enters, but keep my fingers in the page as a bookmark. She tells me she woke Stanley, and she is going to bed. She stands there for an awkward moment.

I wait to see what she wants to say. Finally, I decide maybe she is waiting for me to say something, but I don't know what.

"I'll go to bed shortly."

"How do you McKenzie women do it?"

"Do it?" I question, unclear what she means.

"Someone tried to kill you, and you are sitting there reading a book." She becomes emotionally animated.

"Eleanor, have a seat," I say and motion to a chair near me.

She sits across from me, but scoots the chair a few inches closer. I know it is just a gesture to feel close.

"They caught the man at the gate and he won't be back." I speak softly and calmly.

"When I first saw you, I knew you were just like your grandmother. That Brooke is nothing like Mrs. McKenzie." She takes a deep breath.

"Brooke has problems. I'm not sure what to do to help her." I look directly at her. "I am fine," I nod my head and smile slightly. "We'll get through this. I promise, Eleanor."

"Aren't you afraid?" Her eyes water.

"Yes, of course I am. But I think clearer when I keep my wits about me."

"How do you do that?" she asks—desperately.

I look at the book in my hands. "Here, this is Grandmother's book. Sometimes we have to look to our sisters to know what to do." I hand the book toward her. "We are all going to get through this—and anything else that comes." I say it with strength and calmness—for Eleanor, and for myself.

She rubs her fingers over the book jacket. It is something of Grandmother's that she can touch. I hope it helps. Reading it might make her feel the strength of sisterhood among women—something I think we all seek, even if we don't recognize it.

Dearest Maggie, I have run the gauntlet of emotions. I'm exhausted. Past disappointments have been hard, but I have learned lessons I would not have learned another way. I have to appear strong, even when I don't feel it. That is what is expected of me. That is what I expect of myself.

~~~

The morning shift of officers won't let me venture beyond the patio with my breakfast coffee. These two officers are less personable than the night shift were; arrogant better describes them. Both claim there is no new information about the shooter. I find that hard to believe.

They mock me, "It's Saturday, the sheriff's off for the weekend. Call him Monday."

My second cup of coffee will be taken upstairs to my room. I want some distance from all of this madness. Little people with a gun, amazing.

Since I gave the book I was reading to Eleanor, I add another entry to my diary.
~~~

Dearest Maggie, Yesterday is among the worst days of my life. A stranger tried to kill me. All of the days that rival the experience have the common thread of death and dying—my parents' deaths, the little girl in our case, you and Dave, Monica, and now me. The violence of the stranger's act is the most difficult to understand.

Your words resound in my thoughts, "It isn't how long one lives, it's how wide that matters." I am not sure my life has, to this point, been adequately wide. I look to the women I know and to those who went before for example. I look within myself for strength and wisdom. I look to you.

~~~

Grandfather has decided to spend the day in his room. He wants no company, not even me. Stanley is as steady as any English butler, though he's not English. Eleanor seems in better spirits today.

I'll busy myself attending to business calls, trying to appear "business as usual" for everyone's benefit. Mr. Bradford often works on Saturday. I'll start with him and apologize for missing my appointment. We reschedule for Monday.

Next, the staff. Mrs. Bailey is easy to convince to stay home from work on Monday, with pay. She sounds jumpy. She asks about Grandfather and Brooke, but not about me.

Louise insists on coming in on Monday. Maybe she is correct. Grandfather needs to get back into his regular routine. Louise's meals are a good anchor for him to get back on track. Mr. Li isn't home and doesn't have an answering machine. I'll try him again later. Sam plans on coming to work on Monday, but I tell him I will meet him at Mr. Bradford's office. That saves him a trip to the mansion. I tell him to have Chico wait a couple of days before starting work. Sam can get a purchase order for him and he can hand-pick his equipment; I'll sign it at Mr. Bradford's office when we meet.

Who am I forgetting? Garrett! He'll have to drive me to L.A. since I am without a car. Besides, I doubt I can get a "pass" to leave without him, otherwise I could take the helicopter. All of this would be comical if that guy with the gun hadn't scared me out of my wits.
~~~

~~~

When the helicopter arrives with Karen and Keith, I am at the pad to meet them. I didn't ask the officers' permission to leave the house.

Surely there was only one shooter and he is in jail. There is no reason to think there is some sort of hit ordered.

We hug and get into the golf cart. Karen is wired with excitement about the helicopter ride. It's a blast. I understand how exciting the first ride can be.

"He'll have to take you along the coast on the way home. You've never seen anything that compares!"

The sheriff's officers saw the helicopter land and make a beeline to intercept the golf cart with their Chevy K-5 Blazer. Obviously, it's no contest between our vehicles. A chubby officer gets out, hikes his pants up, and struts to the front of the golf cart. He stands there as a roadblock with his hand on his holster and demands to know what I'm doing. He scolds me about the dangers of being out of the house as if I'm a three-year-old playing with matches, and asks if I think my "friend" can protect me—meaning Keith.

Keith has silently watched the exchange. Once the officer stops chastising me, Keith asks the officer to step aside. The officer takes a defensive stance, showing no intention to yield his authority to a visitor. Keith shows his detective shield and tells the officer to step aside again. The officer opens his mouth to say something, but Keith repeats his request more firmly, "Step aside."

There is no way for the officer to move and save face, but he does move, and we drive past him.

We take our coffee to the library to visit privately. Karen is relieved to see me. Keith is surprised that I know nothing more about the incident. Granted, the sheriff's department shouldn't or wouldn't tell me everything they know. But Keith thinks I should at least know what danger remains, if any. He asks to use a landline phone.

As soon as Keith leaves the room, Karen moves forward in her chair. She wants me to stay with her awhile, but I can't. I need to stay with Grandfather and to be a physical presence for
~~~

the staff. I tell her about coming to L.A. on Monday to get new glasses, see Mr. Bradford, and go to the bank. She welcomes a lunch invitation, but wants to know if my bodyguard, "Bubba" from the sheriff's office, will be joining us.

"You are absolutely awful!"

"I know," she says proudly.

We are still laughing when Keith returns. The officers will be replaced. Keith will register a formal complaint regarding the officer's behavior toward me. I am more relieved than I expected.

Keith has more information about the shooter. "The man thinks God told him to kill the nun who is having the alien baby. He had a letter to the Pope in his pocket. He 'flipped out' in his jail cell this morning. They transferred him to the psych unit—under guard and sedated." Keith looks at Karen for her reaction.

"The guy needs serious help. This also means that there isn't someone else out there waiting to shoot me, if he failed. That's good news, right?"

I won't say it out loud that I had wondered if Brooke was involved. She's absolutely livid about the yacht incident. Besides, she has never

been fond of me. I always sleep with my bedroom door locked when Brooke and Tim are home.

"Good, then it's not Brooke," Karen remarks.

"Why do you say that?" I ask, surprised that she shared my concern.

"To begin with she doesn't like you, but then she lost the drugs on the yacht—that has to be a major problem for her."

"Money is nothing to her," I answer back. "I'm not sure what gives meaning to her life."

"Do you have security?" Keith asks.

"The gate isn't monitored, if that is what you mean," I answer, knowing it isn't what he means.

"I would like to have a friend of mine call you. You need to secure the mansion, and a bodyguard for you wouldn't hurt." He starts to say more, then changes his mind.

"I agree, Katey, you are doing things differently than they were done before, and that will threaten some people. Sooner or later you will need a bodyguard. Now is a good time to start."

"Jim knows what he is doing," Keith adds.

"All right, then. Have him call me," I agree, at least to a meeting. "Now, how about seeing the ballroom—I'm sure Karen told you about it."

Keith doesn't react to the trip back in time as we climb the stairs to the ballroom. I wonder if Karen is disappointed.

He walks around the center of the floor, checks out the chandelier overhead, scuffs at the floor with his shoe. He turns to Karen, smiles, and dramatically takes her into his arms—beginning to dance.

I ponder the scene. This is not the Detective Knight I knew. I stand back, observing Keith and Karen glide across the floor. They move as one person, in perfect unison with each other.

I look around the room, considering restoring, repairing, and basically renovating it. What if I have the skylight above the chandelier reopened—that would be pretty. Besides, it is time to open the light into this room—and into this house.

~~~

Grandfather is convinced to come out of his room briefly to say hello to Karen and to meet Keith. Karen charms him for over an hour. I ask
Stanley to take Karen and Keith back to the helicopter pad for their trip home. I need to attend to Grandfather.

"Grandfather, come on the patio with me." I encourage him, happy that he has finally emerged from his room.

He sighs. But he doesn't protest.

Softly I say, "Come, it will be good to get some fresh air."

He moves his hands to his lap, where he always places them while his chair is being pushed. I take this movement as consent.

It is a pretty spring afternoon. At least, the change in scenery will be good for him. He stares straight ahead, "What have I done to you?"

"You haven't done anything to me. Nothing you did has anything to do with the shooter."

I move closer and unfold the newspaper with the picture of me dressed as a nun that Karen brought for giggles.

He takes the paper and studies it in silence, urgently scanning the photo.
~~~

"Don't worry. I'm not a nun. I don't have an alien boyfriend."

He smiles slightly at the photo. "Have you told his parents about the baby?" he asks with a straight face.

He's doing better. He just needed to get out of that room.

"The man who shot at me is very ill. He thought God told him to kill me because I was a nun who broke the vow of celibacy."

Grandfather turns to look directly at me. Religion is a delicate subject between us, and we have never admitted its existence in relationship to ours.

"He wrote to the Pope that he had been sent by God to purge the Church from evil nuns and priests. It had nothing to do with either of us. You did nothing to me," I say again.

"He's Catholic?" Grandfather turns to look at me with his loaded question.

"No, actually he isn't."

He has a curious expression that I can't decipher.

~~~

We move back to the kitchen where I invite him to stay while we prepare dinner. To the staff's surprise, he agrees.

"Would you like a drink—ice water, tea?"

He decidedly answers, "Something stronger."

While I fix Grandfather's highball, he asks Stanley to join him. At first Stanley hesitates, but I fix him one anyway. They both look adoringly at their glass after the first taste. I'm glad they appreciate the drink; however, I am still not mentioning where I learned to tend bar so exquisitely. The men nurse their drinks. They have never had such a perfect beverage.

Eleanor stops preparing dinner to watch the uncommon activity at the table.

"May I fix you a drink, Eleanor?"

She declines unconvincingly. Clearly, drinking with Mr. McKenzie is not done.

But these are not ordinary times. I pour two glasses of wine, and hand one to Eleanor. If nothing else, it may improve our cooking, I tell her. We touch our glasses together. I join Eleanor cleaning and cutting vegetables for our salad, this time without asking if she wants help. We're no real threat to Louise's job, though our meals have been edible.
~~~

Grandfather pulls the paper out and shows the photo of his granddaughter, the nun, to Stanley. Then he asks, "Have you seen this, Eleanor?"

She has a questioning look after seeing the photo.

"I can explain, honest! I picked up the alien at a bar, ah, when I was in Chicago visiting the factory there." Of course, my explanation doesn't fit the time line when the photo was taken.

Her eyes widen. She pauses a dramatic beat. "We'll have to set up a nursery."

Grandfather smiles, Stanley snickers nervously, and I laugh. The tension of yesterday's shooting is finally broken.

~~~

Rather than change the sheriff's officers as Keith had said, they remove them altogether. The unexpected abruptness of their withdrawal makes me feel uneasy again, but I mention it to no one. It is an irrational fear. I should be back in my proper place working at Spirit of Hope, and none of this should have happened. "Beam me up, Scotty."

After dinner, the cousins disappear again. Grandfather and I move to the library and talk at length about the shooting incident. We openly discuss our concerns, pragmatically. I tell him about Keith's security suggestion. Considering the unlikeliness of another person being "told by God" to shoot me, we decide to have the gate regulated and a monitored alarm system installed. Beyond that, neither of us want full-time bodyguards—perhaps only for special, high-profile occasions.

~~~

Tim is still gone. During the night, Brooke came home. Brooke is in rare form at the breakfast table—almost makes me wish I hadn't waited to eat with the family.

When she says it's too bad the shooter wasn't a better shot, Grandfather tells her that's enough and to apologize to me.

Rather than apologize, she says, "You just don't get it, old man—the only reason she looked you up was for your money!"

She shoots a glaring glance at me as she storms out of the dining room. Garrett came into the room just in time to hear Brooke's comment before she pushed past him. He looks at Grandfather, then at me, but says nothing about Brooke.

"Mr. McKenzie, if I am not needed tomorrow, I would like the day off. Yvonne's mother fell this morning and broke her hip. We need to go to Las Vegas to be with her during surgery. I'll come back tomorrow night," he gets right to the point.

"Kathryn?" Grandfather puts the ball in my court.

"That would be fine. Do you need more time?"

"That should be enough."

"No, on second thought, don't come back tomorrow. Stay a few days."

"Thank you, I will," he agrees easily and is gone.

"You handled that like your grandmother would have." Grandfather smiles.

"Thank you." I'm happy for the approval. I get up from the table, then give him a peck on the forehead. I appreciate his compliment, but more than that, I appreciate that he finally said something to Brooke, even though she didn't listen to him.

Both of us know what Brooke said was untrue. I don't know if Garrett is aware that Grandfather found me, not the other way around, but he probably is. He drove Grandfather to the park to meet me. He doesn't seem to miss much that goes on around here—neither does the rest of the breakfast group. I don't think Garrett believes for one minute that I'm after the money. All that matters is that Grandfather knows the truth. There is no point bothering with trying to straighten out Brooke on the matter.

~~~

Eleanor and Stanley are at the kitchen table sharing the Sunday paper. Two papers are delivered: Grandfather has one and the staff has the other one. While pouring another cup of coffee, I ask, "Is there a car I can use to go to town?"

Eleanor nudges Stanley. "Miss McKenzie wants a ride to town. Didn't you say you were going to town?"

He has no independent recollection of the conversation she is referencing.

She nudges him again, only harder this time. "Stanley, didn't you say you were going to town today?" She is obviously putting words in his mouth.

"Oh, sure. Sure, I'm going to town." He looks at Eleanor, who nods approval.
~~~

Storm Surge

They might as well be married. Sheesh.

~~~

"So, where are we going, Miss McKenzie?" Stanley asks as soon as we clear the front gate.

"I just wanted to go for a short drive," I lie. I had other plans, if I had a car and no chaperone. I lean back and relax into my seat while Stanley drives south along the coast. When we get to town, he pulls into the market. He says he is going to get some, ah, something, and asks if I want anything. Very funny, he couldn't think of what he came to purchase. He is a terrible liar.

I wait, curious to see what he decided to buy once he was in the store. In a few minutes, couldn't have been more than ten, Stanley comes out with a six-pack of root beer, and we go home. A six-pack of root beer? That certainly warranted a trip to town. We are a pitiful bunch when it comes to deceit.

~~~

Night comes, then morning again. It feels good to be free to go outside again for my morning walk. It pales in comparison to the beach, but a person has to make the best of what is available. Today's plan is damage control from the shooting. I just want to make a few mental notes before I go back inside.

Tim and Dan haven't come home. Danny isn't expected back yet. I suspect Tim isn't coming back until Brooke gives him the "all clear" signal—either about the cops or me, I don't know which.

Brooke has steered clear of me. She isn't subtle, though. She slams her bedroom door or the refrigerator door if I'm nearby. Last night, she played her stereo loudly in her bedroom, the one across from mine. It wasn't worth engaging her wrath to get to sleep before she gave up and shut it off on her own.

As requested, Mrs. Bailey calls to inquire about work. She still sounds shook up about the shooting on Friday. I arrange to drop by her house later in the week, but for now she should take the week off. She eagerly agrees, seeming to be relieved not to come to work.

Sam and I confirm our plan to meet at Mr. Bradford's office. Sam in on his way to pick up Chico's purchase order from the corporate office downtown and bring it for my signature. I should visit the corporate office sometime, but frankly I need to take things in measurable steps, I will get to it in its own time.

Without my car or Garrett to drive the limo, I take the helicopter to L.A. It is faster, and parking is easier—but getting around on the surface streets is a problem when I fly. Sam offers to meet me and give me a ride to Mr. Bradford's office for our appointment. I agree.

Mr. Bradford is undeniably happy to see me alive and kicking. The shooting was a bonding of sorts, at least for those who like me and the
neutral parties, like Eleanor, Stanley, and Louise. As for those who aren't all that crazy about me, they were rooting for the shooter. Maybe someday they will get their wish, who knows?

I know Mr. Bradford isn't comfortable with sentimental exchanges, so we get right down to business. As far as I am concerned, Sam should sit in on the whole meeting—he is part of the inner circle now.

Mr. Bradford produces a document for Sam to sign that prohibits him from ever divulging any information he learns about Kathryn McKenzie, the McKenzie family specifically named, and about any business involvements of myself or McKenzie Enterprises. We might as well ask for his first-born child too. All of this legal mumbo jumbo—I hate it, but I appreciate its purpose.

Sam and Mr. Bradford exchange documents. "Here, I know you will have to read it before Ms. McKenzie signs it." They both read the documents, while I soak in the oddness of my new world. Sam signs his papers and hands them to me.

His contract looks a little thick, if you ask me. Mr. Bradford laughs at the bundle of papers. "That's right, Sam. The large print giveth and the small print taketh away!" They both laugh.

Finally, they finish their legal jousting and are ready to work. "Mr. Bradford, I need to know everything you know related to the McKenzie family—or me." That should be specific enough to actually get answers from him.

He leans back in his chair and clears his throat. He looks like he's going to tip over, if he isn't careful. "Where would you like me to start?"

"At the beginning."

Mr. Bradford smiles.

Sam pulls out a legal pad and makes a desk out of his leg. Since I can get a copy of his notes, I am free to listen without distraction.

"Sam's father, your father, and I were friends at USC." He nods at each of us as he mentions our fathers. "I think your two parents were friends in high school. I didn't meet them until later our freshman year." He nods toward Sam. "Garrett had a football scholarship to play for the Trojans." Then, he nods toward me. "Your grandfather is a USC alumni and expected his only son to attend his alma mater—so your fathers roomed together in college. Kathryn, your mother and my wife were roommates, so it worked out that we did things together." Thus, he begins his story.

I wonder if it's strange to have the grown children of his two best friends sitting across the desk from him. He doesn't get sentimental, but

to me it's interesting to hear about my parents from someone who knew them when they were young.

"Mr. McKenzie threw a fit when he found out his heir apparent was going to marry a "heathen" Catholic. He opposed the marriage. Kate, Mrs. McKenzie, didn't care, she loved your mother."

Mr. Bradford chuckles under his breath about her independence from Grandfather's opinions.

"When Mr. McKenzie was in Europe, they had a private wedding and party in the estate ballroom. He was furious when he found out, but Kate stood her ground."

Sam looks a little surprised. He probably didn't know about the ballroom.

"Kate?" I haven't heard Grandmother called Kate.

"Your grandmother. She was named after her mother, Amelia, so they called her by her middle name, Kathryn—Kate." He smiles that he is revealing a secret that I didn't know. "You're named after her. She really liked that." He laughs. "She protested, saying it was confusing, but everyone knew she was proud to have a namesake. She was some lady, that Kate!"

"When she was young, your grandmother was in love with an artist. Her father disapproved—he had someone else in mind to marry his only child. Kate struck a deal with her father, your great-grandfather. Both of the men were given a thousand dollars to invest any way they wanted. In a year's time, Kate would marry the one who made the most money.

I can feel my eyes open wide. "Grandfather is an artist?" I nearly whisper in amazement. I wonder if he painted the portrait of Grandmother.

"No, no, the artist lost. But Kate did well with the family fortune. She had a sixth sense about business."

"The artist lost?" That's sad.

"That was probably why she supported your parents' marriage. I think she regretted the bargain with her father."

"Grandmother ran the businesses?"

"They kept their money separate. They had a friendly competition to see who could make the most money—that Kate was one smart lady. Your grandfather lost most of his money in the first ten years they were married. After that, she just let the world think it was his money." He stops to think about her again.

"Hopefully, I inherited some of her business savvy," I joke. I wonder if that is why Grandfather is the way he is.

"I hope so, too. She left her entire family fortune to you—the only heir. Most of the businesses were hers, the house, yacht, nearly everything." He sits up and looks serious.

~~~

What does one say to that? I am speechless. Managing the corporations for Grandfather is one thing. I thought the cousins and I would divide things someday, and I wouldn't have to live this life. I don't see that the money has done anyone a favor in this family. It is a good thing Sam is taking notes. I don't really understand the implications of the legalese Mr. Bradford lapses into now.

"How much are we talking about?" Sam asks without looking up from his notes.

Mr. Bradford smiles wryly. "Let's just say Kathryn is a multi-billionaire in her own right. I'd have to check the latest quarterly reports—it might be another billion this quarter."
~~~

A what? At the moment I can't even think how many zeros that is. I can't imagine anyone with that much money. My breath is shallow. I don't know what to say.

"Kathryn, you didn't know it was your money?" Mr. Bradford asks.

I shake my head from side to side. "No, Mr. Bradford, I didn't know." I take a deep breath.

"Anything else you want to know, Kathryn?"

"I was going to talk to you about my salary. In a month's time, I will make more than all last year. I suppose this changes even that."

"Yes. There are some complications. You were to inherit next year. Your Grandfather stepped down early."

"Complications, what complications?" I think "oh crap" fits in here someplace.

"You are going to have terrible tax consequences unless you set up a charitable foundation."

"A trust?"

"Not a trust. A charitable foundation has fewer limitations than a trust."

Sam nods agreement.

"You are going to have to give away more money than you already do, now that your wealth has gone through the roof. I've started the papers, you need to decide on a name for the foundation."

"Do you need the name today?" I'm relieved that the complications aren't serious. I expected something worse than naming a foundation and giving away money.

"You have a week or two; we can add it into the document when you decide on something. You'll have to live with the name. Pick a good one. We'll get a logo trademarked."

The meeting with Mr. Bradford was overwhelming. Sam drops me off at Karen's office. I'm glad we are having lunch together. Then she's

loaning me her car to run my errands. I'm getting a headache from all of the stress; besides, I am really hungry.

"Hi, how's your day?" I ask.

"Actually, quiet for us." Karen smiles. "How are you?"

"Things are good. Lunch is on me! Today and every other day."

Karen watches the traffic as she drives to the restaurant, but I can see she is pondering what I just said.

"Remember Grandfather's big announcement?" I ask, watching her think about that night. "It didn't matter. I was going to inherit it all next year anyway. My grandmother left everything she had to me. It was all hers, not his."

That got her. The look on her face is priceless.

She pulls to a stop at the light, and turns toward me. "What? You were getting this anyway and no one told you?"

"I know. Not to mention the questions I have about Grandfather. I had hoped he found me, I don't know—to get to know me. Maybe to atone for his decisions before he died. To atone for wiping me out of his life, sight unseen." I shrug. "I think he just did this to protect his image." I snicker. "I'm sorry, I shouldn't laugh, but this is too funny. I think he didn't want anyone to know that he is only a figurehead."

"Whatever his motive, you love him and have enjoyed getting to know him."

"Yes, I love him. I'm not sure of his motivation. I really wanted it to be me. I wanted him to want to find me—not the family heir."

"What about your cousins?"

"If they ever learn the truth, they are really going to be angry." With a huge grin I add, "I would like to kick them out of the house."

"Really! You wouldn't—would you?" She is amazed at the idea because it doesn't seem like I'd become so power hungry.

"No, not really. I have more options now. The house is mine —the art, statues, grounds—everything."

"And, the ballroom!"

"Yes, and the ballroom. Quit grinning. You know we can't talk about any of this once we get inside. Take a deep breath. Ready?" I ask as we open the door to the restaurant.

~~~

After the bank cashes my paycheck, and I pick up my replacement glasses, I'm on the way to return Karen's car when
~~~

Storm Surge

I drive past a Ford dealership and pull in to look at the new cars. I don't want my Mustang back. I don't really believe that they can get all of the glass fragments removed from it. Besides, I don't want to wait for it to be repaired and have to bum a ride when I want to go somewhere. It might be time for a new Mustang.

At the dealership, the salesman catches me at the first car I stop to peek into. We go through the usual are-you-looking-for-a-car routine, and no, that's not my trade-in. While we play car-buying twenty questions, I move from car to car looking through the window for a five-speed. I'm focused on my search. Clearly, he is going through a script. I like the Thunderbird, but it's a five-speed automatic and the color is all wrong. We reach the Mustang section.

"Do you have authority to sell a car, or do you have to talk with 'someone' else to wear me down?" I ask, deliberately throwing off the rhythm of his script.

"Why, ah, yes. Sure, I can sell you a car."

I write a number on a paper and hand it to him. "I'll give you this amount in cash for this black, convertible Mustang, if you can agree to it now—on the spot. Ten seconds."

He looks at the amount, then the car, then the figure again and hesitates. Take it or get approval? Take it or get approval?

Maybe I shouldn't have put him on the spot, but I don't want to take all day. There are plenty of other dealerships.

Finally, he agrees to the purchase.

He should. It was a fair amount, but not the full sticker price. I've shot myself in the foot if there is a rebate on it.

We go inside. I lay out the cash in stacks of ten one-hundred dollar bills across his desk. The look on his face is priceless. He calls the cashier to come count it. I can tell by his side of the conversation that she doesn't want to be bothered.

"I have $20,000 cash on my desk! You need to count it!"

She's at his desk in seconds, and very pleasant to me.

We have a done deal, I sign on the dotted line. The salesman doesn't know who I am, but the cashier saw my alien baby photo and mentions it—that figures. After we joke about the alien. The car will be ready to go by the time I take Karen's car back and return in a taxi.

~~~

On the way home, I call Sam. He's stuck in traffic and is a captive audience.

"Sam, I just want to make sure I heard correctly. Did Mr. Bradford say that my inheritance from Grandmother is in a trust, or whatever he is managing for me—along with the one from my parents?"

"That's right, why?"

"I'll talk with you about it tomorrow, not on the phone," I say.

Next call is Mr. Bradford's office. "Crystal, is Mr. Bradford available? This is Kathryn."

"Sorry, Miss McKenzie, he is in a pre-trial meeting. I can have him call you when he is finished."

"That's fine, thank you." The conversation concludes as I approach the town south of the mansion.

I locate the hospital parking lot. No, I don't want to see the shooter. There is no point for me to try to talk with someone who is hallucinating, even if the officers would let me see him, which they won't. I am hoping to catch his wife. Rather than ask at the visitors desk, I find the psych unit and see if the shooter's wife is there.

The psych unit is a locked unit, as it should be. I find a seat in the waiting area outside the unit, facing the double doors. I can see through the windows in the doors there is an officer standing outside one room. In about fifteen minutes a woman exits the guarded door. She looks like the weight of the world is on her shoulders. I guess she is the shooter's wife. Laying down my magazine, I join her at the elevator. The door opens and we both enter. We utter token hellos.

"You look like you could use a cup of coffee."

"I don't know what I need," she replies.

I tilt my head slightly and tempt, "Coffee?"

She lets out a deep, weary breath. "All right, thanks."

Her hand shakes uncontrollably, nearly spilling her coffee.

"Let me help you with that." I reach for her cup.

She tries to smile.

We find a table away from the staff on their break. "I am Kathryn McKenzie."
~~~

She is surprised and uneasy with the news. "What do you want?" she whispers defensively.

"I know this is hard for you. How can I help?"

"You just want your name in the paper," she says.

"No, actually I'd rather you tell no one."

"So, what do you want?" She can't figure it out.

"I want to know how can I help."

I expect a flippant comment about curing her husband or something as ridiculous.

"Billy lost his job a couple of months ago. We're behind in our utilities and house payment. It was like something snapped in him. I'm really sorry he shot at you." She stops talking and looks down at her cup. "I don't know how I'm going to manage."

"I'd like to help until you get back on your feet."

"I—I don't know what else to do. A few months ago, I was planning to go back to school this fall, so I could get a better job. Things were finally working out for us." She forces a smile. "He just wasn't the same after his deployment to the Middle East. He can't seem to keep a job, he's restless, irritable. I hardly recognize him." She looks up with all of the pain she feels visible on her face.

Her despair moves me. I can see she is destined to be homeless if something isn't done. "Let me help, so you can still go to school this fall, as a gift—just between us."

She pulls a tissue out of her pocket and wipes a tear. "I just don't know what happened to Billy. Things were going good. We bought a house last year, and, and—" She begins to cry.

"The doctors will figure out what to do for your husband. In the meantime, let me help, okay?" I take out my card and write my cell number on the back. I get her phone and address.

"I'll repay every penny—I promise."

"That's not necessary. Help someone else, sometime."

"I will, but I'll pay you back too. I'm so sorry that Billy tried to kill you, he isn't like that. I don't know what happened to him."

"It's all right. He just needs help right now. And you need to focus on taking care of your family. Here is my number, call me and we will work it out."

~~~
~~~

Calling me for help is probably too hard. I decide to take care of it myself. Tuesday morning, I research who holds the mortgage on the shooter's house and pay twelve month's worth of utilities, in person with cash to hope to be anonymous. I meet with the president of the little bank who holds the deed. I prove my identity to his satisfaction and swear him to secrecy. I know any small bank would be glad for the infusion of cash. I tell him if it leaks out that I've paid off the house, I'll own his bank before sundown the same day. He believes me.

It cost the Foundation less than $186,000 for both transactions. It is a bargain for a mother and children to have a life—it's definitely a bargain.

~~~
~~~

CHAPTER 9

The Stuff Tabloids Are Made Of

Things settle down to normal again. Well, if anything is normal in my world. Mr. Bradford finishes the documents to create a foundation. All that remains is a name. Naming the Foundation is more difficult than I expected. I wonder if Mother Elizabeth had as much trouble naming Spirit of Hope. I tried a variety of practical and boring name ideas. I settle on Amelia Kathryn McKenzie Foundation. Boring, I know. It's a tribute to my grandmother, it's her money.

Mrs. Bailey is thrilled with my offer of an early retirement package, including a retirement party at the mansion—a place usually closed to outsiders. She is thrilled to show her friends where she worked.

I am equally happy that she won't be at the mansion longer. Frankly, I'm surprised by the number of her friends attending her party. The really interesting thing is how easily she laughs as she opens her gifts—that isn't the Mrs. Bailey I know.

Grandfather gives her and three friends a cruise to Alaska. All of the women are woozy at the thought of such a gift. He almost looks embarrassed by the fuss his gift causes. I give her a camera for her trip. We conspired on the gifts, but the cruise was Grandfather's idea. It is a classy gift. Good job, Grandfather.

Chico starts to produce reports and financial analyses that make sense to me—a great improvement over Mrs. Bailey's reports. When Chico needs help to manage all of the data entry, I offer the position to Race. We'll put that computer training to good use.

It's good to see Race again and hear of his progress since he left Spirit of Hope. He wears his confidence well and is a semester away from a bachelor's degree in computer science. He plans to move his family to town, so that he can shorten the commute. I offer to pay him the industry standard and he thinks he is rich.

Later, I learn he and Lana plan to purchase a house next year, the first home they have ever owned—a far cry from the day they came to Spirit of Hope with only a trash bag of belongings for the entire family.

~~~

Grandfather comes out of his room and stays out longer each day. He is his old self again, possibly even more engaged with those around him than before. There is no hiding from Grandfather what we are doing, so we enlist his help. Sometimes it's only advice, other times he helps Sam and me analyze the businesses. We develop a plan to efficiently conduct site visits of each company. Grandfather is a wealth of information on the histories of the businesses and the reasons for their location. I don't think that he knows that I am aware that the businesses belonged to Grandmother all along.

As for the reports, I begin to understand the dynamics of the reports I read. The learning curve is incredible. Sam and I commence with my privately owned companies, saving the public companies for after I get up-to-speed in this new world of mine. We ease into the flow and take Grandfather's counsel by starting with the companies who bid government contracts. That is both interesting and mind-boggling.

~~~

Danny comes home. His mother is doing fine after her surgery. He doesn't volunteer what kind of surgery she had and I don't ask, it's none of my business. He missed all of our recent excitement.

Danny and I need to have a private conversation—sans his brother and sister. Luckily, Tim and Brooke are often away partying somewhere.

In the morning we are the only two in the kitchen, so I seize the opportunity at hand. "Dan, let's take a walk."

He shrugs. "Why not?"

"Bring your coffee."

When we are away from the house so not to be accidentally overheard, I begin.

"Dan, if you could do absolutely anything you wanted, what would you do?"

He stops and looks at me like he is considering whether it's a loaded question.

"You have to want more out of life than passing your days hanging around here."

"Are you kicking me out?"

"Of course not. It is a simple question. Don't complicate it."

He takes a measured breath as he looks away, across the manicured gardens. Then he looks back.

"If you really want to know, I want to have my own architect firm."

"What's stopping you?"

He looks down. "Grandfather. I can't leave him alone with Brooke and Tim."

"I'll look out for Grandfather. Go have a life. Dan, live your dreams—life is too short not to live it well."

We have come full circle on the garden path. "Think about where you want your firm. Stay here as long as you like, but don't stay because you feel a sense of obligation. It's my responsibility now. I'll take care of Grandfather." I make my final point before we reach the patio and go inside.

Dan doesn't think I am after the family money. I genuinely want him to be happy and to have a life—something I want for myself, as well.

Besides, I have already had the opportunity to live as I chose. I have had successes and failures, made good decisions and bad, but I experienced my choices and their ramifications. Dan hasn't had that freedom because of his sense of duty to the family—it is time for that to change.

The next time I go to my beach apartment, I bring back the blueprints and design-idea notebooks that I have from my parents' architectural firm, McKenzie & McKenzie. I offer them to Dan, if he wants them. I want to help him set up his own firm any way that I can. He doesn't have to stay at the mansion any longer to secure his inheritance, or watch over Grandfather's welfare.

~~~

Mr. Bradford said that Grandfather gives each of us an annual allowance of $100,000. Mine was automatically deposited
~~~

into the trust Grandmother for me—and I was blissfully unaware of its existence. If I had been Dan, I would have taken the allowance as soon as it was deposited and started my business without regard for the bulk inheritance, which doesn't exist anyway. No one should have to put their dreams on hold for such nonsense.

When I talk to Dan about his plans, he tells me he is just waiting until he is old enough to access his trust account. I offer him the assurance of five years operating capital—the minimum needed to start a business—if he really wants to start his own firm. If he's half as good as my parents were, he isn't going to need the money for five years. It seems like it had never occurred to him to just go get a job at a firm and work his way to the top, or get a business loan at a bank. He hesitates, then agrees with the promise to pay me back from his trust. I don't tell him that there is no trust for him and his siblings. They will get the annual allowance until they are thirty-five, plenty of time for anyone to get situated in life.

Almost immediately, as he begins to create the life of his dreams, his stuttering stops. He has a new bounce in his step and stands taller now that he is moving out on his own. I feel proud that I set him free. He only needed the encouragement to go.

Tim gets another driving while intoxicated ticket and loses his license. I warn the staff not to tell Grandfather about it. One morning the police are at the front door. They found Tim's car, wrecked. It smells of liquor and they find some drugs. The passenger is severely injured, but expected to live. As far as I know, Tim hasn't come home. I don't ask. I suspect Brooke is hiding him somewhere. She left early this morning, which is an unusual time of day for her to get up.

As for Brooke, she usually steers clear of me, but I can't imagine that lasting forever. It is a pleasant reprieve from her hateful comments. I haven't come up with a foolproof strategy for the next time she lashes out at me. Detox comes to mind.

~~~

Zoe has smoothly made the transition to working for me. She is obviously loyal and has the energy to keep up with the pace
~~~

we are setting. She handles my calendar like a pro, when it comes to giving me a manageable schedule. Zoe understands the importance of things like Shasta's dance recital, and doesn't overbook my trips to tour the companies. Finally, I feel like I can catch my breath. I feel secure that an in-house conspiracy isn't waging while I am away and unable to monitor my affairs.

Sam and I take a day to visit the plants near L.A. and Long Beach, and the second day to take the helicopter to Lancaster to tour that plant. We are beginning to put together what we are seeing on paper with what is at the plants—and faces to the names.

~~~

The next morning, I overhear Zoe on the phone as I approach her office. She is turned with her back to the door and doesn't notice me standing in the doorway.

She whispers desperately, "No! I can't. She would never agree! I can't ask her to do that!" There is silence as she listens to the person on the phone. "Yes, I understand, you know I would help, if I could."

"Agree to what?" I whisper from over her shoulder, startling Zoe who hangs up the phone without saying another word. Containing a grin, I ask again, "I would never agree to what, Zoe?"

"Well, you see, my boyfriend works for someone who wants to meet you."

I tilt my head in a questioning glance.

"He, he wants me to get you to agree to a blind date."

"A blind date? Oh, no, probably not," I agree with Zoe on that.

"My boyfriend's boss likes you. He wants to go to dinner with you," Zoe continues, then hesitates.

This seems a little junior high to me. After the Joseph incident I don't really think much of blind dates. I look at Zoe fidgeting with her pen. There is no reason to say no just because one blind date didn't work out well in the end. Besides, it doesn't require a second date.

"Is this a double date?" I query, watching her eyes grow wide with disbelief, and she nods and smiles big.
~~~

"I'll consider it. Let's get back to work—after you call your boyfriend back."

She jumps up and hugs my neck.

"I only said I would consider it." I caution her optimism. I smile at her zest for life as I return to my office. Oh, gee. A blind date? I hope I don't live to regret this.

~~~

The shooter's court date arrives. It has been a long time since I have been in court. Even though I never saw the shooter, I am on the State's witness list. I have been a witness hundreds of times, but I really don't want to do this. No one is served by putting this mentally ill guy in prison. He needs long-term treatment, and prison isn't where he will get it. Neither do I want him free on bail where he may decide to come after me again. In an ideal world he would be locked up while he receives treatment.

Trusting Keith's advice, I hire his bodyguard friend for the day. If, for some strange reason, the shooter is released after court on a technicality, I'll be ready.

It turned out to be a short hearing. The defense attorney filed a plea of not guilty by reason of insanity. So, now we wait while the shooter is evaluated by both the prosecution and defense psychiatrists.

The thing I tell no one is, the shooter is the guy who sat in his car and watched my apartment with binoculars. This wasn't a sudden onset of craziness. He'd planned this for a while. He had a better shot at me walking the beach, than at the estate. I wonder why he waited? There is something that doesn't ring true about this. There must have been some significance to the date or the location. Otherwise, why wait?

The shooter's wife leaves court alone. I deliberately miss the elevator she takes and take the next one to spare her from the media frenzy that will catch me.

The media catches me and my entourage outside the courthouse. I watch the shooter's wife slowly walk down the front steps—ignored, dejected, and relieved that she is invisible.

"My people" push me through the reporters until I stop when one asks if I am encouraging the prosecutor's office to go for the
~~~

death penalty. My entourage nearly runs into me when I stop suddenly to respond.

I think persons preying upon others and robbing them of life should be permanently removed from society. No one should be condemned to live in fear because known murderers are released among us.

As perverse as their crimes are, I am not prepared to become like them by advocating their murder as recompense. I am not ready to become a poster child in the death penalty debate. I skirt the question.

"What are my thoughts regarding the death penalty?"
I tolerate the question and the photos. "Let me remind everyone that the death penalty doesn't apply to this case. Now, no more questions. Thank you."

~~~

In the vacuum of reality, it is apparent the shooter needs long-term treatment in an environment that protects the safety of society; Brooke and Tim seriously need detox, and to learn the responsibilities that accompany their age and social position; and, as for myself, the media needs to find some other socially redeeming topic to report, not whether I attend baseball games, and with whom. I am out of sorts today.

Overall, there seems to be a waste of the human spirit in our society. It seems too important to play political games, flex perceived power, and to exploit the poor for the benefit of a select few wealthy scum.

Ugh, being in court again has tainted my mood. I need to get out of here and clear my head, and I don't really feel like having Garrett or my bodyguard's company.

"Zoe, I'm going for a drive for a couple of hours."
"Anyone going with you?"
I grimace, because I want to be alone. "I'm only going to Saint Leo's beach. I have my phone." I give more specifics to satisfy her, then take my leave before she can tattle on me.

As I slide behind the wheel, I toss my purse into the passenger seat. It feels good to be out, free, shifting through the gears. I think everyone has their own means to recalibrate their soul. For me it is always the beach, it's naturally honest.
~~~

Standing at the water's edge, I look at the piles of rocks with birds perched on them. Before long, the mood of the waves awakens the emotions I have hidden or ignored.

The sounds of the repetitive advance and retreat slowly strip away the noise in my brain clamoring to be foremost. The artificial world of commerce where I live seems very far away as I sit on Father's Beach. It is only the beginning, yet I am tired of being Kathryn the Great and crave a few moments as Katey the Ordinary.

After an hour of lounging in the warm sand, I feel ready to return to the mansion. I sit up a little fast and make myself dizzy.

Within minutes, I am slipping through the gears into fifth, and on the way home. I have gone back to my own beach less and less often since the shooting.

Zoe reports my blind date is set for Friday night. Friday night seems soon. The last I knew, I said I would think about it.

Zoe and "friend" will join us for drinks, then we will be on our own for dinner, if I give her the signal that things are okay for her to leave.

"So, do I get to know his name?"

"Mark."

"Mark? Does Mark have a last name?"

"Well, yes. But, he doesn't want me to tell you." She smiles, making me all the more curious.

"Okay, then what does Mark do?"

"He is a musician." The phone rings and saves her from additional inquiry.

Garrett has agreed to work Friday night to drive me to Beverly Hills in the limo for my date. I haven't been on a blind date for more than six years, and I feel better having Garrett around, since Zoe and her date won't be staying for the entire evening.

~~~

I look in the mirror one last time at my black cocktail dress. My hair and dress look fine. Surprisingly, I am more excited than nervous. I am fully aware that this is a stupid idea.

We arrive prior to Mark. Garrett sits at a table where he can comfortably observe while he eats his dinner. Zoe looks lovely in
~~~

a very young-styled cocktail dress. Her date admits he won lots of points for making the arrangements for the date. What can I say? We aim to please.

Mark arrives. He is quietly handsome in his charcoal suit with a burgundy shirt—no tie. His manners are impeccable. To my surprise, the conversation between the four of us is easy.

Garrett and I exchange glances. He nods his approval of Mark. Smoothly, Zoe and her date leave. Mark and I begin our dinner. He invites me to attend the preview of a movie for which he wrote the musical score, plus two additional songs. He says it's Oscar-bound. I'm a pushover for movies. I don't have to think twice about accepting. He does warn me that he has to appear in his public persona—Scourge.

Scourge? I can't believe it! Mark is the Bad Boy of Rock? He is so engaging and polite. This can't be true.

On the trip home, Garrett says that first impressions are good. He thinks I should go out with him again. He can't believe Mark is Scourge. Frankly, neither can I. He asks if I have heard Scourge's music, it's loud. Unfortunately, I have heard a couple of his songs, parts of them. Garrett thinks I should still go out with Mark.

~~~

The two weeks since the date with Mark passed quickly. I have thought of him more often than I would like—definitely more than I will admit. Mark is unlike Joseph, who fell into periods of silence while his life carried on without notice of how much I loved him. Mark calls, sends flowers and chocolates—not all at once, but scattered throughout the fourteen days. He makes me smile. I don't feel those giddy feelings about him that I did toward Joseph. I think it is a good thing this is different.

Dana came last weekend to fit the gown she is making for me to wear to the premiere with Mark. We are scheming—I am going to wear something from her holiday line. It is, after all, a Hollywood affair and I am glad to debut one of her designs. The media is sure to be there. If they take my picture, I am hoping for something better than what the tabloids have run so far. ValDana's fashions never suffer when the rich and famous wear them—neither do the rich and famous.
~~~

She is cutting it close in delivering the "dress of my dreams"—as she calls all of her gowns. I do like it. It is hunter green—she also offered cranberry—made out of a shimmery blend of silk and something else. I forget what she said.

Dana and I run upstairs to put on the dress. Ooh, it is beautiful! The fabric is supple, but not limp. Dana wanted to address the alien baby issue by cutting the dress low in the front. It isn't in bad taste, but I hadn't thought of cutting it quite so low. I have to agree, the design works.

We look through Grandmother's jewelry case in the closet. Dana advises me on which to wear. She selects a ruby and diamond necklace and earrings—screw-back earrings. Dana says I need to have them converted to pierced before my date. We locate the matching ring, it is too large. I'll have it sized when I have the earrings done. Dana's keen eye appraises my hair and makeup. She adjusts the necklace to hang perfectly.

I feel beautiful!

Luckily, Mark warned me that he would be in his public persona. When he gets out of his limo with his leather "Bad Boy" outfit, I study the transformed Mark. Frankly, I am not sure anything I own would go with the chains and black leather. What a sight he is! A distasteful sight.

If I don't look at him, it seems like I am with the same man who took me to dinner two weeks ago. His Rod McKuen voice tells me I look lovely. He has a dozen roses in the limo for me. When I look at Mark and see his yellow and red-tipped spiked hair and black eyeliner, I don't know whether to gasp or laugh.

Struggling with his transformation, I try to make casual conversation about the evening without looking at him more than is necessary.

"Tell me about the premiere," I begin, trying desperately not to stare.

He takes my hand in his, looks into my eyes and says, "Go ahead, laugh and get it over, so you can make it through the evening." He opens his eyes and mouth wide and sticks out his tongue, then throws back his head and laughs ferociously.

I laugh nervously at first, then openly. It works. I feel more relaxed. He has champagne chilling in the limo bar.

"Tell me about tonight," I prod again.

"I'm invited because I did the feature song for the movie." He smiles proudly, lifts his glass high, and laughs again.

"That's marvelous."

"Here, listen to this." He slides a CD into the stereo beside the bar.

Music, or rather, loud, obnoxious sounds and screaming lyrics blare harshly from the speakers. The suddenness of the sound causes me to jump.

"Should I assume this is not going to be a chick flick?" I ask loudly.

He turns down the volume of the music. "Actually, it is a touching story. That was my new CD, not the song from the movie," he answers softly. He glides smoothly back and forth between his two personas.

"This one is from the movie."

It is difficult for me to keep up with him. "How many personalities do you have?"

"Just one, Scourge is my manager's creation." He winks.

There were new expectations since Grandfather's announcement, but no one expects me to take on an alternate persona. I am glad I don't have to live like that. All I have had to do is learn new protocols.

We arrive at the theater and wait in the limo line for our turn for the grand entrance. There are fans for the various stars standing behind a barricade. The media is present. This is the first time I have attended a Hollywood affair. The whole scene is overwhelmingly fabulous. Even if Mark is in costume and has this bizarre personality, I am thankful that he is experienced in these matters and I am not making my debut solo.

Mark looks like an actor getting in character before he enters the stage. He says, "We're next. Ready? I'll get out first, then I'll help you out. Take my arm. We will pause for a minute for photos, then walk toward the door. Smile like you just won an Oscar. Try not to get cornered with personal questions from the reporters. Sound bites, you know. I'll keep us moving."

This is it. Mark gets out of the limo, raises his arms in the air like a presidential candidate who just won the Iowa primary, then offers his hand. I place my gloved hand in his, and slide out of the limo.

The cameras flash. An official reporter, invited to cover the premiere, kisses Scourge and asks who is his date. He smiles and gestures toward me. "CeCe, may I introduce Kathryn McKenzie."

Her face lights up. It is entertaining to see her awestruck. She quickly regains her wits, "Miss McKenzie, your gown is beautiful! Which designer made it?"

My cheeks are hot. I feel like I'm blushing. These Hollywood extravaganzas are fun. "It's a ValDana design." I say with pride that Dana is my friend, and turn a bit to show it off.

"You are beautiful! Enjoy the premiere, dears." She moves down the line to the next waiting couple.

This is the ultimate movie experience. All of the cast and principals are present. The producer makes a few remarks. The director thanks everyone he has ever known, or might know in the future. The movie begins. Mark's title song is tame for him. I am a little surprised, as are others who haven't heard it yet.

At the reception, Hollywood stars are mingling. Some are watching the room to see who notices them, most are not concerned with such things. Mark is more popular than I thought he would be since his standard music isn't what I imagine most of these people would listen to regularly. Several people tell him that he should expect an Academy nomination for the song. He seems to take it in stride—no ego problem for him. Everyone he introduces me to is gracious. Some are not quite sober, but still they are gracious.

~~~

Mark sends a dozen roses and a personally written note thanking me for attending the premiere with him. This is much better treatment than I ever had from Joseph.

Monday, the tabloids hit the stands. The most noteworthy is the cover story of "ex-nun dates devil," complete with a photo of Mark and me. At least the picture is better than the last one. The other tabloids are not as rich as the first's headline. I hope this headline is not another invitation to get me shot at, or killed by another mentally ill person.
~~~

~~~

I show Grandfather the paper before he sees it some other way. He asks questions about my intentions with Scourge. Of course, I have no intentions with "Scourge," but Mark is nice. I explain Mark's two personalities to Grandfather. In some ways it's convenient that he is unrecognizable as Mark. However, it won't be long before I am readily recognized by the public at large as Kathryn McKenzie.

Grandfather cautions, "Have him checked out. You'll be sorry if you don't."

I promise Grandfather that I will run a check on Mark. I will be alert regarding him and everyone else I meet. It doesn't take a rocket scientist to know that questions must be asked about anyone who makes the extra effort to get near me now that I have become "Miss McKenzie." No worries, I am not a lonely, rich old maid blinded by the attention of every gold digger that comes my way. Joseph taught me to guard my heart.

Brooke comes into the library with a smug look on her face. She is armed with the tabloids. It was a good decision to show them to Grandfather before Brooke had the chance to cause agitation between us. She masterfully plays the concerned cousin and feigns outrage. Grandfather laughs and shows his stack of them.

"Kathryn was about to autograph these for me. Would you like yours signed, too, Brooke?" He smiles innocently.

She disappears as quickly as she arrived. When she is gone, he offers a chuckle regarding our alliance in warding off Brooke's advance.

I don't see Brooke again for a week, but there are indications that she is in and out of the residence.

Officers are once more at the door looking for Tim. They won't be specific about why they want him. I convince them to allow me to ask Grandfather about Tim, rather than trust the task to them.

I introduce the officers to Grandfather. "These officers are looking for Tim. Have you seen him?"

"I haven't seen Timmy since he came back from Europe," Grandfather says gruffly.
~~~

I don't know whether to believe him or not. Brooke is not likely to give me a straight answer, or a civil one for that matter. There is a slight chance that Mrs. Bailey might know some of Tim's friends; she is obviously fond of Tim and Brooke.

I apologize that I do not know my jet-setting cousins very well. The look on their faces indicates the officers are hesitant to believe me, but it's the truth, whether they believe me or not. I give them the phone number for Mrs. Bailey, and send Zoe upstairs to find Brooke.

I go about my own business. Brooke takes the officers outside the front door. Before long the officers are gone.

Mark calls again for a quiet dinner, but I decline. At the moment I don't have time for a relationship. I need to slow this down a little until I get acclimated to this new job. Of course, it is an excuse and I am simply being cautious. We agree to have dinner in the next week or two instead.

~~~

To further complicate my organizing efforts, Chico found unusual bookkeeping practices in the Seattle company. All we have to go by is the final numbers on the quarterly reports. Chico needs raw numbers to really determine what is happening and hopefully who is responsible. He wants to go to Seattle and infiltrate the company. He starts to explain how he'll do it, but I don't speak "geek" so we bypass that process.

I am not sure about the idea, but Sam thinks it's good. I arrange to send Chico to apply for the mailroom job that is open in the company. Grandfather loves the sleuth idea of spying on the company to determine the extent of the creative accounting. He wishes he had thought of it.

Race is left to hold down the fort while Chico is away. Everyone working at the mansion is told Chico is returning to New Mexico to attend to family matters. We arrange for Chico to move to Seattle and apply for the position. Sam will be Chico's reference, so that we can control the information given out about him. Chico doesn't think his previous boss knows he came to work for me, so we are safe listing him on the application.

As a mailroom worker, Chico will be able to move freely around the office complex delivering the mail and perhaps collect
~~~

information necessary to determine the nature of the problem and hopefully the person responsible.

Sam wants to contact the Feds. I think it's premature. Grandfather agrees with Sam since the company has a lucrative government contract. It takes my best effort to present my case to wait to have something more concrete. They could barge in and tip off the guilty, if there is anyone guilty.

In the end, they both acquiesce to my decision to wait. When Chico is hired, he tells them the reason for moving to Seattle is to attend college in the fall. Just to be safe, he enrolls in photo journalism classes, something he has always wanted to do anyway.

In the meantime, I ask Sam to put together a list of items we need to find before notifying the authorities. When we get hard copies of the information, we can determine if there is a problem requiring reporting to the security regulators. I hate to fuel a witch hunt if there isn't really embezzlement, just sloppy practices. The Chico operation is in place.

~~~

After Chico leaves for the great northwest, Race finds two more companies with similar accounting practices. These people should be artists with all their creative talent. It isn't likely this is a random occurrence or a coincidence. Race is looking for any connections between the three companies. One company is manufacturing, one is an intellectual properties company, and the third is a holding company for four overseas firms.

Even though the companies are outwardly unrelated, if their products interface, then perhaps they intersect somewhere else. Race is also looking for bookkeeping, marketing, auditing firm connections, any connection on a subsurface level. The last thing I can think of is a connection between key personnel in the three companies: relatives, college friends, prior common employment, anything that ties them together. What a task.

I remain hesitant to infiltrate the other two companies, one in Tennessee and the other in Texas, until we have something from Chico about Seattle. It's a tough decision whether to wait to get definitive information. If there is a connection between the three companies, I don't want to tip off the remaining two. It is difficult
~~~

to decide whether to keep the bird in the hand before going after the two in the bush.

Grandfather is shaken by the possibility that there is corruption in the corporation. He misunderstood what I said, but when he mentions his concerns to me, it makes me think we should look closer to home—the McKenzie Enterprises corporate office. Our investigation widens. The added stress is fueling my headaches. I am sure that the anxiety, fatigue, and eyestrain contribute to both the stress and headaches. I need a vacation—and I have only yet to begin my new reign.

~~~

Government probes, tabloids, bad legitimate press, alien babies— my headaches increase exponentially. I have trouble focusing, mentally and visually, on the reams of paper Race is generating. Another visit to the eye doctor reveals that the eyestrain has rewarded me with stronger reading glasses and the promise of full-time bifocals in the near future.

In the meantime, reviewing corporate expenses reveals there is an inordinate number of trips taken on the two company jets. I realize that the jets might be in the company as a tax deductible business expense. However, some of the trips are to locations where we have no holdings.

Until I know who to trust to provide accurate information in the company outside my closest circle, I contact the airport where the jets are hangared. It takes speaking with several people before I find someone at the airport who can provide me with a list of the flight plans filed by the McKenzie jets and helicopter. The catch is that I will have to come, show identification, and sign for the information personally.

~~~

Since I am going to the airport, I arrange for a meeting with all of the pilots and flight staff. Zoe is able to set the meeting for tomorrow. She has spoken with each flight crew member and scheduled a conference room at the hotel across the street from the airport.

The catch is that the meeting will have to be held at noon. Zoe suggests arranging for a light lunch to be served. I only anticipate the meeting to last a half hour, but I agree to a meal.

Until we know where the problems lie, I put the room and the meal on my personal credit card so it doesn't have a corporate record. I'll get reimbursed for the expenses once the corruption question is answered.

Grandfather and Sam agree that Sam to attend the meeting with me. I suggest that Sam comes casually dressed, rather than in a lawyer-looking suit. Since it is getting late, I ride to the city with Sam so we can discuss key issues for tomorrow's meeting. I will spend the night at my apartment. Sam can pick me up in the morning. My mind is racing. The plan is to designate a senior pilot and crew member. It is a perfect excuse to get copies of their résumés and begin to know who these people are flying the McKenzie skies.

LAX is on the way to my apartment, so we stop for the flight records. I'll partially review them tonight and brief Sam before the meeting tomorrow. Hopefully, the records will provide enough insight to get the flight costs under control. Maybe it will reveal a pattern of activity that will lead to answers about who is going where and for what reason, particularly who is jetting between the three companies in question.

~~~

I head for a walk on the beach. It seems like I have been away for months rather than weeks. First thing I do when I reach the beach is draw a deep breath. Then, savor it as it escapes. The ocean smell is rich in memories. It feels good to be home again. The sand, spray of the waves breaking, and the sounds of seagulls intermingled with it all—it is rich.

Summer-people populate the beach. Lifeguard stations are in position to watch over the activities. Children are playing. Sandcastles have sprung up like tulips in spring.

My thoughts are deeply focused on the problems of the Enterprise. This is bigger than me. What if corruption does exist? What if it is not isolated in Seattle, or even three companies? What if there are similar problems in the public companies? All of these are legitimate questions. The hard questions must be asked. And they must be asked now.

I hate corruption. It is nothing more than greed. Sharing, taking turns, using manners is all preschool stuff. But there are
~~~

people who think they are above the basics. In the final analysis, corruption cannot be tolerated in civilized society.

I devise a chart for the flights and begin plugging in data: Who went where, and when. I look for anything that correlates in a less-than-natural manner, including flight crews. Dates are the first element that line up suspiciously.

I run a probability formula and find that it isn't a natural coincidence. There is a destination that keeps coming up oddly. I think we are in big trouble. I am concerned that we have sent Chico into a dangerous situation.

It is time for a meeting with people I trust. I leave Grandfather out of the loop for the moment—deniability. I call Sam and see if he is available for a meeting. Then, I'll call Karen and Keith and see if they are available. That should do it—a lawyer, a politically savvy friend, and a detective. Between the three of them, someone must know someone we can trust not to leak this to the media. The media is watching to see how the first one hundred days go. I don't want to cause an unwarranted hiccup in the public companies' stock prices.

Sam is sitting down to dinner with his family when I call. He agrees to come to my apartment tomorrow evening for a short meeting. Karen will check with Keith, and bring him with her, if he is available. Mostly Karen is moral support.

Sam calls back. Chico caught something that points to a cluster of short selling in another group of our companies. Now we have another problem, or is it a related problem?

Even though I am feeling my way through uncharted territory, I feel more settled about tomorrow now. With a fresh cup of coffee, I sit down to write in my diary.

Dearest Maggie, the older I get, the more circumspect I become about petty people. I do not believe that we are outnumbered, but I think we can be outsmarted, if we don't learn to understand how greed works in the mind of men. I intend to become cunning and braver than they are. I may not have been able to make the Judicial system work for my dead little client, but I can make my empire work as it should. I may not have chosen this path, but I will landscape it! When I'm finished, everyone will know I have arrived.

~~~
~~~

CHAPTER 10

Camelot

Before Sam arrives to go to our lunchtime meeting, I take a morning walk on the beach. The fresh ocean air clears my mind. I have a hunch the flight information will be useful even if we don't detect a connection involving the cooked books theory and the corporate office. Regardless of the data, I want control of the spending on the McKenzie airline, whether or not the people abusing the use of the planes are involved in the creative bookkeeping.

Beginning on Monday, all flights will be cleared by me. It is micro-managing, but I can ease back later. In this age of technology, I can't imagine anyone in McKenzie Enterprises needing to fly around the country as much as our jets are in the air. All flights will be reimbursed from department budgets, so there is accountability for usage.

Personal use will require advance out-of-pocket payment, or better yet, not allowed at all. Foundation use will be paid by the Foundation. It's that simple.

The flight service won't make money, but at least it won't run at a complete loss. Primarily, I will be the only person using the planes and helicopter from now on—but I am not telling them that yet.

Sam agrees with my idea, at least in theory. I see no reason not to trim the fat out of McKenzie Enterprises. Personal use of the air fleet is not a perk that I am willing to offer. With Grandfather aging, everyone has had too much freedom to dictate the operations of the Enterprise, as well as the private companies and corporations.

We probe the flight records with a cup of coffee in hand. Brooke and Tim use the jets as their personal vehicles for their jet-setting. That will stop today. There are several names from the Seattle company that keep appearing. There are a few flights to Tennessee and Texas to pick up passengers at the other two companies in question. They rendevous in the Caribbean. We have no companies in the Caribbean. Didn't they think anyone would notice? Maybe they thought they had one more year —providing they were aware of the trust-vesting age. They were probably not aware, since it is a "secret."

Tomorrow, when I return to the mansion, I'll have Race database the flight information. It will be easier to see patterns in dates, destinations, and passengers. Maybe we will see the less obvious too.

We arrive at the hotel meeting room early enough that Sam can sit next to me. He can write notes to me, if needed.

After everyone arrives, I begin introductions around the table to my right, so that Sam will be the last one introduced. I won't mention that Sam is a lawyer. As each person introduces themselves, I write their name in the margin of my tablet.

Sam introduces himself as my assistant, which is true.

"I am Kathryn McKenzie. I have met a few of you, but I wanted to put faces with your names and get input from you. All of you fly for McKenzie Enterprises; you must have opinions about improvements in our flight division."

Most of the staff come prepared with paper and pen. I take note of the ones who do not by placing a small mark by their names on my notes. Their coworkers give them paper.

After they write their name at the top of the page, I ask the flight team for two nominations each of pilots and flight crew they would like to see as senior pilot and senior flight staff for the jets, and a senior helicopter pilot.

"Also, write suggestions you have regarding operations. Speak now or forever hold your peace, as the saying goes."

A few people laugh. I make note of that, too. They get points for laughing at my jokes. I want staff who are engaged in the process, and with me.

"The last item is, which is the best aircraft and why?"

While the staff write their assignments, the hotel staff indicates lunch is ready to serve.

"Now, ladies and gentlemen, on with the feast!"

I excuse myself to make a phone call, leaving Sam in the room as my eyes and ears. Rather than make a call, I use the time to find something for my headache.

Storm Surge

After the meeting, Sam heads to the corporate office and I take a taxi home to the beach. Finally, I feel like I am making progress in rounding up this stampeding herd.

In the afternoon I read through the comments from the lunch meeting. They offer several good suggestions about staffing and fiscal management. One idea that has merit is static teams. That is, the same people work together as a team, so they are a finely tuned crew. Also, they suggest that those who speak foreign languages be divided among the teams. They request more emergency training. I hadn't realized they didn't have CPR training, unless they did it on their own. They will be happy to hear I have decided to keep both jets. They probably don't have a good resale value anyway. A cross-reference of the notes of who was prepared for the meeting with the suggestions of senior pilot and flight staff suggests the staff nominations is accurate.

I designate senior staff for each aircraft, complete with an increase in pay.

Again I visit the beach before my guests arrive. I won't have time for a walk, but I can go to the beach and stand watching the waves for a few minutes to soak in strength from the energy of the ocean.

The evening breeze is beginning to blow inland. It is still hot out, a July hot. The sand is radiating the heat it accumulated from the day. The breeze is slight and gentle against my cheeks. I almost feel like my parents are here. There are plenty of good people in my life, but I still miss them.

My cell phone rings. Dan is excited about his new office. He wants me to come see it. I explain that I have a meeting in an hour and that I don't have a car in town.

"I don't care, Katey. I'll come get you when your meeting is over. Just call me when you finish."

"It's a deal. I'm at my apartment. I'll give you directions when I call you. And, thanks. Thanks for the invitation, Dan." I respond to his excitement as I begin to walk home, happy to have a developing connection with Dan.

Coffee is brewing and everything looks fine for company. Sam arrives first. He looks around while I pour him a cup. He comments about my movie posters. "I see you are a movie fan."

"My friends would say 'possessed by old movies,' if you asked them." I laugh.

"Really? Calm-under-fire Kathryn—is possessed?" He adds comments about the tabloids of the premiere with Scourge.

"Yes, really. My friend, Maggie, always said that I saw life as one movie after another. Sometimes a romance, sometimes a musical—"

Sam interrupts, "Sometimes a tragedy?"

"Yes. Or a horror!" I add a fake monster laugh.

"You handle them well. I'll have to meet Maggie sometime."

I smile. Sam doesn't need to know Maggie is dead. I appreciate his compliment, though.

~~~

Karen and Keith arrive together. They are openly seeing each other now. I think they are in love. She has never said so, and I am certainly not an expert on such things. They come bearing Chinese takeout. I hadn't realized I was hungry until I smelled the wonderful aroma.

We laugh and relax during dinner. Keith, Karen, and I teach Sam to use chopsticks. He is really funny to watch. I have never seen anyone have such trouble learning to use chopsticks before now.

"I'm Black, you know." He plays the ethnic card to justify his difficulty.

"What does that have to do with anything? We're White, but we can use chopsticks. You know, there isn't a chopstick gene that only Asians have," I say. I don't let him make race excuses, but I offer him a fork. That's all it takes to get him determined to master the chopsticks or starve trying.

Sam gives Karen and Keith an overview of our suspicions. We caution that it is only that, suspicion, at this point. Keith agrees that it would be a federal issue, since we cross state lines conducting business.

Sam says, "It might be a gray area since the companies are all free-standing, but McKenzie Enterprises or Kathryn owns these companies—either way, Kathryn, you are the principal at risk here."

Both men exchange nods of agreement.
~~~

Keith has a friend who is a federal marshall in Chicago. He'll ask who we should contact out here. Karen agrees that we are way out of our league with this, especially if it isn't contained in Seattle, but links to other companies or the corporate office.

If everything goes well with Keith's friend, we should be talking with the local Feds by this time next week. We'll let them figure out what is going on. That's a relief. Conducting internal investigations always makes the findings suspect.

Soon we can bring Chico home. Good thing my companies aren't publically traded. But not so good for the other companies' stockholders.

Karen and I lag behind the guys as we walk out. I can tell she has something on her mind.

"Keith asked me to marry him." She grins a schoolgirl grin.

I reach for her hand to see her ring. It is beautiful. I can't believe I didn't notice it.

I whisper "Congratulations!" when I hug her.

"Katey, I need to get an annulment in the Church first. Will you be a witness for the Church tribunal?"

"Yes, of course I will. Just tell me where and when."

I love the way he treats her. They deserve each other and all the happiness they can catch. Wonder how non-Catholic Keith likes the idea of the tribunal?

~~~

As soon as they leave, I call Dan, as arranged. He is as excited as a kid with a pony when he arrives. He looks around at my humble surroundings. "You live here?"

I'm not sure of the implication of his question. "Yes, this is 'Home Sweet Home.' So, tell me about your new office."

"You'll have to see it for yourself," he answers proudly as he puts his hand on the doorknob, encouraging me to hurry.

Dan has a nice office and a good location. I compliment both.

"Thanks for the push," he says. "I needed a push to get out of Pacific Estates. That place was killing me."

"I know what you mean." I laugh, but it isn't funny.

He uncovers a paper on his drafting table. "I wanted to show you what I'm going to paint on my door. "McKenzie, McKenzie & Anderson Architects" is drafted on the paper.
~~~

I am taken back. He included my parents. They would have been proud to work with him.

"I thought your parents would like it. I just added my name to theirs," he says proudly looking at the paper, then to me. "This is your dad's old drafting table from high school. I found it in the storeroom upstairs—the one down the hall from our rooms."

"Yes, they would be very proud." Not for one minute do I think he is using the McKenzie name for anything other than a tribute to my parents, his uncle and aunt. He is different from his brother and sister. It is almost as if they aren't related, but all three look like McKenzie descendants, even if they don't bear the name.

"I can never thank you properly."

I am not used to such sentimentality from the McKenzie side of the family. It is an awkward moment of silence. Then, he hugs me. Finally, there is a connection with one of my McKenzie cousins. My eyes mist. Maybe I will invite him to Thanksgiving in the park and show him how family can be. I'll think about it.

"Do good with what you have, be happy, that's thanks enough."

~~~

This week seems to go on forever. I'd like to say today is Friday, but it is only Thursday. Keith calls, as Sam and I are on our way north to the mansion. His friend is on vacation, but Keith thinks the FBI might be a better choice than the Justice Department and its federal marshals.

As soon as Keith says it, it rings true. Sam and I agree with his advice. The one thing for sure is, if there is a problem, I don't know its size or its form. I hope that the probe doesn't make things worse.

"There has to be a way to investigate the three companies without tipping our hand and allowing the evidence to be hidden, or worse— destroyed," I confide to Sam.

Another question I have is, "Can the government handle this without making it worse?" I've outgrown my belief that systems work as they should. I know a little dead girl who is proof of that.

Zoe calls. The officers are at the mansion looking for Tim. "Is he home?" *What's next*, I whisper. "Zoe, keep them away from
~~~

Grandfather. See if Brooke is home, and have them talk with her."

"She's not going to like that," Zoe says.

"Yes, I agree, but she will simply have to do it, if she is there. Tell them I am about thirty minutes away. Call me if there is a problem. And, thanks for keeping me informed." I band-aid the situation for thirty minutes.

Sam and I discuss Chico. The first piece of confirmable information Chico finds, he is out of there. Desperate people can be ruthless. At the moment, Chico is my major concern.

Just as we are about to call Chico's cell and see how he is, my cell rings again. This time it is Mark, a pleasant diversion. He wants to get together tomorrow night. I can't make any promises yet—it's too early in the day. However, Mark is willing to be flexible. What a great guy.

"Let's get to the mansion before anything else happens," Sam says.

"No kidding!" I agree.

"Seriously, I think your Grandfather has to be told when we go to the FBI. Don't you?"

"I agree, we need to tell him. We don't have anything more than suspicions. I am not ready to act on the FBI." I look at him squarely. "I'll tell you when the time is right."

"Are you worried about his reaction?" He won't let it go.

"I have no idea how Grandfather will react. He almost always responds differently than I expect. Oh! I forgot to call Chico!"

While I dial Chico's number, Sam has an afterthought. "You don't think your Grandfather is involved, do you?"

That possibility hadn't even crossed my mind. Damn.

"He is definitely ruthless. I can't predict what he is going to do next. He is a 'rule' man. He likes to set the rules, but I can't imagine him cheating. No, I don't think he is involved. He would be stealing from himself." I answer without conviction in my voice. Now I have a new worry. How much information should I trust to Grandfather?

Chico doesn't answer his phone, so I leave a message for him to call me. It will probably be best for him to pick the time and place to make the call.

At the gate to the mansion, a sheriff vehicle meets us. They left a subpoena for me to appear at the next hearing for the shooter. "Oh great! One more thing to juggle."

Sam laughs.

Does he want to trade places with me? Then, we'll see how much he laughs.

~~~

Race is excited about putting the info into the computer. He thinks he'll have it by the end of tomorrow. He has come a long way since his days at Spirit of Hope.

Zoe arranges my schedule for court and the next flight meeting. Grandfather is in the library. I join him and work at the library table, so we will be in proximity to each other.

Race has done a great job mimicking the report on the other two suspect companies like Chico generated on Seattle. The information certainly looks similar to the Seattle information. I take a thoughtful sip of my coffee, and massage the back of my neck—damn headaches. If Chico finds a specific red flag in Seattle, then I think we'll proceed in investigating the other two. Maybe even send him in there under another name. Wonder if we can do that. I mean, legally change his identity temporarily.

~~~

Brooke storms into the library like a whirlwind. "What do you think you're doing, helping the police find Timmy, you gold-digging bitc—" her admonishment is cut short by Grandfather.

"That is enough, Brooke," Grandfather says forcefully as he lowers his newspaper to his lap.

Brooke stops short. "But, Grandfather—"

"Where is Timmy, and what has he done this time?" He coldly looks at Brooke, and I wouldn't want to mess with him in the mood he's in.

"I'm not telling you, old man!"

"If you can't be civil, pack your things and get out." He settles the matter without so much as batting an eye.

"Well, maybe I will."

"Yes. You will. And, you will today."

It's clear she pushed him as far as he is going to let her push. Grandfather looks directly at her.

Brooke looks at me with a hateful glare, questions my parentage again, then leaves angrily—not saying another word to Grandfather.

I let out a deep breath. I can tell she is as hurt as angry. She doesn't really hate me, just the threat she perceives. I had hoped to show her that I wasn't a threat, and also trim her jet-setting life of drugs and lack of direction. She needs a role model, but now I won't have the opportunity to reach her.

"Kathryn, she has no right to talk to you like she does."

"I understand. She's just afraid that I'm going to disrupt her world."

"She is out of line. I thought you would put her in her place the first time, but you didn't. Now, I have had enough." He opens his paper again with a bit of a jerk, obviously finished with the conversation.

I'm not finished yet. "I was hoping to reach her. She's scared." I talk to the back of the newspaper—since I can only see the top of his head.

He lowers the paper enough to look directly at me.

"Tell Eleanor to have the locks changed today and change the code on the gate." He is obviously finished with the discussion and not willing to give Brooke another chance.

"All right." I leave to follow his wishes.

~~~

Eleanor understands the situation. She says that is what happened with his daughter, Brooke's mother. I tuck away the new information on my aunt. We decide that only the house staff, Eleanor, James, and Louise need keys—and me of course. There is always someone in the mansion to let everyone else in. Grandfather is never left alone.

Since Eleanor is in the mood to provide family history, I ask about Grandfather's confinement to the wheelchair.

"Eleanor, did Grandfather have a stroke?"

"When your grandmother died, he stopped making an effort to walk. Before that he used the wheelchair only when out of the house, as necessary. Why do you ask?"

"Just curious."

~~~

Grandfather may be ready to shut the door on Brooke, but I'm not. He should learn that his way of excommunicating his family doesn't work very well. It's what he did with my father too.

I climb the stairs to the third floor and knock on Brooke's door.

"Go away!" she screams.

"Brooke, I want to talk to you." The door isn't locked. I doubt she really wants to be left alone. I open her door partway.

"I don't want to talk to you."

"Then listen—I'll talk," I say, entering the room.

It's obvious she has been crying. She isn't as hardcore as she would like everyone to think. She drops the clothes she is packing, and looks submissive—something I hadn't expected.

"Brooke, let's not burn bridges between us. You know what happened to our parents. We don't have to continue that tradition. Like it or not, we're family. We just need time to get to know each other."

She sniffs and wipes her nose. She's embarrassed, but she says nothing.

"You deserve a life better than this." I pull a Maggie-trick and get right to the heart of the matter. "When the party ends, it feels empty, doesn't it? What do you really want to do with your life?" The question is more for her to consider than to be answered.

Brooke lets out a whimpering breath. "I don't know," she says in a frustrated tone.

"If you like the beach, we can see if there is an apartment near mine. You can sort out what you want from life. It's peaceful, healthy. You don't have to stay there permanently. Just a thought."

"I'd like that." She smiles slightly and wipes her eyes.

"You can stay at my apartment a day or two while you get your own apartment. There are several complexes in the same neighborhood. Pack your stuff. Put some of it in my car. After work, I'll help you move and show you my neighborhood, okay?"

"Okay."

She responds to me better than she ever has. Brooke just needs a big sister right now. This is my chance to show her what family is supposed to be. And, I'm not going to let Grandfather continue to wipe out all the members of his family, one by one, except Dan and me.

"I need to get back to work. Catch me later, okay?" I want to pat her shoulder. I have pushed my luck enough, so I restrain the urge of further connect. I know that we will still have ups and downs. I just caught her with her defenses down. I know we'll have a big issue when I broach her drug problem. As matriarch of the family, I want to fulfill my duties well.

I turn back to say something about Tim, but think better of it. She's right. I did give the police Mrs. Bailey's contact information. How was I to know he was staying with her?

~~~

"Grandfather, I'm going to stay at the beach tonight and this weekend."

He lips his paper slightly, then goes back to reading. He still pours over the financial pages, and watches the hard news for coming trends that will benefit him financially. He has his investments and two companies of his own, but the bulk of the McKenzie empire is mine. I can't understand why Grandmother left everything to me, and nothing to her daughter or other grandchildren. My maternal Grandmother would have never behaved that way. With her, it is share and share alike. One for all and all that.

~~~

I'll see if dinner tomorrow night will work for Mark. Since I am going to be at the beach it is much easier for us to go out, than when I am at Pacific Estates. I am relieved he is available. In light of everything else, Mark seems to be rather tame—even with his alternate persona. I wonder if Brooke would like to meet Scourge.

~~~

There are apartments available in my complex. I don't have the numbers to the complexes in the neighborhood. Brooke might not want to be my immediate neighbor. I hope she will make friends with the beach and somehow find herself there. We can have dinner at the pier tonight. In the morning, I'll teach her to walk the beach. I hope the beach and the ocean become her new drug of choice.
~~~

~~~

The day with Brooke has gone surprisingly well. She decides to get an apartment at the complex one street away, rather than where I live—lived. Dan comes and helps move her things to her apartment. They decide to go shopping for furniture for her new beginning. She hasn't squandered all of her allowance, since the planes and the yacht were on my tab.

It was a surprise that Brooke seems to enjoy the beach this morning. She looks around with an abandon that I had not expected from her. She collects a pocketful of shells. I risk discussing her new beginning and suggesting new friends that aren't rich brats idling away their life with drugs and parties. Of course, I said it better than that. She denies a drug problem, which is a typical response.

Brooke confides she has always wanted to be a grade school teacher, like her mother. Both items are news to me. I would like to meet her parents sometime. I suppose that, too, will come. It almost seems my larger duty as heir is to bring the family back together. Could Grandmother McKenzie had hoped for this, or had she only desired managing the money?

With an allowance of one hundred thousand dollars a year, Brooke doesn't have to work. In theory, she could go to school full-time and live comfortably. Dan encourages his sister to have a worthwhile life.

Dan and Brooke go out to dinner, while Mark and I go elsewhere. Mark really is a nice person. When I get through the initial crisis period of the first couple of quarterly reports, I will spend more energy getting to know him.

We go to a little out-of-the-way restaurant. It is nice and quiet. Mark talks about taking his music in another direction —thank God. The hard part is to ditch the Scourge persona. Scourge is extremely popular and the music, such as it is, has been lucrative.

Someone, a tourist, I think, takes our snapshot. Mark leans over to smile for the camera. The lady is delighted that we allow the photo. She asks for an autograph. I decline, but allow a photo of her with me. It's strange that anyone would want a photo with me.
~~~

"How do you like being a celebrity?"

"Oh, Mark! It's a thrill a minute, an absolute thrill!"

"It is harder than it looks, isn't it?" His voice becomes consoling.

"How do you manage it so well?" I ask, truly hoping for a clue to survival.

He smiles a cheesy grin. "For a musician, it's a dream come true. It sells CDs!" He leans forward. "Without fans, there is no one to hear the music. I might as well sit in my room and play to the walls."

"That's true for you, but I don't need fans."

"It is part of the responsibility of being who you are. They need to have people to dream about, to reach for, to make sense of things that life is—that it can be better than it is now." He trumps me.

"Isn't that sad? Living vicariously, I mean?"

"Support charities that make life better for people. You'll feel better. A person really doesn't need the kind of money we have. It only makes sense out of things, if you use it to help others."

"I agree. I've been so busy, that I haven't had the time to do more than I was doing before the big announcement." I say it as if it is the black plague—"big announcement."

"It will come. You'll get things under control, soon. Be patient with yourself and the new world you're in."

We talk nothing more about the duty of being rich. I can't believe I confided in him. Even more so, I am surprised he understood what I am going through.

The food is good. I decline the wine, since I have taken so much medication for my nagging headache. When we get up to leave, I am a little dizzy. Mark grabs me to keep me from going to the floor. The dizziness passes quickly. I just needed some air.

"Okay, what was that about?" he asks when we get to his car.

"I don't know, low blood sugar or something."

"Right. You just ate. It isn't low blood sugar."

"Practicing medicine now, are you?"

"Yes," he says.

He drives away from the direction of my apartment.

"Where are you going?"

"To my parents' house. My dad is a doctor."

I set him straight. "I don't need a doctor. A good night's sleep and a few days at the beach is what I need."

"Don't bother to argue. We're going—that's all there is to it."

~~~

Oh cute. Mark's dad, Dr. Armstrong, has a happy face sticker on his stethoscope. Good Lord, he's a pediatrician. All that aside, he thinks my blood pressure may have dropped suddenly, but it's temporary. It's still slightly low, but nothing to worry about for now. Mark tells him that I've been having headaches—the big blabbermouth. Dr. Armstrong's brow furrows. He tells me to see my physician as soon as possible. I promise that I will.

~~~

Mark takes me to my apartment. He makes me promise again to call my doctor on Monday. The timing isn't good, but the advice probably is. Mark insists he should stay with me for a while. I am worn out—he has to leave—I'm going to bed.

Brooke calls and says she is staying with Dan tonight. I get the rest of the evening in peace. I take a deep breath and enjoy the quiet. I consider shutting off my cell phone. I'll do it when I get up. It feels good to sit here with my feet resting on the coffee table, sipping coffee. My main thought is on walking the beach in the morning. Ah, this is restful.

~~~

Sunday morning on the beach is unusually chilly. A summer rain comes early, before daybreak. I welcome the fresh, new-earth smell after a rain. When I was growing up, the air was choked with smog; we call it haze now, and rain clears the air. The memories are a pleasant escape from the present.

In many ways, I am standing on the threshold of a new beginning—not only for me, but for the McKenzie legacy. An added bonus is that two of my three cousins are embarking on a new life—I guess Tim is, too, in his own way. What is ahead, I can't imagine. Maggie says I interpret life as a movie; always wanting a knight in shining armor to gallop in and save the day, for good to triumph over the bad guys. Sometimes I do think it
~~~

would be easier if the good guys wore white hats, so I can tell who they are.

As I walk back to my apartment, it begins to sprinkle again. Life is good, not always easy, but life is very good. Before I head north to the other side of my life, I stop to attend Mass in our neighborhood church.

~~~

Monday reminds me of the stunt where the actor is dancing and runs up the wall and does a back flip, and keeps dancing as if any of us could do the same without missing a beat. I set the beat at the mansion. And, if necessary, I will run up the wall, flip, and land on my feet.

Chico finally returns my call while I am in the garden with my coffee. He thinks he can infiltrate the mailroom computer for remote access, and carve a backdoor into the server. He has created a specific program that will activate tonight when the Seattle company uploads their end-of-the-month reports to the corporate office computer system.

If I understand him, the program will go into the corporate system along with the Seattle reports. Basically, it acts like very specific spyware. From his laptop, Chico will be able to monitor the Seattle computer system. From within the corporate office system, he can send the same program to any of our companies as they link with corporate.

The backdoor can give Chico access to anywhere in the McKenzie Enterprises computers. As soon as he knows it works, he'll be on a plane for home. Good work, Chico. Hurry home!

He cautions if the in-house security notices it, it'll be short-lived. We'll have to download as much as possible tonight and get the less important files next. I don't know how long it will take to dissect the information, but I am hoping to know soon whether to turn over the info to higher powers or institute new accounting protocols. We definitely need to hire a new auditing firm.

Once it's determined which computer in the L.A. office is exchanging cooked books for the real ones, Chico will link to that computer and monitor all information exchanges from it. If there are no obvious triggers, then we'll begin with the companies with government contracts.
~~~

Let's see, there was Mrs. Bailey, the press, the yacht, Mark, the cousins, the shooting, the conspiracy: I'd say that was a full test. It seems I pass my ninety-day probation in this new life, figuratively speaking.

No contact from Brooke today, but that isn't uncommon for her. At least she is doing something besides getting into trouble. Dan makes me the most proud. I think the only two things unfinished are the shooter's trial and Tim. Maybe things will settle down to a normal roar.

~~~

Karen calls. "Oh, Karen, I'm sorry. I haven't written your reference yet. Oh, okay. I'll wait to hear from the tribunal first."

"Actually, I called to remind you about Linda and Todd's Halloween party. I thought you might want to get started now, if you wanted Dana to make something."

"I totally forgot, thanks for reminding me."

"You're going, aren't you?" She catches on quickly.

"I haven't given it any thought. What's the theme?" I ask.

"You'll love this—favorite movie character!"

"That is a very good theme! Who are you going as?"

"There are so many great choices, I don't know yet. What about you, any ideas off the top of your head?"

"Ah, maybe Katharine Hepburn or I might take a trip to Casablanca—I'm not sure."

"You do a good Katharine Hepburn impression. Dana won't tell me who she is going to be." Karen laughs. "Are you going with Scourge?"

"No, I'll go solo." I can't believe she asked that. We are definitely not an item.

"Good. Andy will be there." She tries to be coy, but isn't.

"I know—'he's dreamy.' That is probably why he was married last Valentine's Day. You are too much, I need to get back to work before you start trouble," I say to end this matchmaking discussion.

"Oh, all right. See you later."

~~~

Every time I think things are perfect, something happens. I do my best to mind my own business, and here comes trouble.

Karen has been as giddy as a schoolgirl since she and Keith became engaged. She wears love well, but some of us have work to do. I don't need her help to get into trouble.

~~~

My phone rings again. Now what is Karen up to? It's Mark wanting to know if I have called my doctor. Mark is an annoying mother hen.

"Sorry, I forgot, but I will do it as soon as we hang up," I promise.

True to my word, I call my doctor and tell the nurse the reason for the appointment. If there's a cancellation, I'll take it. Otherwise, it will be three weeks before they can get me in to see the doctor. Fine with me.

~~~

For the last three days, Chico has been generating reams of raw data. His little virus, mole, or whatever it is, is working perfectly and he is downloading the accounting department's records. The firewall hasn't stopped the intrusion. That's certainly something we'll have to fix in all our computer systems.

I'm not sure there is enough coffee on the planet for this job, but Louise is keeping up with the demand for the steamy brew. I review this year's numbers from Seattle. Sam has last year's, and Grandfather is going over the year before that.

Grandfather seems to enjoy being in the thick of things. His suggestions of what line items to cross-reference first is extremely helpful. He has cut at least a week off of the process already. He loves it too. He has a sparkle in his eyes, and if he could walk, I bet he would have a bounce in his step. He remarks he feels ten years younger. He looks it too.

The only two correlations Chico finds in the companies Race red-flagged are they both have government contracts for the same project and are owned by McKenzie Enterprises. One manufactures microchip components, the other has a secretive military contract.

There's nothing suspicious on the third company. We are unable to find connections among senior staff. There isn't obviously questionable emails among the companies. Chico thinks they must be using an encrypted tag file piggybacked onto innocent-looking email. It sounds mysteriously sophisticated for a gang of thieves.

When a fourth company, one in Kentucky, shows the same financial problems with cost overruns and bookkeeping practices, we begin to look more intensely toward the corporate office. Chico gets Race independent on running the downloads. Sam focuses on the Texas plant, while Chico takes Tennessee and Kentucky. We test our new phone system and pull Zoe from her desk to help Chico.

~~~

Eleanor catches me on the way to the patio for fresh air and a cup of coffee. She starts with returning the book I loaned her. She knows something is "afoot" and wants to know if we need her help. I hesitate for a moment under the guise of thoughtfully sipping my coffee, not sure what to say.

She points to the book and says Grandmother has written a note to me inside.

I look inside the first few pages. Nothing is there, so I hand the book to Eleanor to find the page.

She quickly flips through the pages and easily finds it. We put our heads together and read:

> "Kathryn, the key to your question is in this book."
> She signs the note with her initials.

I look at Eleanor. She shrugs and shakes her head.

"Kathryn, your grandmother confided in me that she was putting everything in your name—the mansion, everything. If something happened to Mr. McKenzie, I was to contact an attorney, B-something, Branson, Bradley—I have his name in my room. I can show you her note, if you like." She pleads the case of her trustworthiness.

"Mr. Bradford?"

"Yes, that sounds right."

I know she is telling the truth, because I have told no one that I own Pacific Estates. It is unlikely Grandfather would have told anyone that all of this is not his.
~~~

"We could use the help. Let me finish this coffee. What about Stanley?"

"Stanley is as good as gold, miss." She vouches for the butler with a calm, but proud stance. I know she loves to read mysteries, so vouching for the butler is saying a lot. I am sure she hopes to see herself as a female Dr. Watson in what is occurring in the library. We need a Dr. Watson.

"Good. I need Stanley and Garrett to cover the windows in the library. Chico has some kind of film that is difficult to detect, but no one can electronically eavesdrop through the glass. I have something you can help with, too." I want to confirm her usefulness. She beams with excited loyalty.

"You can trust all the house staff; Mrs. McKenzie hired us."

"What about Conner?"

"He isn't very bright, but he is good with Mr. McKenzie."

"All right, then. Thank you."

Garrett passed inspection the first time I met him. So, we have our knights of the McKenzie round table—or library tables. These are "Kathryn the Great's knights," no Lancelot among them. Grandfather beams approval of my realm.

Stanley and Garrett cover the library windows with Chico's special film. Then they cover the lower half of the library windows with butcher paper donated by Louise. The thick, waxy paper is perfect. It's opaque, but the white color still lets in light. I'm guessing the point of the butcher paper is to make it harder for a sharpshooter. I don't ask.

Eleanor supervises Garrett and Stanley as they set up the easels and place the huge tablets on them. The two whiteboards are hung where priceless art hung only an hour ago. We'll rehang the art after each meeting and lock everything in my office at all times, when we aren't using it.

After lunch we have a meeting in the library where Chico outlines assignments. Only Chico, Sam, Grandfather, and I know the purpose behind our activity.

Eleanor has the neatest handwriting, so she is designated the official scribe. Grandfather watches Eleanor organize her markers, and all of the other activity in the room. It obviously energizes him.

Garrett was a business major in college, until his football injury his senior year ended his education a semester short of graduation. He becomes my designated hitter, and takes my place with the Seattle data once Sam gets him orientated. Zoe gets Stanley, "her apprentice," settled with the new phone system, and he is temporarily in charge of the house.

Eleanor doesn't seem to mind Stanley in her domain, now that she is involved in something mysterious. As for me, I free myself to oversee the process, check on Race, and eventually substitute for Grandfather if he tires—not to mention, my eyes could use the break.

By the time of our afternoon break, we have gathered enough information for Sam and me to see a pattern emerging in the administration of the government contracts in the Seattle company.

Chico focuses on a couple of glaring line items found in the other three companies. We direct the focus exclusively on the administration of government contracts with the four companies.

We continue to collect information from other McKenzie Enterprise companies and Kathryn McKenzie companies. Chico spends time with Race to re-adjust his computer searches, but we will hold that information until we complete the in-house, informal audits on the four companies we have started. Zoe checks on Stanley, who is proudly sitting at her desk, then helps Eleanor set up for what's next, after we all have a break and some of Louise's hot apple crisp, fresh from the oven.

The sinfully delicious aroma is probably what encouraged us to find a stopping place. Congregated around the kitchen table and the kitchen island, my knights are all beaming with pride of purpose. Even though most of my knights have no idea what we are doing, they are eager to be engaged in the process. This activity, even more than the shooting incident, has forged us into a single-minded unit.

~~~

Mark calls. I go out to the patio with my coffee and cell phone for a bit of privacy and sunshine. His youngest brother is in a theatre group, and the dinner theatre is hosting a fund-raising dinner on Sunday evening.
~~~

"We can take him to dress rehearsal Saturday afternoon, then find something to do that evening. You could spend the weekend at the beach." Mark, the tempter, doesn't ask about the doctor.

With the week I foresee, he wouldn't have had to go to such dramatics to convince me to take the weekend off and away from the mansion. I accept his offer of a diversion.

"Sounds great, but I won't get down there until late Friday night. I have a full week ahead of me."

"Did you call your doctor?"

Ah, I knew it was too good to be true that he wouldn't pester me.

"Yes sir, I did. Three weeks at the latest, sooner if there is a cancellation."

"Okay, okay. You win," he says.

"Sorry, I didn't mean to be so abrupt."

"You sound stressed."

"I am, a little. But—"

"Do you want me to come and take you to dinner?" Mark interrupts.

"Thanks, you're sweet. I'm going to bed early tonight."

"Sure?"

"Yes, I'm sure. Thanks though."

After dinner, I return to the library. My mind is too tired to work, but I sit with a cup of coffee looking over the fruits of our labors. My eyes move from one easel to the next, hoping I will see something we missed before. God bless Eleanor, she has everything color coded and very neat. She was a perfect choice for scribe.

~~~

Tuesday and Wednesday are carbon copies of Monday. We make great progress. We are organized and engaged in our tasks. Thursday, I have Eleanor use the whiteboards to create graphs of the boiled-down data. We graph the materials cost and overruns, delivery deadlines and tardiness of the companies in question. She catches on quickly. We could have used the software to do the graphs, but walking through it is better, less likely to miss something by manually creating them.
~~~

I begin to list the people at each of the four companies whose names appear on the email address lists at any other of the four companies. The first and second list have one name in common, simple enough if the pattern is consistent throughout the sample. The third company shares one name with each of the first two lists, but they are different names. If I am correct, the fourth will have a name in common with each of the other companies, but again there will be no duplication.

My hypothesis is correct. There are three people at one company, each communicating with one person at one of the other companies.

I remove all the names and start a Venn diagram with the Seattle name that communicates to Texas, the second who communicates with Kentucky, and the third Seattle person who communicates with Tennessee. I do the same with the other three companies. I am left with three names in each company.

The McKenzie employee list on the laptop is by department. I sort them alphabetically. There are no matching names to whom "the twelve" send emails.

I'm disappointed. I thought we were onto something. That's enough for today. We are all tired and stop an hour early.

Grandfather asks me to stay after the others leave the library. We look at the charts and lists posted around the room.

"Kathryn, what do you see?"

"I see patterns, but I can't put together the centralized element."

"Do you think it is a random pattern?" he asks.

"No, I think there is some connection. I just don't know what."

"Then, let's call the FBI, the Justice Department, whoever Sam and Keith say we should call. We know enough to know that there is a problem. Let them take it from there. Otherwise, someone will pitch a fit because we waited to call them."

"Yes, you're right. I'll call them tomorrow," I say.

"You did a good job on this project. I'm proud of you."

"Thanks, Grandfather." I turn his wheelchair toward the door.

After dinner, I return to the locked library. I lean back in the leather chair and sip my coffee—looking at the schematics on the walls and thinking about the activity of the week.

Storm Surge

With my cup drained, I replace the whiteboards with the art that had been temporarily removed—erasing any sign of the week's activities. I stash all our evidence in the office and lock the door. I think we have all earned a short day tomorrow. And, I am spending the weekend at the beach.

This alleged corruption in the companies has taught me that I don't want my life full of complications. This has not been enjoyable. The only good from it is that the household staff are now my staff. Since I am paying the expenses of the house and the staff, it is nice to know that they are loyal to me.

Zoe makes copies of the materials to give the FBI. Chico moves his operation upstairs to his office. Since we still have the backdoor open, he and Race will continue compiling information on all of the McKenzie properties, manufacturing and intellectual. We don't mention that we haven't removed our hidden portal. I don't want any more surprises, I have to get control of this conglomeration—it has been on autopilot far too long.

~~~

While I'm walking in the garden with my morning coffee, I visit Garrett in the garage. He is hand-washing my limo. Garrett always brings my Mustang to the front when I'm going out. I've never been to the garage, and this seems like the prefect time to check out the place.

He proudly gives me the nickel tour. It is no surprise that everything is in its place and orderly. Garrett utilizes his business sense to manage his corner of the realm.

"Wow, what are all of these cars?" I ask in amazement at the fleet as I survey the lot of them.

"This one was your grandmother's car." He points to a Bentley relic. "This was your grandfather's until he bought the new limo," he points to it. "That is, of course, your limo. But, this is the prize."

He removes the cover from a cream-colored Jag with crimson and biscuit interior.

"What is this?" I ask looking at the gleaming chrome of the beautiful two-seat convertible.

"This," he extends his hand proudly, "this, is a '53 Jaguar roadster XK," he says as if he is speaking of his first love.
~~~

He walks around the car, touching it as if it is a beautiful goddess, opening the engine compartment, the trunk complete with the stock toolbox from the factory, and finally the driver's door. "Try her out."

I slide behind the large steering wheel, rubbing my hand across the leather seat beside me. It truly is a marvelous vehicle. I can't reach the clutch when I sit back in the seat, and the seat isn't adjustable. I guess, one size fits all.

"Your father drove this in college." He beams, gently touching it on the door he opened for me.

"Really!" I look at the car again with more admiration.

He grins widely. "We had a lot of fun with this car."

Opening the door and sliding out, I ask, "Does she run?"

"Oh yes, I keep her in perfect shape."

"Then, let's take her for a spin," I say needlessly, since he already has slid into the driver seat and has her fired up the minute I got out.

I set my coffee on the workbench and call the house to report to Zoe our impending disappearance.

The passenger seat is surprisingly roomy for a sports car. The gauges in the wooden dashboard are streamlined and sleek, with overstated chrome typical for the '50s. Exempt from the seat belt laws, it is strange to sit without a lap and shoulder belt.

Garrett proceeds down the drive, turns right to head north up the hill, across the WPA bridge, and along winding Highway One, with the Pacific Ocean dropping below to our left. Garrett doesn't seem to notice the lack of power steering as we take the narrow curves on the two-lane PCH in considerable excess of the speed limit. There is only one way to drive this car on this road, and that is fast. If I had a scarf over my hair, trailing behind me and rhinestone sunglasses, we could be out of an old movie.

I don't ask, but I can imagine Father walked away from this car that he loved when Grandfather disapproved of Mother. I imagine them in this car. I try not to think about the fun Dad and Garrett had with it before their wives arrived on the scene. But I see those two cruising Sunset Strip in style, slow enough to catch the girls' attention.

When we return to the garage, I look over the fleet again. "Who owns all of these vehicles?"

"You do," he answers and pulls out the registration. It reads, "A. Kathryn McKenzie and/or Kathryn McKenzie Trust."

"All of them? Are you serious?"

My eyes widen and my jaw drops. It makes sense, but I still can't quite grasp all this wealth is mine. "Wow."

"Yes, ma'am."

"We don't need all of these cars. We'll keep Grandfather's limo, my Mustang and limo, and the Jag. I do like Grandmother's Bentley, maybe we'll keep it too. Garrett, I need advice on selling everything else."

"There's Barrett-Jackson auction in Phoenix or there are companies that purchase cars to lease to movie companies."

"I like the possibilities of the cars being in a movie. Let's take that route. And, thanks for the drive. It was fun! We will definitely do that again." I recover my abandoned coffee.

Today seems like a good day to deliberately begin to simplify the excess that started with the sale of the yacht.

Liquidating a few companies isn't going to happen over night, more like five to ten years. We'll have to consider tax consequences, sale prices, and what to do with the cash. Most of the money will go into my Foundation, but I have to consider the operating cost of the mansion. It's much too large for me, not to mention it is too far from my beach, but I will keep it as long as Grandfather is alive. It isn't an immediate problem, but I need to be apprised on the household expenses.

The alleged conspiracy theory in the companies still entices me to want to sell my stock in the public companies where things are even more out of control, but I'll wait, the timing is off for that. I'm sure it would make the news if I did anything to my stock portfolio right now. We don't need that kind of press.

~~~
~~~

~ **CHAPTER 11** ~

Bellwether

Things are back to normal at the mansion, if normal is an adjective that should be used in the same sentence as anything "McKenzie." Rather, I should say that everything is back in the comfort zone for those of us who are connected to the mansion.

I'm happy to take time to go home to the beach. As the mansion disappears from my rearview mirror and the miles between me and the beach decrease, I think about what I leave behind me: the McKenzie money curse. Grandmother wasn't able to marry her artist lover because he was from a lesser social class. Who knows what the story is about my aunt and uncle who live in a commune—one way or another, it suggests an abandonment of the family money.

Dan, though educated, was trapped in the mansion like he had an albatross around his neck. The limitless wealth hasn't served Brooke or Tim well. Drugs, booze, and who knows what else as they jet-set around the world robbed them of purpose, direction, and meaning to their lives.

Grandfather has no intimate relationships with his family. I am the closest to him, yet he keeps me at arm's length. As for me, the family money took my life away, and I terribly miss the simplicity it had.

~~~

The weekend with Mark goes well. We have a casual dress rehearsal. Of course, the actual production is adorable, and Scourge is nowhere to be seen. Being with Mark is less complicated, since he isn't switching between both personalities.

Mark gives me a signed copy of his new CD. How sweet is that? Not only is the cover art in questionable taste, I hope I'm not struck deaf by the content of the lyrics.

~~~

The Monday morning meeting with the FBI agent is less intimidating than I expected. Agent Dexter is a young, clean-cut, bright-looking kid —probably only one year out of law school. He listens carefully as I explain my purpose for contacting the agency. He seems clueless until I point out that each of the companies are having "trouble" with creative bookkeeping when it comes to their government contracts. He brings in his supervisor, Agent Davies.

Agent Davies is a woman a little older than I am. She is wearing a government-issue-looking black suit. Instantly she bristles and takes command. Her primary interest is questioning why I have brought this problem to them. She is skeptical of my motives and doesn't bother to hide her skepticism. I guess I should have taken this to the securities people. It figures. Oh well.

"Thank you for your time." I stand and extend my hand to Agent Davies, then to Agent Dexter, and gather my stuff.

"What are you trying to pull here?" Agent Davies asks in a condescending tone.

"I am not '*pulling*' anything. Now, if you'll excuse me, I have another meeting." Sam opens the door, into a big room where we walk between the row of cubicles. An older, balding man is approaching in the narrow walkway. He hesitates when he sees me, seemingly recognizing my now-public face. After we pass each other, I overhear him ask Agent Davies what "Miss McKenzie wanted?"

As the elevator doors close, Agent Davies is hurriedly walking toward us. The look on her face is priceless when the doors close before she reaches them. I was not going to push the button to hold the door for her. It was hard not to smile until we started down.

During the descent to the lobby, we discuss the need to document our attempt to solicit their help to figure out what to do about the apparent embezzlement of government funds. Sam is sure this is going to blow up and get ugly before it's done. I just expected more fiscal responsibility for tax dollars. I thought the FBI would want to be involved in the process. At least she didn't scold me for our rudimentary in-house investigation.

Two men in black suits approach Sam and me as we leave the building. "Miss McKenzie?" the shorter man asks.

"Yes."

"Come with us."

I think of a quip remark about being kidnaped, but neither man strikes me as having a sense of humor. While we are waved through the security screening, Agent Davies walks out of the elevator.

She apologizes for her disregard as if she has been told to make reparations, and invites us back upstairs.

"I'm sorry, I really must go. Here is the information I brought. Call if you have questions."

I smile and hand her the file folder. She had her chance to pay attention the first time I presented the information, but oh no, she wasn't going to give us the time of day. There is no apparent reason for me to sit through another meeting. I had expected to be asked to leave the file anyway, so it's no great loss. The original is under lock and key at the mansion, she is welcome to the copy I brought.

~~~

On the trip back to the mansion, I try to listen to Mark's new CD. It is a good thing Sam is in his own car. The first song is crude and rather loud, even at the volume level still set for the previous CD. I skip forward to the second song and decrease the volume. The song is heavy metal, revisited. I skip to the next song. I grimace. It is the worst song yet. I can't hear myself think. That's enough for now.

The silence is a welcome relief. I wonder if the FBI is going to assign much priority to the information we compiled. Perhaps we should continue to figure out what is going on with the creative bookkeeping for ourselves.

Damn! I had hoped to give this problem to someone with the experience and resources to get to the bottom of what is going on in the four companies in question, and possibly the corporate office. One would think there would be more interest in how the government money is spent. I'll figure this problem out, but I am not spending the rest of my life babysitting these companies—or the FBI.

My doctor's office calls, they have a cancellation for today. I look at the clock on the dashboard. I suppose I can make it on
~~~

time if I turn back to the city now and don't run into any freeway snags. I call Zoe and Sam about the change in my plan, without being clear it is a doctor.

~~~

"Hello, Doc!" I hide my dislike for doctor appointments, although I do like my doctor.

"Katey, I ran into Dr. Armstrong at the hospital this morning. I hear you are having headaches—" his voice trails off as he palpates my neck below my ears, looks into my eyes, then pulls a penlight out of his pocket to check my pupillary reaction.

"Yes. Headaches, dizziness, my visual acuity is diminishing." Might as well put all my cards on the table and figure out what we can do about these headaches.

"Open, say 'Ah.' Any trouble swallowing?" He continues his rudimentary examination.

When he finishes poking and palpating to his satisfaction, he excuses himself and leaves the room. He returns with a list of tests he wants done as soon as possible. He is referring me to a neurologist, and these are the tests they have agreed are necessary.

I call and check in with Zoe and Sam. With the fasting lab work early tomorrow, I'll stay at the beach tonight rather than at the mansion. Everything seems under control there. I tell them it is personal business and I will be back on Wednesday afternoon. There is no need to mention the word "doctor" yet.

~~~

Spending the afternoon on the beach will clear my mind from this morning's meeting and the problems behind it. It will help keep my mind off of the lab work and the MRI of my brain. Wednesday promises to be equally entertaining with a trip to the nuclear medicine department for more brain-investigating tests.

~~~

Thursday offers the shooter's court date. The prosecution hasn't had time to go through a witness prep with me. But I'm not worried about the witness stand—I have been on the stand a million times. The only questions that he can ask are relatively clear cut. I didn't see anything since I was lying across the front seat while bullets broke the windshield.
~~~

That leaves Friday to catch any urgent business I've missed this week. Grandfather will be due for some extra attention by then. He would never admit the need for family, but I can tell he enjoys the attention I give him. Maybe we will have time for a game of chess. It's been a long while since our last game.

~~~

The September beach is lovely. The weather is warm. With school's resumption, the tourists are few. The sky is clear and a crisp, rich blue. There are no clouds or smog today. The warm sand feels good on my feet as I carry my shoes. After a while, I turn and walk back in the direction I've come—this time at the water's edge.

There are three people in the water wind sailing. They glide effortlessly over the water's surface. I imagine that I am gliding over the water, free of worry. The truth is that in addition to everything else, and as dismissive as I act, I am concerned about my headaches now that the doctors are alert about the situation. Their concern seems honest. I don't think it has anything to do with special treatment because of who I am.

~~~

After two days of tests, court is a welcomed change. Due to the media interest in the case—I suspect because of my involvement—Grandfather wants James to drive me to court. He still calls Garrett, "James." The darkened limo windows provide added privacy.

Neither the prosecution nor defense attorneys represent the interest of the witness, so Sam accompanies me to court. Lastly, Jim, my part-time bodyguard, rides in front with Garrett.

My cell phone rings as we are leaving the Pacific Estate driveway. It is the neurologist's office, they want me to come in today. Because I have court, the office staff settles for an appointment on Monday. She won't tell me the nature of the urgency, other than it's to go over my test results.

The phone call certainly upstages the court appearance. I hardly notice the swarming reporters who meet my limo at the courthouse steps. Jim moves them back while Sam guides me safely through without letting the media push me to answer their questions. I struggle to refocus my thoughts to the trial.

Storm Surge

An Asian woman, in her mid-fifties, stops the prosecutor just before he enters the courtroom. She is speaking earnestly in a quiet voice. The prosecutor looks surprised, rubs his beard a minute, then asks her something. The scene holds my attention. The prosecutor seems troubled, but grateful for the information. The woman nods her head in agreement, then leaves hastily.

I have a feeling that was bad news. For a brief moment—I'm not sure why—I fear the shooter is going to get released today.

Inside the courtroom, the sketch artist is quickly catching the defendant and the Judge. Watching the sure, quick strokes distracts me from my concerns. The shooter has shed his disheveled appearance, but has a dull look of pharmaceutical influence on his demeanor. We are told to rise, court is in session.

After the docket is read and the preliminary statements are made by the Judge, she tells the court that the shooter was found competent to stand trial.

Sam filed a notice of appearance. The Judge remarks though it is unusual for a witness to be represented by an attorney, it will be allowed if there are no objections. Neither the prosecution or defense object. I feel better with Sam officially involved.

The State puts on its case, calling the officers and myself as witnesses. None of the State's witnesses are qualified to clearly address the insanity defense. To me, it seems like a gap in the prosecutor's case. Maybe it was covered adequately in the competency hearing, or some agreement was struck to stipulate to his mental health status. Clearly, I am more familiar with Juvenile Court. The only criminal cases I have experience with were putting away the worst child abusers.

The defense attorney cunningly cross-examines each witness, careful not to appear to attack me, the victim. It seems that he is still pursuing an insanity defense and doing a fairly decent job. I think he has won the jury's sympathy.

Since depositions weren't taken, Sam listens carefully to both sides to learn what would have been revealed during discovery.

The prosecution looks around the gallery, hesitates, then rests his case.

The defense makes a half-hearted motion for a directed verdict, citing the prosecution failed to make a prima facie case.

The Judge denies his motion to dismiss, thus requiring the defense to proceed. Their case is largely a parade of doctors explaining the shooter's mental illness and how he is no longer a threat, since he is on psychotropic medication and is stable. I have a different definition of "stable." But there is no hint of a technical error or mistrial to set him free today.

Just to be sure, I write a note to Sam that many mentally ill patients respond well to medication, so well, in fact, that they often stop taking their medication, thinking they no longer need it. Then, they are prone to another episode of their illness, and this guy is a threat to society when he is psychotic, especially when his auditory hallucinations tell him God says to kill me.

The prosecution's cross-examination is feeble attempts to discredit the defense witnesses, rather than to question the extent of the illness on the afternoon the shots were fired, or highlight that the shooter wasn't out-of-control crazy until the day after the shooting, or even that he has the real potential to be a threat again. Apparently, the young prosecutor was unaware of the propensity to stop taking psych drugs by psych patients.

Just as the defense rests, the Asian woman appears and quietly takes a seat on the prosecution side of the gallery.

The prosecutor sees her entrance, rises from his seat, then asks to re-cross the defense witness who administered the psychological tests.

"Now, Doctor—that's a Ph.D., isn't it?"

The witness answers affirmatively.

"Refresh my memory. The tests revealed the responses of someone with schizophrenia, is that correct?"

"Yes, there's no doubt he has schizophrenia."

"No doubt? No doubt whatsoever?"

"Absolutely none."

"Would it be accurate to say that there were no test answers that indicated anything, but schizophrenia?"

"Every answer pointed to schizophrenia, as I have already said." The witness' voice rises. He looks offended by the question and isn't hiding it.

I know from experience, the witness is close to being designated as hostile, if he doesn't watch his tone with the prosecutor. That is not something he wants to do. The questions can become more pressing and harsh after that. Even though the witness is in his late thirties, he should know to be careful. He should be more experienced than to fall into the prosecutor's trap. Didn't the defense prep their witnesses?

A strange look comes over the witness' face. He must have realized how close to the line he was.

"Would it be correct to say that, in fact, the test answers were letter perfect? Even the questions built-in to weed out false test results?" The prosecutor shows where his questions are going.

The witness hesitates, ponders, his eyes open wide before he replies, "Why, yes. Yes, all the answers were perfect!"

The prosecutor has managed to get the psychologist to repeat his words. Well done. The witness is putty in his hands now. He is acting like a novice on the stand.

"Isn't that unusual? What conclusion would you draw from that?" The prosecutor is on a roll.

"Um, I would say that the test was invalidated," the doctor answers, his cheeks turn beet red.

"Invalidated by false answers, deliberate, planned answers?"

"I would venture that he studied the test and memorized the answers to look schizophrenic." He fidgets in his seat. "I should have noticed that he answered all the questions to look schizophrenic, paranoid schizophrenia." The witness foolishly volunteers information.

The prosecutor says, "That's it for this witness, Your Honor."

So, he faked schizophrenia? Why would anyone do that? I don't understand what just happened. I understand that the shooter is not really mentally ill—I don't understand why he would fake schizophrenia, or why he shot at me.

The shooter's wife's expression changes from concern to confusion. I watch as she looks toward her husband with questioning eyes, even though he is facing away from her.

The Judge is obviously pondering this new information. Her expression is neutral, but her eyes reveal she is thinking seriously about this new development.

Based on their expressions, most of the jury realize something just happened. Several have the look that "something isn't right here," but I am not sure they have moved beyond the schizophrenia question to the shooting question. I'm not sure what lies behind all of this information, but I hope the jury gets that things have drastically changed, that this was a deliberate shooting. The Church, the Pope, all of it was a ruse. I wish at least one of the jurors would have a spark of understanding on their faces. But they don't. They hardly look like they were paying attention.

At least the shooter is not going anywhere today. The Judge won't let him loose with this new information in evidence. It suits me fine, because I know he is the guy who was watching me and it makes a bit more sense that he faked mental illness than that he is mentally ill. The question remains: Why?

Court adjourns for the day. We'll be back tomorrow. The prisoner is ordered returned to his cell. The gavel falls. We rise. The Judge leaves. They remove the jury as we walk out in the other direction.

~~~

The sky has become overcast while we were in court. Sam and I walk down the stairs together. Jim is on the alert, walking slightly ahead of us. He keeps the journalists at bay, but they still shout questions at me until the prosecutor appears at the top of the stairs behind us. Then they go after him.

My thoughts land on the question of the shooter's fake mental illness. Then, on my health. This has been a draining week. During the ride back to the mansion, I should ask Sam for an update on the corporate conspiracy we have going on, but I'm too tired. It can wait.

~~~

Jim stays at the mansion. He has taken up residence in the guest room that I used before I came to live here. He seems calm and deliberate. He is cunning. I can almost see his mind working as he secures the house for the night.

Eleanor made it a point of privately mentioning to me how thorough Jim is. I think she is attracted to him. They are polite and businesslike toward each other, but their mutual attraction is apparent to anyone paying attention. He is younger than Eleanor, but I don't think she should let that get in the way.

~~~

Court starts with the prosecution calling a rebuttal witness, the Asian lady from the hallway yesterday. Basically, she is covering for the person who did the psychological testing for the State. The original tester is on their honeymoon. When reviewing the file for court prep, she noticed the test oddity. That's what sent the prosecution down the road that his cross-examination took yesterday.

There is no explanation for the shooting, which I find glaring —and unsettling. The one thing that is apparent is that it was not borne out of a hallucinogenic episode. Both sides deliver their closing statements, and we are done. But it doesn't feel finished.

The Judge instructs the jury and recesses for the weekend. In my opinion, the State didn't do an extraordinary job of addressing the motive for the shooting. We will have to wait and see how it turns out.

Of course, I am afraid that he may actually shoot me next time he gets the chance. In open spaces around the house, it would be hard to protect me from someone with a rifle. Almost all of his shots hit my car. Without the car for protection, I could have been killed. I turn to whisper to Jim, who keeps watching everyone rather than look at me. He agrees to work for me full-time until I stop listening to him. Then he will be gone. Fair enough.

It's not necessary that I'm in court when the verdict is read. I'll tell Jim I have an important meeting on Monday. I'll keep my doctor's appointment with the neurologist, instead of waiting for the jury at the courthouse. There is no guarantee that the jury will finish deliberating on Monday. I don't think they got whether or not this guy is guilty of attempted murder. Perry Mason could have done better and he isn't real. God, this is frustrating.

Again, we descend the stairs outside the courthouse. Jim takes the point. Garrett has the limo waiting. Sam walks beside me. None of us speak.

I watch the shooter's wife leave ahead of us. This time she is not able to escape the press. She desperately tries to move
~~~

forward and ignore their hounding. Her husband has set her life in turmoil. Her sadness shows on her face and in the weight her body seems to carry from this place.

Suddenly, we hear a gunshot. Sam and Jim have me to the ground instantly—Jim covering me with his body. Everyone is down flat or crouched behind a car. A second, then a third shot echoes off the buildings. Officers are alert, scanning the crowd for a shooter. Quickly, someone is at the side of the shooter's wife, helping her up. It looks as if one of the reporters had pulled her down, then dropped to her side when the shots continued. An officer rushes to her. She looks shaken. Sam and Jim rush me to the limo where Garrett has left the door open and is back in the driver's seat for a quick escape.

I think about the shooter's wife. I remember how shaken I was when I heard the shots being fired at me by her husband. Was someone now shooting at her?

~~~

As soon as we return to the mansion, I tell Grandfather about hiring Jim full-time. He seems relieved.

However, Grandfather is disappointed the jury didn't finish what he considers a clear-cut decision. Either way, it's up to the jury now, and that's plenty reason for celebration. Grandfather agrees and has Sam mix highballs for them, while I mix myself a Cuba Libre, rum and Coke with lime. Libre, liberation! I wish.

I know Jim will be hard-pressed to protect me if the shooter is set free and proceeds to gun me down. He can fortify our defenses and educate us how to be more careful. There's not a lot more he can do. Our only hope is to catch the shooter before he gets to me. But I don't mention this. This shooter isn't the only nut in this fruitcake world. If he can come this close to killing me, then someone else may do the same—or worse, be a better shot. Remove one and there will always be another to take his place.

~~~

It has been a hectic week and I feel the need for another weekend at the beach. I feel safe there, though it is wide open for a sniper, and the other guy was there watching me. Jim pitches a fit and gets to come with me.

Storm Surge

Saturday morning early, I forgo the walk in the garden and drive directly home. I arrive in plenty of time to prepare Chicken Kiev with steamed fresh vegetables. Mark is visibly impressed with lunch. I remind him that I have not always been rich, and I have many useful skills. It is a harmless dig at his silver-spoon existence. He grins a sheepish little boy grin. He doesn't get any mileage out of the grin, but he is cute.

The afternoon is another clear-sky day. The water is enticing on this summer-warm fall afternoon. We walk close enough to the water's edge to feel the waves' spray. It is too much like a romantic movie to take off my shoes and walk in the water. I don't want to hint at romance, since Mark is becoming a comfortable friend. Besides, Jim is following us.

One minute we are walking and the next I feel dizzy. Not exactly dizzy, I feel hot and motion-sick. My face must have turned white or flushed, there is something about the way I look that prompts Mark to stop his story and ask if I am all right.

"I'm fine, just a little dizzy." I stop walking.

He turns squarely toward me. "Are you sure? This is the second or third time you have been dizzy lately."

With a forced smile I say, "I'm all right, really, I'm just a little tired. It was a long week."

~~~

The next thing I know, I feel hands on me, laying me flat on my back on a gurney of some sort. I want to tell them that my left ankle is turned funny and is hurting, but I can't speak. I can see them and myself in a detached third-person sort of way. I remember it being dark. My eyes are shut and I can't open them. I think, this must be what dying is like, then I hear Mark talking, muffled. My whole body and soul is straining to focus on his voice.

"Doctor, how is she? Is she all right?"

"She is resting now, Mr. McKenzie," another voice says.

"Mark, call me Mark, and this is her mother, Karen."

He is lying, that little sneak, I think inside my misty head.

"What can you tell us about her condition?" Karen asks.

I struggle to force open my eyes. I'm frightened and I want to see Karen. If I can see her, I can focus on her calmness. I
~~~

must be in a coma. My mind screams, I'm here, Karen, I'm here—I just can't open my eyes.

The conversation catches my attention again. "I want to keep her tonight, then rest at home for a week. We'll run some tests after she is rested," says an unfamiliar voice.

I feel like I am eavesdropping. "Home," I whisper inside myself. If I will go home, then I must be going to be all right.

In the background, I hear the rhythmic beep-beep-beep of a medical machine somewhere above my head. It slows to a calmer pace. It is kind of weird being so acute to the sounds around me. I feel someone let go of my hand. I wasn't even aware anyone had been holding it. I contract my fingers, but I can't tell if they respond. There is a kiss on my forehead just as I drift off to sleep.

When I wake up, Karen is sitting by my bed. "Hey, sleepy-head, you gave us a scare." She tells me that Mark took the night shift, and now it's her turn. She also tells me that my physician came in this morning. He's going to tell the neurologist where I am. "What is this about a neurologist?" she asks.

I ask about Grandfather. I am relieved to hear he hasn't been called. The last thing I want is a McKenzie entourage descending upon the hospital—then the media is sure to follow.

"The neurologist?" Karen presses.

"Oh, just tests because of my headaches." I brush past an answer.

"Headaches?" Karen questions, but seems to decide not to push for an answer right now.

I know Karen, like Maggie, does not let go of anything so easily. I predict she will bring the conversation back to the neurologist before she leaves.

"Do you want to call your family, maybe Aunt Grace?"

"No, we don't parade our illnesses in front of each other, we show off our children." I attempt to change the conversation into a joking mood. "Seriously, it will probably be cured with a good dose of rest. I'll be fine by Thanksgiving, and no one will have to know about this little dizzy spell."

Karen's face shows that she doesn't like my answers, but she will have to live with them for the time being.

Storm Surge
<center>~~~</center>

The doctor dismisses me from the hospital during his early-morning rounds. I have time to go home to my apartment, clean up, and make it to my original doctor appointment to get the results of my tests.

I call a taxi and slip out while Jim isn't here to say otherwise.

I'm surprised to see Karen enter the doctor's waiting room. I called her from my apartment to tell her I had been discharged from the hospital and would catch up with her later in the week.

"Hello?" I greet her.

"Hello. I came to be with you," she says softly. "Don't look so worried, someone accidentally called my number when they were trying to reach you. They think I am your mother," she whispers, then grins, probably with the thought of the deception —the deception she doesn't know that I overheard.

"My mother?" I look quizzingly. "You aren't old enough."

"As far as they are concerned, I am."

"I don't suppose you would settle for waiting out here, would you?" I ask, already knowing the answer. I'm relieved that she is here with me, though I would have never asked her to come.

In my heart, I know I am ill. I have never admitted it out loud, nor how worried I am becoming. I just don't feel well. I have headaches, eye problems, dizziness, and memory problems. I know it is more than fatigue. I had things to accomplish before I could take time to be ill. But, the illness seems unwilling to wait.

"If you really want me to leave, I will." She jumps to the extreme to force me to admit that I want her to stay with me.

"No, it's all right. Come in with me," I whisper with a forced grin on my lips that feel as if they are trembling like I am inside. That is as close as I can come to admitting that I don't want to go through this appointment alone.

Inside the doctor's office, he has my brain scans on the x-ray film light board. The look on his face makes it obvious that he doesn't like what he sees. He points at various films, making circular motions with the end of his ink pen as he explains generalities about the films.

He asks, "How many headaches?"

"I've had quite a few. Almost constant now." I might as well tell him everything. "Lately it's not only an ache, it is more of a stabbing pain—like a sharp letter opener stabbed swiftly in my head, then pulled out. It is a strong pain, but it only lasts seconds."

At first, he has his back to me, looking at the back-lit films. He turns partially as he listens to my symptoms. Now he is looking directly at me.

"It disables me for a moment, but it passes quickly. And, I have vision problems, stronger glasses—actually bifocals, but I thought that was eyestrain from the increase in reading I've been doing the last couple of months." I pause, reconstructing other symptoms from my recent past. "I've had some memory problems too."

"Short-term or long-term memory?" He asks a clarifying question as he studies me for a moment, then turns back to the cross-section scans of my brain.

"Nothing out of the ordinary—it's just fatigue. I have been pushing myself lately."

"That might be a factor, but it's more serious than that."

"The memory loss is more of a loss for words. I can't think of the name of common things like 'glass of water'—but it isn't that often. It may happen several times in one day, then not again for days."

"The headaches and vision problems are likely to increase," he speaks softly, as he looks at both Karen and me. He begins to rub his forehead, while he searches for the words to explain the situation.

"What is it, Dr. Billingsworth?" Karen asks when the pause seems to linger too long.

"See this area here?" He points to a specific spot on the film that he has moved to the center of the screen. "This mass is the problem." He pauses again, but only slightly.

"Mass?" Karen and I say nearly in unison.

He faces us. "It looks to be a tumor, astrocytoma. It's growing, causing more and more pressure on these areas." He points on the film with his pen. "That is why you are having headaches. That pressure is the problem. I just don't like the kind of pain you describe."

"Tumor? Is it cancer?" Karen whispers the word "cancer."

I feel disoriented the minute the word leaves her lips. Mother died of breast cancer. It can't be cancer. I listen numbly as he speaks, unable to ask questions of my own. I am intent on his words, but hear none of them.

"It may or may not be malignant. It's hard to tell from a scan, but it is definitely there, and it is definitely a problem."

"So, so, what happens next?" I rejoin the conversation. "A biopsy?"

"That would be the usual option," he says.

"But?" Karen encourages.

"But, the position of the mass is the problem. I don't like where it is. It is dangerous to probe in this location." He points to the location on the film, like seeing it would mean something to us. "I can't recommend going in there. If the surgery doesn't kill you, it's very likely to leave you in a vegetative state."

"Can you treat the mass as if it is cancer with chemo or radiation, shrink it somehow or even kill it?" Karen asks.

"Either of those would only be marginally successful."

"What would you do, if it were you?" Karen isn't leaving without a treatment plan better than nothing can be done.

"It needs to be removed. The surgery isn't usually successful. It's not even done in the U.S." He raises one eyebrow.

"Where is it done?" Karen asks.

He explains a new procedure being tested in Sweden. He's been following the study with a great deal of interest.

"The study is in its fifth year. Early results are promising. It is several years away from FDA approval. I think you are a pretty good match for the profile, but you can't wait long. The surgery is showing good results on young, otherwise healthy patients."

Clearly there is only one cure, regardless how risky, it's my only choice, my only hope is experimental surgery.

Dr. Billingsworth wants to refer me to the medical team in Sweden as soon as possible. He'll make the contacts and get back to me. They might be pleased to have such a prominent patient in their test group.

"It will likely take months to get in, but I think surgery is your best choice. Considering that you wouldn't be a charity case, they might be more willing to consider you for a test subject and streamline getting on the list." Finally, being Kathryn McKenzie is a good thing.

"So, what do we do first?" I ask.

"Let me get you into the study group. We can do the preliminary lab tests here and send them with the referral. You must be ready to go at a moment's notice." He tries to smile, but looks grim.

"I see. Then, let's do it." I nod agreement.

"I'll call Dr. Klienfelter and get back to you."

"Thank you, Doctor," Karen is saying as she puts her hand on my wrist.

"Yes, thank you." I get to my feet, feeling wobbly.

"Make sure we have your cell phone number," he adds, as I sling my purse strap to my shoulder.

My hand shakes. It takes two attempts for the strap to stay in position. By then, Karen is handing him her business card. "We'll be there—just say when and where," she confirms.

I feel numb. "Cancer" I repeat over in my head. I can't breathe.

Karen's hand is on my elbow. She moves me through the waiting room and outside. I fumble in my purse for my keys.

Gently, she places her hand on mine and pushes the keys back toward my purse. "You look pale. I'll drive," she says. It isn't a request or an inquiry, it is final. In no uncertain terms, she is driving. Keith can help her get my car later.

Vanity can't force me to protest. I feel faint and can't wait for the elevator to reach the ground, so I can get into the fresh air. Once we are in the car, Karen starts the engine, runs the power windows down, and starts the A/C on full for more air. "Lean forward, put your head down," she instructs as she puts her hand on my shoulder.

I begin to gulp in the cool air. She brushes the hair out of my face and makes an audible, "Shuu-u, shu-u-u" sound.

"Katey, don't hyperventilate. We'll get through this one step at a time." She continues to stroke my hair away from my face.

Slowly the blood returns to my head and I don't feel so lightheaded. Karen's hand is on my upper arm. When I open my eyes, I can see she is leaning forward to look in my face. I take a deep breath and begin to sit up. Her hand slips away, but not her gaze.

"I know you are frightened, but we will do this together, understand? I better not find out that you have gone to any appointments without me or that you didn't call me when you needed to talk."

I intend to answer affirmatively, but whisper, "Cancer."

"I know," she says softly.

Tears run shamelessly down my cheeks. "My mother died of cancer," I whisper.

"We are not going to let you die. We are going to tackle this." She takes a breath. "Katey, I know you're frightened. I would be. But you aren't alone. Don't ever think you're alone." She looks intensely at me to make sure I understand.

"I know," I whisper and grasp the back of her hand.

"Stay with me tonight," she says as she begins to back out of the clinic parking garage.

"All right," I agree—relieved.

After we clear the parking garage, I phone the mansion and tell them I am staying in L.A. for the night. By now, no one thinks much about me staying in the city. Things at the mansion are in the hands of the capable staff. If it takes too long to get into the Sweden program, I may have to rely on them more in the future.

~~~

Karen fixes a pot of coffee, then wonders if I am allowed to have coffee. I assure her that, of course, I can have coffee. I'm not giving up coffee at this stage of the game—after everything else I have given up these last six months. It would be horrible to spend my last months without coffee or the beach. I hope that I am not disabled and have to spend all of my time at the mansion. No coffee, no beach, that would be a horrible death.

We sit, talk, and have coffee. Karen has taken the day off from work. We finally decide my situation is better than an incurable malignant cancer that would course throughout my body and eat away at me from the inside out. This, in time, will kill me by crowding my brain, but there is one possible cure.

"Please, don't tell anyone about this," I ask.

"Why the secrecy?"
~~~

I turn to make sure she understands that I do not want her sneaking around behind my back on this one. "The media. I don't want pity. I want privacy. I want everyone to behave normally. If they are angry with me, I want them to tell me, to yell at me, if that is what they need to do." I searched for words to express my thoughts. "Karen, if this surgery doesn't work—I, I want the time I have to be real," I say softly, raising my glance to meet her eyes. "Including coffee," I add for good measure.

She shifts in her chair, a little uneasy. "Tell Mark, and I promise not to tell anyone, except in a medical emergency."

That compromise is probably the best I am going to get. I agree. We lean in for a hug. No tears, just a hug. I hope I am accepted into the test group, so that I can live many more of these moments with my friends.

I prepare her for what might happen."Karen, I am going to designate you as my Power of Attorney and Executor of my estate."

"We'll get through this. You're going to be fine." Karen attempts to reassure me of the future.

"Still, will you do it?" I face her squarely.

~~~

In the morning, Karen drops me at my car. I feel fine now. I just want a few minutes at the beach that I don't have to be the heiress McKenzie before I get back to work.

The sun is beginning to turn the sky into sunrise colors. The beach is waking. The waves seem fresh. The birds, seagulls and sandpipers, are busily going about their morning routine. There are two men running side by side along the beach. Otherwise, the beach is deserted. The beach patrol drives by as I walk past the pier. I am trying to memorize all of the sights and smells of the beach, and the feel of the water on my bare feet.

I brought my camera to take photos of everything I love about the beach, the waves, the pier, the seagulls in hovering flight, all of it. I fill a small California wine bottle with sand. I know it is childish. I know sand in a bottle cannot replace the feel of the sand on my feet or the spray on my face or the sounds and smells, but I have to take a bit of the beach with me as long as my heart cannot leave this place.
~~~

I would rather stay here and concentrate on getting well—or preparing to die. But I feel a sense of duty to my father's family.

Father's face and the soothing sound of his voice comes into the forefront of my memories.

There are business matters that need set to autopilot for the near future. There are arrangements to make for my private and public lives. I need to call Mr. Bradford and tell him I am having surgery, and, as always with surgery, something could go wrong. He'll need to prepare a will naming Karen as the executor of my estate, and Power of Attorney. There is no heir. I trust her judgment. The bulk of the estate will go to the Foundation, and I want it set up in a way that the McKenzie cousins and possibly their parents will not contest my will. Obviously, they would have no claim to the money my parents left me in the trusts, or that I have made from my investments. Mr. Bradford will figure out a way to set up a trust for Spirit of Hope, so that the Church can't get their hands on that money.

I had hoped to establish a place similar to Spirit of Hope for families with a family member with AIDS. I planned to call it "Monica's House." I had so many ideas, hopes, and dreams. I wonder how many of them I can accomplish in the time I have left. And I want to establish a college scholarship fund for the children who go through the Spirit of Hope doors.

Sam will have to have a Power of Attorney to run the business aspects of the McKenzie Enterprise while I have surgery. If I die, it will all revert to Karen in six months. I need to tell him of my plan to trim the fat through attrition at the corporate office. I want to give Father's Jag to Garrett. He looked perfect behind the wheel. Zoe can have my Mustang—her car is a piece of junk. I wonder if she can drive a stick shift? I don't have the time or stamina to teach her to drive it. Wouldn't it be funny if Sister Theresa taught her. Pay backs! No, I'm sure Garrett will help her. I begin to feel ready to face the uncertain future.

Mr. Bradford promises to get started on the documents this afternoon. He doesn't press for details about the surgery. Maybe he thinks it's something female and asks no questions. He does seem to understand the sense of urgency to get this done now.

~~~
~~~

CHAPTER 12

The Verdict

By the time I arrive at the mansion I have told my face not to reveal my worries. There is a lot to do before my surgery, and no time for further self-pity. I'll either live through this or I won't.

As soon as I hit the door, Sam warns me:"Kathryn, Jim is looking for you. He is furious you didn't check in with him after the shooting!"

"The shooting?" I'm clueless. The last that I saw Jim we were on the beach.

"The shots when we left the courthouse on Friday. Didn't you hear what happened?" He sounds surprised as I turn and see Sam standing in the doorway.

"What happened?"

"Your shooter was killed by a sniper as they were exiting the side door to go back to jail! He's gone. It's over!" Sam says, happily relieved.

"I haven't listened to the news since then. But it leaves a lot of questions about why he faked schizophrenia. What about his wife? How is she?" How did I escape the media?

~~~

"Jim, good morning. I hear it's over." I'm trying to get him past the part about not checking in with him before he scolds me. I'm not ready to discuss it with anyone.

"Good morning. It isn't over yet, Miss McKenzie."

"Oh, I must have misunderstood."

"The shooter is dead, but who shot the shooter? And the bigger question—WHY? No offense, but I don't think you have a loyal fan out there revenging you."

His words make me uneasy."What do you think?"

"There are many aspects to consider. I think there is a correlation to the testimony that he faked his illness and the shooting. Before that, he was not much of a threat. But who is he a threat to?" He looks questioningly at me.
~~~

"Me?" I say the obvious answer that he expects. And I expect that he is attempting to make a point from it.

"Yes, he was a threat to you, but you were not a threat to him. You wouldn't retaliate for what he did. Although, I bet you are a suspect. Is there anything you need to tell me?" he asks suspiciously, looking between Sam and me, and back again.

"I haven't hired a mercenary, if that is what you mean. I don't want to be shot at, but I would never kill anyone," I add softly.

"If you think of anything let me know. I'll keep checking. Someone wanted him dead before he could talk."

Maggie, The jury may not have decided the fate of the shooter, but the verdict is in for me. I am dying at a more rapid rate than the general population. I knew the McKenzie money carried a curse! Not literally in a spiritual sense — bad luck certainly follows the money in this family. I have a tumor.

There's a lot to do in an unarguably short amount of time. Surprisingly, I have been thinking clearly about my personal business, and even about some of my McKenzie duties. There is nothing like adversity to make one rise to the occasion. This is the greatest test of my character to date. I can only imagine what lies ahead. I hope I'm ready for it.

Tuesday always seems an odd day to start the work week, especially when everyone else worked Monday. I'm already a day behind. I hadn't realized how upset the staff was with the shooting. There is a noticeable relief now that he is gone. There's no point in telling them that Jim is staying on the payroll because he still has an uneasiness about the shooter's death. Maybe I'll hint to Eleanor that I am keeping Jim around so she can spend more time with him.

I begin to join Jim's uneasiness about the shooter's death. I don't think his wife was involved. Clearly, she wasn't expecting the shots. I truly doubt it has anything to do with her. So, who does that leave? Not me, not her. Another crazy person? Honestly, that seems unlikely.

So who wanted the shooter dead? Who can hire a sniper? Who would my shooter be a risk to, if he lived and spilled his guts to someone, and it leaked to the media? Is that person going to come after me and finish what the shooter didn't?

I can't worry about another threat. It is possible I am not going to live anyway. I need to advise Sam of the Power of Attorney. There is no reason to give him the specifics behind my decision. He doesn't usually question my business decisions. I am sure I can waltz past this one without missing a beat.

After the safeguards are in place in my official life, I can take a breath while I wait for the call to fly to Sweden. This isn't a good time for regrets, but I wish I had made time to attend more Dodgers games this summer. I don't even know who won the World Series this year. That is most unusual for me. The funny thing is that I could have afforded box seats at the games and gone to all seven of them.

One thing I can't put off is to tell Grandfather that I am planning to have surgery. There is no need to give him every detail, but I do need to be candid about the big picture. I'll start with generalities, then go from there. That way, he will understand when I suddenly fly off without advance notice.

While we finish the bottle of wine from dinner, I decide this is as good of a time as any to talk with Grandfather. Unless he insists, I have no plans to relinquish my position as Kathryn the Great. He made his decision to step down. When the need arises, he is welcome to advise Sam, but after my recovery I am going to fulfill my duty—if I recover. Besides, that is what Grandmother set in motion all these years ago, and he is well aware of that.

"Grandfather, I'm going to have surgery and I wanted to tell you about it now, since I don't know when it will be. The procedure isn't available here, so I have to go to Europe." I dive right in. After all, he did the same to me with his retirement announcement, I think he expects things to be done in that fashion.

He takes another drink. "I suppose it is not a routine matter, since you can't have the procedure done here."

"No, it isn't routine. I don't have the information about what to expect yet, but I have to be ready to go at a moment's notice."

Grandfather tilts his head to ponder my answer.

"I've asked Mr. Bradford to make a Power of Attorney for Sam to handle anything that can't wait for my return. The FBI is taking the point on the corruption enquiry. Still, Chico, Race, and Sam are going to continue with our in-house investigation."

He nods approval, while I tick through the items on my list of McKenzie duties. He is a patient listener.

"A friend is having a Halloween Masquerade party in San Francisco, but before that I am thinking about taking one of the McKenzie jets to visit a friend in Austria. I need the jet so that I can go to Sweden, if I am called for the surgery while I am in Vienna." I smile and squeeze his hand.

"Are you all right?" he asks softly, reaching his other hand out to touch mine.

"It's pretty serious, but I'll be all right. I'm a McKenzie."

"Yes, yes, you are. Your grandmother would be proud of you." He smiles, but his eyes are unaware of the smile and have filled with tears. I can only imagine what he must be thinking, but I don't dare minimize the situation too much.

I stand to bend over him with an affectionate hug. That went well, but I think he will need a little more attention from me than usual for the next few days.

As far as my McKenzie cousins, I have neither the time or the energy to worry about telling them. That would leave the door open for trouble—trouble that I don't have time to squash.

Grandfather's approval of what I have done, and more so that Grandmother McKenzie would be proud of me touches me. More than I realized, I needed his and Grandmother's approval.

The only way I can think of to tell the staff to call Karen in a medical emergency is to have Zoe make up an emergency call list for all of the people who live and work at the mansion. That way Karen's phone number can be listed for me.

Zoe loves to make documents. She takes on the task with youthful enthusiasm, and has the list completed in no time. She gives a copy of the emergency phone list to everyone and places one in her master notebook in her office. If she gets any more organized I will have to move her to the corporate office and unleash her on that mess.

~~~

Mr. Bradford's secretary, Crystal, calls to say the first wave of documents are ready for my signature. The documents will
~~~

have to wait a day or two, I have work to do here. Monthly reports are coming in, and the third-quarter reports should come on their heels.

I'm not cleared to run around and get fatigued. Sam will have to attend the board of directors' meeting in Chicago next month. It's getting cool in Chicago this time of year, but Sam is welcome to take his wife with him for a mini vacation. Chicago is a marvelous city anytime.

Sam has been putting in long hours since he came to work for me. They are probably due for time away, together. The board meeting won't take much time. The only downside to the trip is that it isn't baseball season. With the Cubs and the White Sox in town, it could have been fun to send them to a game at each field. I am sure they will find other ways to be entertained in a city as grand as Chicago.

Thursday evening, I head to the city after work. First thing in the morning I have tests to add to my surgery profile.

<p style="text-align:center">~~~</p>

"The latest news is the surgery is past test status in Europe," I tell Karen. I look from my coffee cup to Karen's concerned eyes.

It takes a moment before Karen responds, but she understood immediately.

"That opens up the surgery for you without being accepted in the test group." Her eyes water and her voice softens to a whisper.

"Finally, a break my direction," I admit, also in a whisper. I am relieved and feel exhausted.

We wait outside for the tests to be printed, so they can be added to the medical file I have to keep in my briefcase, so that I can be ready to go at a moment's notice. Karen breaks into tears. That is all it takes for me to burst into tears of relief too.

I am a million miles away, thinking about living and dying. I certainly have a new perspective on my life now that I am ill.

Karen is quiet, obviously lost in thought. She startles me when she suddenly speaks.

"Katey!" she reaches for my hand. "Katey, you don't have to be on-call. You can schedule your surgery. You can choose the time. Why don't you call your doctor and get your surgery scheduled as soon as possible?"

Karen catches me off guard. Wow! She is absolutely correct. Her words are liberating. This illness, this tumor, has been outside my control. However, the thought that I can select a date for the surgery gives me a piece of control over this thing that otherwise scares the beejeebies out of me.

I look up to meet her eyes. "You're right! Thank you. I can't tell you how relieved I feel with the idea of having a little control in this, this situation. I'll call the neurologist in the morning and let you know when it's scheduled. Do you want to fly on my personal jet?" We both laugh, finally.

~~~

The tests, except those of my head, are normal. My doctor sent the results and interpretation files via email to Sweden. They have requested the films, but have made a tentative appointment for early December. That gives me slightly less than two months to get everything ready for my absence. I still don't know how long it will take to be back to normal. There is much to do. Regardless of what happens to me, the businesses will continue on with their own momentum.

What worries me is time for seeing everyone again if something goes wrong with this risky procedure. Mr. Goldstein is covered. We have the arrangements made for my visit to Austria next weekend.

Signing the documents with Mr. Bradford makes it crystal clear in my mind that this health problem is a problem. I call it many things just to avoid saying tumor or cancer. I don't want to face it, but I cannot not face it. Quickly, I make a mental list of the people I want to see this weekend before I return to the mansion on Sunday evening.

"Mr. Bradford, thank you for doing all of this work on short notice."

"Kathryn, I am happy to do it. I know your father would look after my family if the situation had been reversed."

"I just want to make sure you know I appreciate what you do for me—what you have always done for me."

Mr. Bradford never seems to pay full attention to what is said
~~~

He is always shuffling papers or reading a document. But this time he isn't multitasking. He is listening completely without distraction. His eyes narrow and his brow wrinkles.

"Is everything all right, Kathryn?"

"As right as rain."

Mr. Bradford nods in acknowledgment—relieved to hear the answer he was hoping for.

~~~

I go to see Mother Elizabeth and everyone at Spirit of Hope —Mother, the nuns, the clients, and that place were pivotal in my recovery of self after returning from Nebraska, not to mention a change of professional direction.

Standing before the heavy-weathered door, looking at the metal door-knocker brings a myriad of memories of my first impression of Sister Theresa. The image of her speeding through the hallway brings a smile. I should have known she had a lead foot when driving, but I never figured it out until she was behind the wheel. I smile.

Inside the convent doors, the cool air is noticeably cooler than the fall weather outside. Sister Theresa is wearing a sweater, something I have never seen her do before. The older sisters sometimes wore sweaters over their habits, but Sister Theresa never did.

After our greetings, I ask Sister Theresa, "What's going on?" I look around and notice everyone is wearing a sweater or jacket, and I am beginning to get a chill.

"The boiler went out last week. We are trying to get it repaired. Every company that looked at it has a different opinion about what is wrong with it."

I touch her wrist. "Where is Mother Elizabeth?" Obviously, Karen doesn't know about the boiler or she would have mentioned it.

"She's looking at the boiler with another contractor. You can wait in her office."

We walk down the hall, past the statues in their alcoves, and into the waiting area outside Mother's office. When we pass the chapel doors, we both genuflect, as we should.

~~~

While I wait alone for Mother Elizabeth, I call one of my cousins. He is from my "real" family, the one I grew up with, attended family dinners with, and watched his children learn to walk. He is a builder—multi-million-dollar homes. Possibly he will know someone in the boiler business even though his homes don't have boilers.

Luckily, I reach him on his cell phone. "Mike, this is Katey. I need your expertise."

I laugh at his comment about my questionable mental health and his doubt there is a cure. "I am certainly glad that you aren't a shrink. Seriously, the boiler is out at Spirit of Hope. I need someone I can trust to look at it. Got any contacts in that area?"

"I don't put boilers in my houses."

His heating and air conditioning contractor might know someone who specializes in boilers. I just have to wait for him to call me back.

Mother Elizabeth comes into the room. She looks tired and frustrated, until she sees me sitting on the sofa, then she greets me with a cheery smile, as if she hasn't a care in the world.

"Hello, Mother Elizabeth. What's this about your boiler?"

"I think it is shot—or should be shot."

"It's that bad?"

"Unfortunately, I think it is. Everyone who has looked at it has found something else wrong with it." She pauses for a long, deep breath. "We used up most of our reserves with Spirit of Hope. We are a Diocesan Community. The Bishop is in Rome for a month, and the bank won't give us a loan." She humbles herself to explain her situation. She is a formidable, independent person. She prefers to be self-reliant. I'm sure it was difficult to tell me her problem.

"It is supposed to dip down into the forties tonight, and it's already cold in here." I state the obvious. "How long have you been without heat?"

"It is almost a week now." She looks away as she speaks.

My cousin calls back with a phone number of a boiler expert. I excuse myself to make the call in the adjacent conference room. He tells me that he is booked. There is no way he can look at the boiler before next Tuesday.

That won't do. I tell him there are women and children, and elderly nuns here. They can't go without heat that long. Apparently, my cousin didn't tell him that I am Kathryn McKenzie.

To my mother's family, being a McKenzie is not a big deal. My aunts and uncles knew of the connection with the McKenzie fortune, but no one ever hinted that it made any difference, and so it never did. To them, I am Katey.

However, I am not above playing the McKenzie card if it will get heat for these people. I ask who he would use, if he couldn't use his own company. He hesitates to give me his competitor's name.

"All right then, how much do you want for your company?" I ask, quite annoyed with him.

"What?"

"How much will it take to get you here, or to buy your company?"

"What are you talking about?" He is sounding angry.

"Look, my cousin says you are the best. If you won't tell me the name of your biggest competitor, and you won't come, then, I will buy your company or whatever it takes to get heat for these people—it is that simple."

"Is this a joke?" he snaps back at me.

"No. No joke. I'm Kathryn McKenzie and quite willing to pay you full market value of your company, if that's what it takes."

"McKenzie Enterprises—that McKenzie? I have a bid in on the new plant you are planning for Long Beach—" his voice trails off into silence.

He probably thinks I already knew that, but I didn't. His humanitarian side is certainly not making a good impression.

"Where can I reach you? I have to call you back with the number." He seems more interested now that he hopes to influence the bid letting for Long Beach.

I give him my phone number. Though I know better than to burn bridges, I certainly am angry with his attitude.

~~~

Mother Elizabeth is sitting at her desk when I tap on the open door to her office. She looks like she has the weight of the world on her shoulders.
~~~

"Mother, do you have someone who can replace the boiler right away, if you had the money?"

Her eyes light up. It seems that she forgot that money is not an issue for me. She still sees me as a former staff person, not Kathryn the Great—ruler of an empire.

"The last fellow thought that he could get the boiler in the Spirit of Hope center running tonight with a patch job. The two systems are linked, but he thinks he can isolate the shelter's system and get it going. It doesn't seem to be in as bad of shape as the convent boiler."

"Do you think you can have him come back and talk with both of us?"

"Sure, why not?" she beams.

The boiler man and his father return to the convent within thirty minutes. They meet with Mother Elizabeth and me. The father looks at the system with his son and they come up with a plan to get the heat on, and hopes it will last until they can correctly fix the boiler by replacing it. The father is retired, but he started the company forty years ago. He is the expert on these ancient boilers.

I ask about switching the system to heat pumps and duct it for heat and air conditioning, something they don't presently have. It gets hot in here during the summer. The problem is that running that kind of system without an in-house generator would be astronomical. Solar panels can't carry the load. The best we can do is to replace the boilers. The major catch is that a hazmat company will have to come and remove the asbestos covering the pipes and boilers, before they can be replaced. Currently, the covering poses no threat. Once the coating is disturbed, the asbestos will become airborne, and that's a problem.

The old man says there is room in the old high school, currently Spirit of Hope, to set the new boiler beside the old one. That way as soon as the asbestos is peeled off, bagged, and the air exchange has been completed, the new system can be hooked up. The old boiler can be removed later.

The convent boiler is an entirely different story. The current boiler is a monstrosity. There isn't room to set a new one beside it and make the switch. The old boiler has to be removed before the new boiler can be installed. The only catch is, it has to be cut into pieces to get it out of the building.

That is the best we can do. Hopefully the boiler will run until the new one arrives. I guarantee payment and write him a deposit check from the Foundation for twenty thousand dollars to get the new boilers ordered and shipped in the most expedient fashion. The men proceed to the Spirit of Hope boiler room to get the old boiler to fire up and run.

The whole system will have to be flushed and all of the radiators checked, something that can be done while the hazat team works in the boiler room. I ask Mother if she needs cots to move the nuns into the auditorium until the convent system is repaired, but she says they will manage in their cells.

I write another check, this time for fifty thousand dollars and warn her that the Diocese is not to get a penny of the money, if it exceeds the boiler expenses. I know that I won't be here next week, so I am hoping the check will cover all of her expenses and purchase the extra blankets they need in the meantime.

With the situation at Spirit of Hope on the mend, I leave without addressing my desire for one last personal moment with Mother Elizabeth. The opportunity for a heart-to-heart did not present itself. It is probably better that things worked out this way. Besides, I think she knows my feelings toward her.

We hug goodbye. It is a hug that lingers a moment longer than usual. I suppose for her it is gratitude for the boiler, but for me, it very well may be a final goodbye.

~~~
~~~

CHAPTER 13

Life in Review

Threatening to purchase the boiler company to get what I want embarrasses me. That's something Grandfather would do. My behavior surprises me. I have to take a long hard look at how I behaved. The question is, "Am I less constrained now that I am dying?" Am I really a rich spoiled brat when I need to be? Or am I in such a hurry to pack as many accomplishments in the time I have, that I abandon who I am?

The concept of dying Is new to me only in the sense of perspective. I remember Mother's approach to both, living and dying. I was sixteen toward the end of her life. She shared some of her thoughts about life with me. However, considering my desire to keep this illness to myself, I am now questioning how many of her thoughts she kept to herself.

On the way back to the beach, I call Dana to see if there is a time in her weekend when we can get together. She opts to come over tonight for a nightcap and a walk on the beach. I am not sure how to go about saying what I would like to say to her, and allowing her the opportunity to say what she would say if she knew I was dying.

The thought of her gratitude embarrasses me. However, I realize she may need to express her appreciation for getting her off of the street and in a position to reclaim her life as a fashion designer.

Yet, I'm not ready to say aloud that I might be dying. It is a choreographed dance to not leave anyone with the regret of unspoken words, like I was left when Maggie died.

"So, what is the reason for this sudden get-together?" Dana asks as the evening gets underway.

She's intuitive. It must be the artistic spirit in her.

"I didn't know we needed a reason!" I smile sheepishly. "I am losing touch with everyone. I decided this is the week to start catching up—so, here we are!" I smile and squint at her.

She laughs a vigorous laugh that is reserved for special occasions —occasions outside the fashion arena. Dana seems to accept my explanation.

We catch up quickly as if we'd seen each other regularly over the past months.

"Oh, before I forget, I am going to Austria and will miss Linda and Todd's big Halloween party—" I begin, but Dana interrupts.

"Don't even think I am going to tell you what character I'm going to be. If you want to know, you have to show up!" Dana laughs again.

"Artists!" I feign dismay.

Dana tells me she has her spring collection finished and is nearly finished with her summer line. She exaggerates her words and hand motions—making fun of me. What she doesn't realize is how I appreciate her skill. She is so ahead of the game that she is beginning to work on her fall line for next year. Dana laughs again and says she isn't organized—she is driven.

She stops walking and looks into the distance. "Shh, listen to the waves!" Our conversation falls dead silent. Then, just as suddenly she throws back her head and laughs.

I don't know what that was all about, but the laughter is nice. It is another facet to add to my experience of the beach with friends. I stow images of Dana into my memory for later.

"I have the perfect holiday collection just for you." Dana grins as she draws me back into a conversation.

I catch myself from saying my thought aloud—I may not be here for the holidays this year, or any other year.

"Really? I'll have to stop by," I say.

Maggie, I am pragmatic about my life now. I have moments of regret that life could be so short. There are also times when I feel absolutely certain that the surgery will be successful and this will all seem like a bad dream. However, all of the time I feel driven to get everything to a place that it can continue on without me. Now, if I can only allow everyone a chance to say goodbye without knowing this might be the end.

~~~
~~~

Storm Surge

Saturday morning, I drive to my aunt and uncle's house. We reminisce about family experiences. My aunt starts telling stories about my childhood, including the home perm one of my older cousins gave me, without adult supervision or permission.

It didn't take long for the smell of the mix to make the perm obvious to the adults who had been visiting on the patio. It was disastrous. There wasn't any fix for the tight frizzy curls. Unfortunately for me, the next week was school photos and mine was unusually bad that year. That was first grade.

~~~

In third grade I had a black eye for my school photo because my older cousins let me play baseball with them. We all were in trouble when I walked into the bat during a practice swing. I don't remember them trying to run me off, that wasn't the way things were done in this family—everyone is included In everything. And I had a black eye to prove it! I do hope they have better memories of me than those.

~~~

For lunch, I go back to the beach and rest before my next visit. I have been trying to pace myself. It is unnerving to know that at any minute, it could be my last. I try not to become too pensive. Hasn't it always been—no guarantees of tomorrow? The only difference is that, because of the headaches, I am acutely aware of it now. "It isn't how long one lives, it's how wide."

~~~

I visit another aunt and uncle. He is such a ham that he keeps us laughing so much that my sides begin to hurt. It is a nice hurt, though. He is full of family stories of things he and his siblings did growing up. Some of them can't possibly be true. He has a full dose of blarney. Luckily, most of them are not about embarrassing things that I did.

When the laughter dies, my aunt asks how I am since Grandfather McKenzie's announcement. I confide to her that being wealthy is greatly overrated.

She smiles. She agrees that there are other kinds of wealth—the kind I already had. I almost tell her about the surgery, but at the last minute I change my mind. It just doesn't fit into the conversation.

On the way back to the beach a headache starts. This time it's a dull headache, not the shooting pain headache. It is probably an ordinary headache, the kind everyone gets from time to time, but it reminds me of my situation. Those thoughts are never far away.
~~~

Storm Surge

After not finding my camera, I walk to the store two blocks away and purchase a disposable one. I am sappy-sentimental as I walk through Main Street of my hometown toward the beach to take photos.

The waves seem exceptionally dramatic today, full of white foam that rushes toward the beach with an uncommonly loud roar. I think of Dana and how she laughed at the waves last night. I never did see what made her laugh, but I do have the memory of the laugh to savor.

The sun sets early since it is late fall, so I cut short my walk and head home. About the time I am at the place where I turn away from the ocean to go home, the sun breaks through the clouds and bathes the beach in magnificent colors.

The sunset is absolutely beautiful. Turning to the west, I notice the birds have begun to congregate on the beach behind me. When a wave recedes, the birds are silhouetted on the mirror image of the sunset. I have never seen anything like this sunset in all of my years on the beach. I shoot the rest of the roll of film as the sunset changes from minute to minute.

Just as I finish dinner, Mark calls to tell me he is going to London this week for a recording session. He invites me to join him. Mark has everything figured out: We'll fly together Wednesday, spend the night in Paris, he'll go to London while I go to Vienna. We will meet in Paris a week later, after his recording set. The only "catch" is that it will take several days for him to show me his favorite spots in Paris. He rattles off the list of places he wants to take me, enticing me into agreeing with his scheme.

"Katey, think of it, Le Quartier Latin, Centre Georges Pompidou—"

I interrupt his litany with a laugh. "Okay, okay! I give in. It sounds wonderful—I get my own room."

"Ah." He pretends to pout. "If you insist."

"I do." I like our relationship just fine. Besides, I note, he didn't protest strongly.

It's worth having the extra time and a traveling companion. I don't mind running around L.A. alone. I'd rather not travel to Europe alone with a ticking bomb in my head.

~~~

Sunday morning is the last of the time I can devote to visiting family. Everyone else will have to wait until Thanksgiving dinner. Catching three sets of aunts and uncles, Mother Elizabeth, Dana, and Karen is a lot to accomplish in such short time. Even Mr. Bradford can technically be added to the list.

The morning traffic is light, and I arrive before my uncle returns with fresh pastries. Aunt Grace, the one who came to pick me up at Karen's
~~~

house so we could go to the beach, takes one look at me and asks, "What's wrong, Katey?"

"I just haven't seen you for a while."

"That is the official story. What's the truth?"

My eyes water. She holds my hands in hers and looks straight at me. I hug her and she holds me tightly.

"I have a brain tumor."

She tilts her head lovingly.

"I have to go to Europe for surgery after Thanksgiving, and I wanted to thank you for everything you have done for me, for all of the times you made time to help me, for—" my voice gives under the great well of the emotion I feel.

Aunt Grace holds me again in a motherly hug. She has always understood me, especially when words fail. We move to the sofa and sit in soft silence. When my uncle returns, he is surprised to see two teary-eyed women in the living room.

Aunt Grace tells him the news of my surgery. The three of us have a long talk. I feel almost as if my parents are here. We drink coffee and eat the light, flaky pastry that melts when it touches my tongue.

~~~

On the way home, I drive through Forest Lawn Cemetery where the McKenzie family is buried. Impressive copies of statues by Renaissance masters are sentinels throughout the grounds. Most, I recognize— Michelangelo's David and Pieta (from Latin for "dutifulness").

Gently, I pull to a stop and walk for a while. "Dutifulness," I whisper the name. It saddens me. Not so much for the dead Christ across His mother's lap, but for Mary. Dying is really hard for the people left living. I feel gravely sad about all of the things I haven't accomplished, and I may not to be able to accomplish now. There are so many humanitarian projects that I haven't had time to begin. I feel cheated.

Maggie's words come to mind, but I haven't lived nearly wide enough yet. I need reassurance that all of my projects will continue. At least Grandmother had that hope in knowing I existed and the child she watched grow for a while.

When I reach the McKenzie section of the cemetery, I sit at the foot of Grandmother's grave. I wonder if I should plan my Requiem Mass? I want my parish priest to have my Mass, as he had each of my parents' Masses. He was the one who gave me the Sacrament of the Sick—Last Rites—as a precautionary measure. My Dear Father, I will miss you.

Silently, my body shakes with tears of grief. I don't try to bargain with God, there are still five weeks for bargaining. Today, I am sad. Tomorrow, who knows?
~~~

The one consolation is this will be the last funeral I must attend. I do hate funerals. That's when it struck me. "Oh, God! They aren't Catholic!" My hand covers my gasping mouth. "Will Grandfather allow me a Catholic burial? Does it matter what I plan or he will turn this into one of his media events?

My posture slumps with the weight of silently deep-into-the-soul sobbing. This ground hasn't been disturbed for a long time. It feels hard and unyielding, even though the lawn is hardy. The grass should be cushioning, but it's not.

Self-pity, Katey? There isn't time for that. Wiping my eyes, I get up and walk to my car.

Pulling away from the curb, I catch a glimpse of myself in the rearview mirror. My face is red. The mascara held up, but I must not have put on waterproof eyeliner. Now I have puffy, raccoon-looking eyes. I can't go home looking like this. Where can I go?

Ignoring the occasional glances of other drivers, glances caused by my black-smudged eyes, I move north toward the mansion. When I reach Father's Beach, I know one more place I must go.

Almost as if a second Baptism, I reach my cupped hands into the Pacific. Over and over again, I fill my hands with the icy water and put it to my face. The heat in my skin is subsiding, and maybe even some of the puffiness around my eyes too.

~~~

When I return to the mansion, Grandfather and I spend the evening together. He's glad that Mark is accompanying me to Europe. I take advantage of the opportunity to tell him of the legal arrangements I've made. It surprises me that he approves of my decisions. He tells me how proud he is of me and the decisions I have made since I became "Miss McKenzie"—my words, not his. He talks of his disappointment with his other three grandchildren. I remind him how well Dan is doing and suggests he visit Dan's new office and look at his drawings.

Grandfather promises to pay Dan a visit. He says the police found Tim in a L.A. bar last night. It seems one of his friends set him up to be at the bar, so the police could pick him up there—in front of people he knows. The police found a kilo of cocaine in his car the night of the wreck. Grandfather is convinced that Tim is the one who got Brooke addicted to drugs. He plans to not intervene in the natural unfolding of Tim's case.

Even though Grandfather is ruthless, he never drinks to excess and has no tolerance for drugs. He has, as is his custom, cut off all ties with Brooke and Tim. Another generation (except me) is cut out of his life.
~~~

I hope he seeks a relationship with Dan. And so the family legacy continues.

~~~

~~~

~ **CHAPTER 14** ~

Bon Voyage

It is funny how the important things become little, and the little things are important to me now. I have started walking in the garden more often. I don't think about anything in particular, certainly nothing enlightened enough to bring about world peace. Mostly, my mind is busy making memories of the dew on the flowers, the busy ladybugs, and recalling the ocean spray at the beach during a winter storm.

~~~

In two days I'm off across the Atlantic. All I can think of during today's morning walk in the rose garden is about seeing Mr. Goldstein again. I love that old man. The memories come over me with the warmth of a blanket: His first attempt to walk the beach, Hanukkah, unsolicited decorating advice, stories about the women at the Senior Center, the internet experience —every memory brings a fond smile.

I return to the patio to sit mindlessly watching the sun come up. The purple, pink, and finally the first glimpse of yellow appear on the horizon. With the sunrise, regret creeps into my mood. My emotions run the gamut with absolutely no warning of their changing.

My coffee has grown cold. Tears well up in my eyes. It is almost as if I am physically reliving the events of yesterday as I think about them. Louise comes to the patio to refill my cup—awakening me from the memories. She joins me for a few moments in the fresh morning air. The sun has finished its birthing and has fully cleared the horizon.

"Miss McKenzie, there is a gentleman here to see you," she says as she hands me his business card.

I stare at the card. Eleanor is awaiting instructions per Louise. We never have guests arrive before the office staff. "Thank you. I will see him in the library."

I take a minute to finish my coffee and collect my thoughts. I wonder what he wants?
~~~

I would like to refill my coffee again, but I set it down and walk to the library. No coffee, this is not a casual visit by my definition, no coffee cups in hand for this one.

"Hello, Joseph," I say.

Joseph turns away from the window when I speak. He looks older than the years since I have seen him. I can see he is fumbling for words—oh, how the mighty fall. Ordinarily, I would help smooth an awkward moment, but I haven't quite figured out the purpose of his visit. He stutters a hello.

I move to one of the chairs and motion for him to sit across from me. I briefly study him. His behavior is self-consciousness.

Strangely, seeing Joseph doesn't rekindle any of the emotions I once had for him. I had wondered what I would feel if I saw him again. Confession worked. I realize the silence and remember my role as hostess. "How have you been?"

Joseph smiles warily. "Divorced." There is a slight hint of sadness combined with bitterness in his tone. The divorce is either recent or was brutal.

"Sorry to hear that," I say softly, genuinely.

"If that is true, will you have dinner with me tonight?" He reverts back to his former self-absorbed style.

"No, but thank you," I say, remembering how he treated me.

He looks annoyed, but it passes quickly.

"Come with me, let's go for a walk in the garden." I rise from my chair, so that there is no misunderstanding that this is not a negotiable request. No one could have overheard us in the library, but I wanted the feel of privacy.

Joseph looks out across the garden, then remarks that it is a far cry from a walk on the beach that I loved so much. His tone verges on sarcasm.

"Yes, it is a different world, in a different time." I turn to face him. "Joseph, what are you doing here?"

"I can explain." He takes a defensive step backward.

Explain? Explain what? Explain why I didn't deserve to be told you were married, and not to come to Ireland? Explain why you think you can waltz back into my life now and expect me to clear my schedule to have dinner with you without a moment's notice? I maintain my best witness-stand poker face.

"Just give me a chance to explain." He continues, though I have said nothing.

That is enough of this nonsense. If he is more interested in the McKenzie money than me, I hope he is smart enough to keep it to himself. I have work to do and two days to get it done. He is not going to disrupt my life for one minute more.

"Joseph, this is life, not a baseball game. There is no three-strike rule. I don't know how many 'chances' you think you get." I move the conversation to a swift conclusion.

"Katey," he pleads.

"Joseph. It was over between us a long time ago." I have timed my final comment to coincide with our return to the house.

Joseph almost looks as if he is weighing the option of kissing me goodbye.

"Goodbye, Joseph," I say in a formal tone.

He nods and softly says, "Goodbye, Kathryn."

~~~

Joseph's unexpected visit is only a momentary distraction from work. I'm pleased he didn't stir romantic emotions when I saw him. It is finally finished, and I'm glad for the confirmation that there is nothing there to return to. I appreciate having that conclusion, especially now.

I have a lot to do. First, is to write a letter to Linda and Todd with my regrets about bowing out of their par—Oh, what bad timing for a headache to strike! I shut my eyes and lean over my desk, breathing slow, shallow breaths until the shooting pain subsides. I think my headaches are getting worse. Only a few more weeks until my surgery. I can endure them that long. Either way, live or die, the headaches will end soon.

My staff thinks that my illness is exhaustion. They are a little more pampering than when I first came to live at the mansion, but most of that comes from the shooting incident. I do like the calmer and kinder environment since Mrs. Bailey left. I'd rather have it this way. I can live with mild pampering, but not morbid sympathy.

I'm glad Karen told me to tell Mark about my brain tumor. He took it well, as far as I know. At least, he never mentioned it again. I saw very little change in his behavior, other than he was
~~~

careful to keep our outings to a reasonable length. He behaved as if I had fatigue and needed to slow down—that was all.

I think preparing to die is very private. Up until the end, I want everyone to behave naturally. After I return from Austria, I'll make contact one more time with the people who are most important to me, the people who have contributed to the richness of my life.

Being sick, incurably sick is a bit like going crazy. I can rationalize anything I want to simply by twirling it around in my mind enough times. The world of dying is a fantasy world that allows me the liberty of any thought I want to have. There is a sane logic to this insanity. I feel like I am living a double life, but I want the luxury of privacy in dying.

~~~

Grandfather goes to bed early, I finish packing, then sit in the chair by the window. Across the room, in the place on the dresser where Grandmother's photos once stood, are photos of my friends. Surveying the lot of them is a reminder of how rich my life has been. There is little Shasta in her tutu, Karen with Mother Elizabeth, Sister Theresa in her habit holding up her new driver's license, and one of the beach photos of Mr. Goldstein. The tabloid photo of Scourge and me is oddly one of my favorites. We had fun toying with the media that night. Mark is such a nut, it will be fun to run around Paris with him.

~~~

Tuesday morning, I feel much better. Not only has my headache not been back, I have more energy and a much more upbeat attitude. Zoe and I have been on a roll cranking out documents and letters for two hours.

I look up from my desk to see Zoe and Mother Elizabeth standing in the doorway. Quickly, I shut the file and set it aside.

"Hello, Mother Elizabeth!" I nod to Zoe, as I get up to greet Mother Elizabeth.

"Hello, Kathryn," she replies softly.

"We will be more comfortable in here, Mother." I gesture toward the library.

"How have you been, Kathryn?" Mother Elizabeth asks in a gentle tone.

"Fine, Mother, and yourself?"

We approach the library door. I am becoming more and more comfortable in being the "Mother Superior" of the mansion. She looks good, but worried.

"Mother, may I offer you a cold drink?" I ask as I go to the wet bar and she seats herself in the rich leather chair.

"Yes, that would be nice—tea, if you have it."

"That sounds good," I say and get two glasses.

She looks around at her surroundings as I prepare our drinks. My house is as rich as hers is poor. I am sure she knows that in actuality, she is the rich one between the two of us.

"I know that you couldn't possibly have been in the neighborhood. What brings you all the way out here?"

Mother shifts slightly in her chair. She takes a drink and sets down her glass. She takes a breath.

"What is it, Mother?" I ask softly, concerned.

She looks down to her hands in her lap, then straight at me in her Mother Superior style. "I came to tell you thank you for the new boilers." It's obvious she has something else on her mind.

"Mother?" I try to encourage her without making her uncomfortable. The woman goes to confession weekly— something I could never do—yet, she finds talking to me difficult.

"Do you have heat? Do you have everything you need?"

Sitting in my house, she has to realize that helping her was no sacrifice for me, and certainly not the slightest hardship. Her presence, full traditional habit embarrasses me to be surrounded by such wealth.

"Yes, yes. Thank you. We have everything we need—thanks to your generosity." She sounds like a nun again.

I smile. "Anytime you need something—great or small—call me. I have more than enough, and it is a pleasure to help you any way I can."

She thanks me again and moves forward in her chair, as if she is preparing to leave. She hesitates, then sits up straight at the edge of her chair. Her soft blue eyes begin to fill with tears.

"Kathryn, Karen and I were talking about you. I told her what you did about our heat problem. We talked about different things you did, the baseball game with the kids, Shasta, and sneaking around with Sister Theresa, so she could learn to drive. Karen started to cry. Don't be angry with her. I made her tell me why she was crying." She hesitates, choosing and timing her words. "Kathryn, I am so sorry about your brain tumor. I prayed all night before the Blessed Sacrament for you and your health—" Her voice breaks.

It is all I can do not to cry with her. Watching her, I am reminded how she took the news of Monica's illness. I can see her in the garden, praying her rosary and Karen coming to her, holding her Sister-sister in her arms as she cried.

"Mother Elizabeth, there is a very promising surgery for this type of tumor. It's not at all like with Monica."

When tears run down her face, I move closer to her to comfort her.

"And there is such a thing as miracles," I add.

~~~

After a while, Mother Elizabeth and I walk out the front door together. I'm surprised to see Sister Theresa sitting in the driver's seat. She could have come inside, but the way she is smiling and holding on the steering wheel it looks like she is guarding her position as driver. Now that she has her license, I doubt anyone would challenge her right to the wheel.

As soon as Mother Elizabeth shuts the car door, they are off in a flash heading for the gate. I doubt Mother has her seat belt on yet. It almost looked like she had a whiplash when Sister took off. I would never ride with that nun after all the driving lessons I sat through with her.

Ordinarily, it is a two-hour drive back to the convent. The way Sister Theresa barely stops at the gate before she pulls onto the Coast Highway, I doubt it will take them that long to get home. I created a monster when I taught her to drive! Maybe not. As I recall, Sister Theresa drove that way from the beginning.

~~~

~ CHAPTER 15 ~

Flight to Paris

Flying has become such a large part of my life that I rarely notice the whine of the engines preparing to thrust us into the atmosphere. Turbulence is insignificant. In a way, it's sad I have forgotten the thrill.

Mark looks up from his guitar and smiles. I put down Grandmother's book, sit back on the sofa and look out the window at the sun shining up through holes in the clouds as it sets on the Earth far below. My martini tastes better than usual with nothing competing with it for my attention. Mark continues to pick out a rhythm on his twelve-string Fender.

"Is that one of the songs for your new album?" I ask, actually liking the melody.

"Yes, do you like it?"

"I do. It seems different from your last album."

"It is—very different. I like the softer sounds. This will be on the new album I'm putting together in London." He begins to play slightly louder and adds the lyrics.

When he finishes I comment, "That's nice. It almost has a Rod McKuen sound to it."

"Rod McKuen? You know Rod McKuen?"

"My mother wore out one of his albums. She loved him!"

"My mother does too!"

"How are you going to sneak that on Scourge's album?"

"Scourge was my last manager's idea. I'm going to record this album under my own name." He beams sheepishly.

I sit up, interested. "Really?"

"Yes. Scourge might have to retire, if this CD sells!"

I study him in surprise. "Let me hear your other songs."

The pilot says we are in French airspace.

Without warning, a sharp pain shoots through my head. My eyes hurt. I close them, but it doesn't help. I feel myself begin to slump off the sofa in slow motion.

Mark moves my body back onto the sofa. He is speaking loudly in a panicked tone to the cabin page.

"Put the pilot on the intercom! Quick! Do it!"

"Yes, sir?" I hear the pilot's voice.

Everything swirls around me like a Van Gogh painting. Through my blurry vision things seem to be in a third-person view. I can see and hear everything, but not quite.

"Miss McKenzie needs a doctor, IMMEDIATELY! Where is the nearest airport?"

~~~

Everything is quiet, dark. Funny, so this is dying? Not that I'm complaining, but I thought dying should be catastrophic, spiritual, musical, maybe in someway a movie-moment. I've had an interesting life, I can't complain about dying. I drift in and out of consciousness.

I hear voices that are human-sounding, no angels. I feel hands lifting and moving me. I smell hospital smells. There is an annoying buzzing sound. Oh, I get it, someone is shaving my head. Hey! Careful, I'm not dead yet! The inside of my head is pounding to burst through my confining skull. It is hot, burning my brain. Dark again, then nothing.

~~~

I can hear muffled voices. I reach up to feel my eyes to see why they aren't opening, but my arms don't move. There is a steady whooshing sound and clicking commingled with beeping sounds. I'm cold. I ask for a blanket, but no words come out.

Concentrating, I make out the sound of Karen's voice. "Mark, you've been here for a week. I'll stay with Katey—go get some rest." She is using her motherly tone—which is legitimate now that they had lied about their identity the first time I passed out.

Karen's voice talks to me about the beach, Livingston, Mr. Goldstein, Maggie, the sunsets, the mist from the waves. I drift off to sleep.

~~~

The days that follow are painful days. It's hard to think with the throbbing in my brain. Finally, it's quiet on the day the respirator is permanently disconnected, and wheeled out of my room. The dainty beeping machine is removed the next day.
~~~

When I finally am able to force my eyelids to respond to my wishes, I see a blurry light. There is a stir in the room. Mark notices my eyes are open. He wakes Karen. When they lean over me just right to block the bright light, I can make out the fuzzy outline of their silhouettes.

It's hard to grasp the passage of time. What day is it? What time is it? How'd the surgery go? I had surgery, didn't I? I can't speak, so my questions are left unasked. I can't tell for certain which things I remember and which I remember because I was told about them.

Even though I am awake, the staff talk around me as if I am not in the room. They tell Mark that nothing is wrong with my vocal chords or my trachea from the respirator tube. They think my aphasia is a result of the swelling in my brain and it will pass. I know what is wrong. It is a deep black void between my brain and my lips.

Karen has to return to the States. There is so much I want to tell her. It will have to wait. Before she leaves, she takes my motionless hand gently in her hand. With all of my might, I will a finger to move. When I lightly squeeze her hand, tears run down her cheeks. She tries to hide them at first, but once tears spilled out the corner of my eye, she releases hers too.

We both know that I will be okay.

~~~
~~~

~ CHAPTER 16 ~

Do You Wanna Dance?

Mark is at my side every time I open my eyes. For me, time passes in disjointed intervals while I am in the hospital. Mark struggles through my breathing treatments, physical therapy, and painful tests. I think it's worse that I am not able to speak, than unable to move—from his prospective and mine. I would like to complain. I think that would ease my frustration.

~~~

When I can speak again, I don't feel like complaining, rather, I squeak Mark's name. He is delighted. Eventually, my speech begins to return. Sometimes I am aphasic. Sometimes I misuse words. But in time, sentences begin to form more often than not. And more often than not, I say what I meant to say.

One Thursday morning during physical therapy, tingling begins in my left shoulder. In a few days the tingling travels down my arm. I am able to clumsily move my arm to a more comfortable position with several flailing attempts. No one knows, or at least admits to knowing, why my recovery has been slower than anticipated.

I surmise it is because the physicians familiar with the surgery did not preform it. Mark says the expert had to advise a local neurosurgeon, Dr. Nidhi, via video conferencing during the surgery. No one hinted that the surgery team had to improvise with neuro-clamps and retractors, rather than the instruments developed for the new procedure.

My recuperation has been slower than anyone else's recovery. My right arm and leg are still numb and move only when it is their choice. For reasons no one seems to understand, my right side resists the passive physical therapy. I wish for anything encouraging from my right side—even pain. It looks like I'll have to learn to write with my left hand. Well, it could be worse in many ways.

Before occupational therapy begins to work on my fine motor skills, I need to get reliable gross motor responses from my left
~~~

side. Progress is slow and discouraging. Mark and I fake that we aren't concerned.

~~~

The McKenzie jet brings Karen to visit again. Not only have I missed the Halloween party as expected, Thanksgiving has passed, and Christmas is threatening. Karen says she copied names and phone numbers from the address book in my purse, and made the necessary calls after her last visit.

"What calls?—Sorry. Thank you. Who were you able to reach?" I rephrase my question.

"I called your Aunt Grace, because she is the only one of your family I know. I told her your basic situation, and we discussed what she would tell everyone else at Thanksgiving. We have spoken often since then. She loves you a great deal." Karen takes a minute to check her mental list. I don't interrupt.

"I called Zoe and told her you were detained in Europe. She had me speak with Sam. He wasn't aware of your condition—I don't know how you hid it. I thought it would be better for him to tell your grandfather about the emergency surgery."

I nod agreement with her triage of the situation. By now, "detained" in Europe probably doesn't work. That would have been only a temporary bluff.

"I forgot to tell you that I brought someone with me." She smiles mischievously, as she gets up from the chair.

"Wait! Who is it? How do I look?" I ask as I run my hand across the inch-long stubble on my head.

Karen leans over me with a comb and careful not to injure the tender incision line with the teeth, she combs my hair into fluff. She re-combs it again, apparently unsatisfied with the first outcome. It is uncertain how truthful Karen is when she says my hair is "fine."

"Fine?" I ask under my breath as she goes out the door.

"Oh, my God! Mr. Goldstein!" I whisper in awe when Karen opens the door and Mr. Goldstein steps into the open doorway.

Mr. Goldstein's expression explodes, his eyes twinkle, his grin is full and continues to widen—hiding any concern he has.

Karen has kept him informed, but I think he is relieved to see me for himself.
~~~

Mark and Karen excuse themselves under the guise of needing coffee, leaving Mr. Goldstein and me to visit privately.

"How are you, Katerina?" he asks softly, patting my hand.

"I am getting better. I can't walk yet, but I will."

"Goodt, goodt," he says, and pats my hand again.

"I am so happy to see you! Sorry I missed our visit, but I will come in the spring."

~~~

When the time arrives for my discharge from the hospital, Mark makes arrangements to move me to a seacoast house in Scotland belonging to his friend, Jake.

I am excited to be leaving the hospital, though I had hoped to be recovered enough to go home. I never mention to Mark my concern that I might live the rest of my life like this—unable to move on my own, a future that discourages me. I tell him, "It is all bridge under the water now."

He looks at me strangely as he lifts me from the wheelchair to the bed that has been placed in the living room. The bed was moved out of the bedroom, because the seizures continue, though they are more infrequent as time passes. I think the idea is that I'll be less discouraged not cooped up in the bedroom.

I grin to turn my remark into a joke. In a way it is true my bridge is underwater. But at the time, I misspoke.

Mark has coordinated with Zoe and Frank the "spin" on my disappearance from the public eye.

The stories are varied with conflicting accounts of my whereabouts. The (planted) leaks work to our benefit, as they had planned. Mark has a copy of the tabloid photo of us, framed and by the bed. It is obvious that he tries to keep my spirits up, so I don't want to disappoint him by telling him how discouraged I am. I remind myself that I could be dead if I hadn't had the surgery. I long for an explanation for the seizures and the paralysis, so we can find a remedy.

Mark waits on me and anticipates my needs. He sleeps beside me, so he will awaken if I have a seizure. He makes jokes about my (loss of) weight when he lifts me in and out of the bed. I am sure taking care of me is impeding his new CD promotion tours, but he never mentions it.
~~~

~~~

In a week, Jake joins us at the cottage. He's a songwriter by trade, sometimes he's Mark's songwriter. He's going to help Mark nursemaid me while working on a new project. This should be interesting, a romantic setting, two men pampering me, and I can barely move.

I didn't make it to Sweden for the new surgery, but the doctor thought it had gone well. My hair is about two and a half inches long, but it has grown back in blotches. I am assured that it would eventually all come back, but for now, I look like a dog with mange.

The second day after Jake's arrival, a Kawai baby grand piano arrives for the guys and a hot tub for my rehabilitation. Jake appears to be able to compose music in his sleep. The house is filled with nearly constant music. The piano seems to sense what Jake's mind hears and his fingers dance across the keys at all hours of the day and night. He has the recorder going nonstop, burning CD after CD of perfect songs on the first take.

When Jake takes a walk above the rocky shoreline, Mark picks out tunes in his mind as he puts on his "ballad" persona. Just imagine if it was Scourge's music! I'd lose what I have left of my mind. I like his softer side of music far better than his Scourge music. His new music reflects the romantic, gentle person that every woman longs to fall in love with. When I listen, becoming lost in his words—half sung, half spoken—I almost forget that I am not my old self. He sings of Camelot and princes and queens in Scotland, loves not lost, chivalry, steeds, and royal banquets. My mind drifts into the fictitious romantic past. I remember Mother's Rod McKuen songs, and can almost hear her sing along.

When the physical therapy hurts, Mark makes up ditties to entertain me. I never complain, but I easily could have in other circumstances. I'm not used to being dependent. It is humbling. In a way, it is probably good for me. Slowly, I ease into wellness.

~~~

February. One day after a discouraging failed attempt to stand, the guys decide to polish my toenails to cheer me. I can't feel them rubbing lotion on my feet, but I imagine the feel of it.

They enter into a disagreement about the correct way to apply the polish, which, by the way, is bright red. Whose idea was that? I would never wear red polish. Besides, they really are clueless about this process.

"You two sound like an old married couple!"

They are surprised and quit fighting immediately. That's not what I meant, and I feel bad for saying anything.

Mark decides to let Jake polish my toenails, because he is going to give me a facial. Great! Where am I going with four-inch-long hair that I'll need a facial? Nevertheless, he massages cream into my face with the confidence of a baker kneading bread dough. Strangely, it feels good. I lean deeper in my pillow. Life is good, definitely not easy, but good.

Sam, Zoe, and Frank keep busy lying to the press. Who knows what they tell Grandfather. Karen keeps my family, Mr. Goldstein, and the nuns informed of my status. I'm bored, discouraged, and restless. I have trouble imagining the future in worse shape than Grandfather. I am in desperate need to get outside and away from this bed and all the rehab paraphernalia.

~~~

In April, the guys use fishing line to hang various shapes of crystals in the windows. The breeze moves them gently, causing flashes of rainbows to dance across the walls and ceilings. They add to the mood of Mark's new music. The days blend easily from one to another.

The facials are now as much of the routine as the range-of-motion exercises. One rainy afternoon, Jake decides they should apply makeup. My aim is improving, but they both jump out of my reach.

"Wait until I get my hands on you two crazed musicians!"

There is a method to their madness. They are trying to make me presentable for a visit from Karen without spoiling the surprise arrival.

When I see Karen, I forget my threat. Mark has a concert engagement in London, and Karen is the relief nurse. She says she is assigned to take care of Jake.

These are nice people, but they are terrible liars. I know that my care is a burden, one they appear to accept willing, but still
~~~

more than enough for one person. My right side begins to recover faster than my left. Still, I can't hold a pen if my life depended on it.

~~~

My ego is adjusting to being dependent on my friends. However, sometimes at night, I can't help crying quietly about how good they are to me. I always took care of everyone else; this is a hard lesson for me. Mark and Jake do their best not to make it obvious they have put their careers in a holding pattern to help me recover. Jake keeps saying he might have to do all his projects here, since he gets more done than when in his London studio. I don't believe him, but don't mention it.

~~~

Someone always sleeps beside me. I haven't had a seizure in months, but they still wake easily if I move abruptly in my sleep. Then they wake me to make sure I'm okay.

Like a child, eventually I learned to sit up on my own. I am beginning to have deliberate movement in my arms. The guys put disposable gloves on me, tape a spoon to my gloved hand and make me feed myself. It is a messy endeavor.

My sense of humor slowly returns with their constant antics. Mark tapes the spoon to my gloved hand with white medical tape as usual. There's a slight problem. I don't say anything. Finally, Jake tells him that I am right-handed.

He lifts his right hand and says, "This is the right hand." He mocks Jake's ignorance.

"Yes, that is YOUR right hand, but THAT is Katey's left hand!" Jake wins.

"Oh, Katey, why didn't you tell me?" Mark looks like there has been a mutiny.

I laugh as he cuts the tape and glove off my left hand. He hadn't realized that the way we were sitting, we were opposite of each other. What a dope!

~~~

Things continue on as usual. Well, usual for us. The day I announced that my legs are beginning to tingle was nothing short of a miracle in their eyes. Mark lifts me to a standing position beside him and tries to talk my feet into walking. We
~~~

have been through this a million times at the parallel bars as I work thought my therapy routine. It still doesn't work.

Not to be disappointed, he enlists Jake to stand on the other side of me and they drag me around the room and say I am walking. They walk me right out of my slipper. From then on, when I need to move, they walk (drag) me around the room—even to move to the chair near the bed. Eventually, their efforts pay off. I begin a stuttered step, as long as one of them steadies me.

As I become stronger, Mark pulls me around in front of him. "Stand on my feet, Katey," he instructs as he moves my arm around his neck. I move the other one around his neck, while he holds me at my waist. Swaying slightly, he begins singing a love song he says he wrote for me. Slowly, he begins to dance with me like an adult dances with a child standing on their shoes. Jake plays the music to the song Mark is singing. It is a nice slow-dance song. I can almost feel the beat in my feet. More than dancing, I like the words to the song.

Jake turns on the stereo and comes to cut in. He is stronger than Mark and lifts me at the waist, relieving some of my weight from my feet. I never imagined that I would ever dance again.

Mark cuts in, but Jake wouldn't bow out. I have an arm on each of their shoulders and the three of us dance together. Life is good. It is certainly not what I expected, but it is good.

~~~

I begin to make phone calls to the mansion. Grandfather is glad to hear from me, so I call him daily. During this time, Sam and Zoe hold down the fort at home, under the careful watch of the house women. I'm getting simplified reports about our internal investigation. Danny and Susan, his love interest, are setting up housekeeping.

By the time my hair is nearly touching my shoulders, I can walk tentatively on my own. I work at it every chance I get. Winter and spring are gone and summer has arrived. I am able to walk outside, but never alone. Often Mark and I sit in the garden listening to the new CD of his authentic persona. It is good. Much richer than Scourge's. It's more hopeful, more loving. This is the Mark I know and love. Jake approves.
~~~

One afternoon while we are walking outside, I watch my shadow's gait. I hadn't realized how crippled I walk. It seemed like such an improvement from being paralyzed, that I hadn't noticed and no one mentioned it.

"Mark!" I gasp as I grab his arm.

"What!" I startled him and it showed in his voice.

"Did I have a stroke? I walk like I had a stroke!" My voice reflects the tears inside my heart. I know I should be happy that I am still alive—and I am. I really am happy to be alive. I just hadn't realized how I looked when I walked.

"Not exactly a stroke, you'll be fine."

I leave it at that. Either it is an unknown or no one wants to say what happened. I guess it doesn't matter what it is called or what happened. I have to keep going.

Later that evening, Frank faxes the latest headlines. The media has been silent about Kathryn McKenzie for months. Zoe fed them a steady diet of tidbits about my donations while I was ill. She failed to mention my illness. Finally, someone in the media noticed that no one had actually seen me for a while. One of the scandal sheets asked in big bold letters, "WHERE IS KATHRYN McKENZIE???"

Because of my obvious limp, Mark and I agree with Frank to leak that I had been in an auto accident and "was recovering nicely."

The wire services pick up the story and run with it as if it were true. Apparently, I had a car accident in a remote (unspecified) location in Europe, and "Miss McKenzie expressed gratitude to her well-wishers for the flowers and gifts that were showered on her."

"Really? And they believed that?" I ask, surprised at the details that have been added to our press release.

Mark shrugs his shoulders and smiles as he reads further. "Scourge was driving and was killed instantly in the accident." No one ever mentioned that he had been giving concerts on and off all the time I was recovering from "the accident." That was Scourge's last concert. That worked out well.

~~~
~~~

CHAPTER 17

The Journey Home

Now that Mark is free of Scourge, he cuts his hair and lets it return to its natural blond color. Without the greasepaint, no one recognizes his former identity. I can't say that I miss Scourge, but the media is sure to miss his staged antics.

One morning, Mark and Jake decide—without consulting me—that a walk to the ocean is in order. As in the days when we sit in the garden, the sunscreen is generously applied, as well as my floppy hat to keep from sunburning the incision scar on my head. Even though the guys are wearing short sleeves, I must wear a jacket. Still frail in comparison to my former self, I tend to easily get a chill.

The beach is rocky. I can only imagine a sure-footed goat walking to the water's edge with ease. Mark and Jake tightly hold my arms. There is zero possibility I will fall, even if I trip over a rock. I feel like an old woman being helped to the car for a trip to the local care home. I struggle with the terrain and my concept of self. When I sit in the sun with the guys, I can delude myself that I am the same as I was.

Walking to the beach is an entirely different story—a difficult story. But the smell of the water is a refreshing coming-home smell that I have missed tremendously these last eight months. I love the sound of the water crashing on the rocky shore and the water fowl squawking at each other. I haven't seen much of Scotland, since I am sequestered on Jake's property, but I am in love with Scotland now.

When I'm totally recovered and have everything that requires my attention at home caught up, I am hopping on the McKenzie jet and coming back to Scotland. I am going to visit the highlands, castles, and the people.

~~~

The next afternoon, I am reading near the window, comfortable to be alone with my thoughts. It is peaceful. I could stay here forever, but I know that I have to go home and take
~~~

care of business sometime soon. As humble as it makes me feel, I am going to fully embrace being "Kathryn the Great" when I get home. Finally I understand my purpose on Earth.

Jake is off to London for a recording session with one of his clients. Mark is out for a walk along the bluff above the ocean. He says it gives him inspiration. And I am here quietly redefining my self-image.

I practically have Grandmother's book memorized. I could read others, but I'm still in pursuit of the key she mentioned. Certainly there is a lot of wisdom and encouragement within these pages, but I don't know the question or the answer. As I straighten the cover jacket of the book to lay it down, I feel something in the spine. I remove the jacket completely, but see nothing. Closing my eyes and running my fingers slowly up and down the spine, I feel something under the cloth backing.

Mark bursts in the house breathless. "Katey! I have an idea!" He takes the book and helps me out of the chair.

"What?" I have learned to expect wild ideas from this man. Ask first, always ask before trying any of Mark's ideas—that is the number one rule when dealing with him!

"Come walk the beach with me. The tide is out. I think the sand will help strengthen your lower legs and feet, so you will walk normally again!" He is delighted with his idea.

So am I.

Quickly, I go along with his scheme. I bet it will work—the sand will provide gentle resistance, passive resistance, the physical therapist used to say. I would beat him to the beach, but I am not that steady on my own over open ground. He holds my hand with the other arm around my back.

We have to walk inside the water's edge to get to the sandy area. The waves splash up our legs—more on Mark than me, because he is deeper in the water than I. As we walk in the sand, I can feel the back of my heel and my calf pull. My stamina for walking is shot from months of inactivity. It makes me think of the first time I took Mr. Goldstein for a walk on a faraway and very different beach from this. If nothing else, being in the water is fueling my soul.

~~~
~~~

When we return to the house, I am tired and cold, but happy. After I change into dry clothes, Mark helps me pull my feet under the covers and I begin to drift off to sleep.

Mark insists on a full week of walking on the beach before he pronounces me ready to return to the States. Little does he know, that I have all ready decided it is time for me to go home.

Besides, Dan is engaged to Susan and I have offered them the mansion for their wedding and reception. He teased that he would have used the yacht for a honeymoon on the Mediterranean, if I hadn't sold it. I'll rent a yacht for him, if that is the wedding gift they would like.

~~~

When we arrive on the tarmac, the reporters are waiting inside. I suspect that Frank tipped them off that I was returning. I don't ask.

"Miss McKenzie! Miss McKenzie! Welcome home, Miss McKenzie!" reporters shout.

"Miss McKenzie, how are you?" asks another.

"I'm fine, Sheila, thank you. Thank you all. It is good to get home again." I stretch out my arm and wave.

The cameras flash in my face. Defensively, my hand goes up to shield my eyes from the light. That is one thing no one had thought about. The light hurt my eyes with a sharp pain.

Mark quickly pulls my face to his chest and holds up his hand to halt the reporters.

"Please, please, no flashes, PLEASE!" Everyone falls silent and stands still—an eerie still.

When they lower their cameras, Mark releases his hold on my head.

I turn around. No more media games. I am going to tell the truth. They can spin it as they will. I am not my grandfather, and I no longer admire the sport of spinning the media.

~~~

"Thank you for coming to greet me. I am recovering from brain surgery. I had a brain tumor." I drop my eyes to the floor for a second to think of what to say.

There is a shuffling sound while the reporters wait respectfully.

"I am fine. I had a stroke during the surgery and have had seizures —that is why your flash hurt my eyes. I am fine, but we will have to take it slow at first." I turn to leave, then turn back. "If I may, I would like to offer my condolences to all of Scourge's fans. We will miss him." I take Mark's arm and he helps me off the small step that I had been speaking from.

~~~

Garrett is standing beside the limousine in his chauffeur's uniform that Grandfather made him wear after he decided to call him "James." Garrett looks very proper standing at the ready, except for when his large lips burst apart into a wide, toothy grin. The contrast between his white teeth and dark skin accent the size of his smile all the more.

Garrett opens the limo door for me, vying with Mark for his rightful position as my attendant.

As I lean down to enter the limo, my attention is moved from the chivalrous men in my life to a pair of legs with black high heels attached to the feet. Moving into the vehicle more, I see a gray suit skirt, and quickly look up to see Karen's grinning smile.

"Katey, welcome home!" She warmly reaches to help me into the limo.

"Oh, Karen!" I reach to hug her.

Mark moves a newspaper and slides to the seat facing us.

"Where to, ma'am?" Garrett looks back over his shoulder with a grin.

"Home, let's go home." I feign seriousness.

"The Coast Highway, ma'am?"

"Yes, absolutely—the Coast Highway."

The newspaper headline catches my attention, though I make no move to retrieve the paper. It reads that one of the McKenzie company's CEOs is being indicted for embezzlement of the pension fund, and something about government contracts that I can't make out because it is at the fold of the front page.

Karen squeezes my hand in excitement. The paper can wait until I get home and Sam fills in the details. For now, I am going to enjoy the ride up the coast with my friends. I smile at Karen and squeeze her hand in response.

~~~

"Katey, we decided to wait until you were home to tell you—" She pauses long enough for me to glance at the headline again in anticipation.

"Your grandfather is not well," she says softly.

Dazed by the unexpected news, I ask, "What?" in confusion.

"He took to his bed three months ago. Brooke was picked up on drug charges on New Year's Eve. She gave up Tim to deal her own release and lured him into a trap. Then, while Tim was in jail awaiting his bail appearance, he was stabbed and died. After Brooke heard what happened, she took an overdose." Karen pauses.

"I'm so sorry, Katey. Your grandfather took the funerals hard. Eventually, he just stayed in bed." She looks at me, then at Mark. Then, she says softly, "I think he was afraid he had lost you, too."

"They are both—" I pause before saying the word, "they are dead?" I ask, then look at Mark who is stirring in his seat.

It is obvious Mark was aware of the situation and the decision had been made not to tell me about it. There is no point in accusing him, for I am, after all, Kathryn the Great again.

"How is Grandfather now? Does he know I am returning?"

"Zoe told him you were coming today, but she doesn't know if he understood. He's depressed and refuses to take medication for the depression because of how it makes him feel. She showed him the video of your birthday that Jake and Mark shot, and he seemed to do a little better."

I look in Mark's direction. I had forgotten about that silly movie. We were being giddy. We danced, laughed and horsed around with party hats on our heads. A deep fondness comes over me for my friends. Mark and Jake are sweet. And Karen has gone beyond the call of duty keeping my aunt and Mr. Goldstein apprised of my condition.

Garrett looks over his shoulder at me. "Missy, I told Mr. McKenzie he had to get himself out of that bed today for your homecoming. I told him you would be disappointed if he wasn't in that chair of his and on the front porch where he belongs."

We all laugh at Garrett's sincerity and enthusiasm—and daring. We will know if his lecture worked as soon as we drive into the gate. I would ordinarily ask to stop at Father's Beach, but considering Grandfather's condition, I say nothing about stopping. Garrett looks in the rearview mirror and catches my attention as we approach the turnoff. I shake my head slightly. He gets the message, and nods his head to acknowledge.

~~~

As we move up the drive and the front of the mansion comes into full view, I can see the staff assembling on the front steps. Everyone is there. Zoe is wearing a young person's business suit. Sam has on a suit and tie. Chico has on black slacks and black shirt—open partway down his chest—and his hair is pulled back into a ponytail. Both flight crews and the helicopter pilots are to the right of the stairs in their uniforms. Louise is wearing her white jacket and chef's hat that she wears only for formal occasions. Danny and a woman, who must be Susan, are there on the top step. Race, his wife, and their children—all cleaned and polished—are standing opposite of Dan and Susan. Juan is at the bottom of the steps with a bouquet of roses in hand. Stanley, always dressed as a butler, is standing in the forefront of everyone, white-gloved hands ready to assist me.

Eleanor is wearing a pretty dress that distinguishes her as the head of the house. She stops in the center of the porch. Everyone stands at a civilian version of attention.

The flight personnel salute as the limo pulls slowly past them. That's pretty slick that they got here ahead of me. Good thing I have a helicopter, isn't it?

Grandfather is missing, but he likes to make an entrance.

I reserve comment.

Garrett pulls the limo to a gentle, perfectly executed stop in front of Stanley, then gets out and goes around the front of the car to open my door. Stanley reaches in his white-gloved hand to assist me. When I am fully standing, he hands me a cane. As I take it in my hand, I notice it feels as if it were made especially for me. It is a beautifully balanced cane. As Garrett assists Karen and Mark out of the vehicle, I wait, using my new cane to steady myself.

Karen and Mark stand on either side of me to help me up the stairs. Stanley walks one step ahead of us and Garrett one step
~~~

behind. I smile warmly at each member of the welcoming committee that has gathered. At the top step, Karen moves to the side to stand with Keith.

As if on cue, Conner—dressed in his white orderly uniform, rather than his standard beach-boy look—wheels Grandfather out the door. He parks the chair beside and a little forward of Eleanor. We are, after all, very particular about rank at these welcoming ceremonies.

Grandfather beams at the sight of me. I love that old man. I swoop down to hug him and kiss his cheek.

"Kathryn, I have missed you," he whispers.

"I love you very much, Grandfather," I whisper.

I stand beside him, holding his hand, facing the welcoming party. Stanley, Garrett, and the flight people have moved in along the bottom step. Juan ascends the steps and sheepishly hands me the roses, tips his hat and blends into the crowd on the sidelines, collecting their approving giggle at his sense of style.

I smell the roses and say to all, "Thank you. Thank you so much. It is very good to be home."

Eleanor whispers from her side of Grandfather's chair that there are cookies and punch on the patio.

"I am told there are cookies and punch awaiting us." I motion for everyone to join in the fun.

The party doesn't last long. Slowly everyone has said "welcome back" and left to enjoy their weekend. Karen says that the doctor has prescribed rest after the party. Grandfather nods and agrees that it is what he is going to do. Eleanor says she'll turn down my bed and tells Stanley to bring my luggage up to my room. Mark and Karen can walk me up the stairs.

Keith says that he will give Mark a ride home when I'm settled.

Mark nods his head in agreement.

"Thank you for everything you have done," I say and give each of them a sentimental hug, and Mark a kiss on the cheek.

I am tired. A nap before dinner sounds good. I stand at the bottom of the stairs and look up. I know that I can take it slow and get to my room, but coming back down alone might be an entirely different story. I have grown accustomed to having Mark and Jake at my side all these months. I feel a little wobbly at the thought of Mark leaving, but I don't mention it.

Slowly, we embark on the assent of the stairs. Because of my "gimp" leg, we have to step on each tread with both feet, rather than alternating as most people climb stairs. The cane slows the process, so Karen carries it and Mark and Keith promise to carry me, if necessary.

Eleanor is coming out of my room as we reach the third and last landing of the stairs.

"Kathryn, we put in the skylight in the ballroom that you talked about wanting. Would you like to see it?"

"Oh, yes!" answers Karen before I can speak.

I say nothing about having to manage another set of stairs to see the skylight. Eleanor opens the ballroom's double doors.

"Oh, it is already dark! Let me get the lights. Wait right there," she says as she walks to the light panel for the switch.

Eleanor has barely had time to reach the light switch when the chandelier comes on.

"Surprise!!!" yells everyone who is hiding in the room.

One by one, they must have slipped up the back servant stairs after they left the cookie reception. Such is the richness of my life! Most of them laugh with nervous excitement. The hand-carved Italian crystals of the palace-size chandelier have been cleaned. There are thousands of twinkling rainbows on every surface of the room. I thought artificial light didn't refract into a rainbow. Ah, who cares? It is beautiful! I am touched by all of this. Words can't describe how I feel.

Standing around the room, and beginning to congregate behind Grandfather's wheelchair is everyone from the original welcoming committee. They must have carried his wheelchair up the back stairs. They were quick!

In addition, Dana, Sister Theresa, Mother Elizabeth, some of the original Spirit of Hope staff and clients, Danny and Susan, Jake, Aunt Grace and most of my uncles, aunts, and cousins are there as I look from face-to-face, and back again.

"I can't believe it!" I keep repeating, tears streaming down my face. I'm no longer thinking about a nap.

From the back of the crowd someone is moving forward. People move aside until I can see Shasta. She is leading Mr. Goldstein to me.

"Katerina! Katerina!" he shouts. Everyone laughs again. We hug, and I kiss him on the cheek.

Shasta gives a full body, tight hug.

My face hurts from smiling so hard. Louise and her crew have set up a buffet table. The ballroom is decorated for a party to rival any other party ever held in it.

It takes a few minutes to greet everyone. Each person comes to me with a hug and well wishes. Karen even flew in Dr. Nidhi and some of my therapists in the McKenzie jets. Karen stands near me in the reception line, hand on my arm to help steady me. I reach for her hand and give it a squeeze.

We turn around when music starts. Jake is conducting an eight-piece band. Race has his sax and begins to move in front of the other band members. I recognize the sweet, sweet sounds of New Orleans.

A trumpet player begins to echo Race's notes. They get into a musical dialogue playing off of each other in the most magnificent rendition of the song as I have ever heard. I wish we were taping this!

The eager applause is well-deserved. Jake announces that I have missed a very special Christmas recital. The music starts. Shasta comes out dressed as the Fairy Queen and dances the ballet beautifully—to the delight of her audience.

Mark leads me to the dance floor, directly under the center chandelier. The perimeter lights dim when the music begins.

Jake, with his husky, sexy voice, begins to sing Mark's latest love song. Mark and I dance. No longer standing on his shoes, I close my eyes and enjoy being alive.

Toward the end of the song, the lights come up. Taking the cue, I motion everyone to join us on the dance floor. I sit out the next couple of dances. Shasta dances with Mother Elizabeth, then Mr. Goldstein, then Stanley. She loves to dance and is "in her element" in the ballroom.

Grandfather seems to be enjoying the party he arranged for me. As friends and family come to our table, I introduce them to him. He is a little overwhelmed with the variety of people in my life at the party.

He is in awe at meeting my mother's family. It wasn't the response I had expected. I thought, at best, he would be properly polite. Instead, he seemed to be longing to be part of a family. I think I will include him in some of my family outings in the future.

Mr. Goldstein is staying for two weeks, and he is in the downstairs guest room until he goes to visit Karl. Karen and I meet eyes and I nod approval of her scheme to bring him to the States. It is a good thing that I own two jets to bring all of my distant friends and family together.

What a day this has been. I am looking forward to spending time with everyone.

I'm tired, a good tired.

~~~
~~~

~ CHAPTER 18 ~

Phoenix Rises

Karen and Keith stayed in the room that connects with mine, with the door ajar—just in case I called for her to help me. Dan and Susan stayed in Dan's old room. Jake gave Mark a ride home. They had everything planed down to the minute details. I suspect Zoe was the mastermind behind the logistics.

~~~

Eleanor comes upstairs to see if I need any assistance this morning and was surprised to find me showered and dressed. I did allow her to help me down the stairs, since this was the first time I faced descending three flights of stairs.

Louise has a fabulous breakfast prepared for her houseful of people. If she had her way, the house would always be full of guests. I propose we eat in the kitchen or even the patio to ease her work, but she will have none of my idea. We will eat in the dining room. And that is that.

Grandfather, who hasn't eaten in the dining room for months, sits at the head of the table surveying his guests: Dan and Susan, Karen and Keith, Mr. Goldstein, and me.

We visit intermittently while Grandfather drinks in every bit of our being together. Grandfather loves Dan's girlfriend, Susan. Maybe he is finally learning a bit about family and acceptance.

Susan is a recent transplant to L.A. from Denver, they knew each other at the university and reconnected on Facebook. Dan promises to be back in a couple of days after visiting Disneyland, the Huntington Library, and the beach. He wants to take Susan to San Francisco and ride a cable car. I offer the use of the McKenzie jet and he accepts, then thinks better of it and decides to drive, since PCH gives such a splendid view of the ocean.

As for Mr. Goldstein, Garrett and I are taking him to the city to visit his Senior Center friends for a few days. Then, I will be back to give Grandfather my undivided attention. Mr. Goldstein and I can resume our beach walks, at least for a week.

~~~

We finish our breakfast and everyone else takes off, seeming to suspect Grandfather, Dan, and I need a moment alone.

When they are gone, I offer Grandfather and Dan my condolences for Brooke and Tim.

Grandfather wipes his mouth with his napkin and stirs in his chair.

Dan interrupts whatever Grandfather was preparing to say. "Thank you. I miss them, but they chose the direction for their lives and no one could stop them," he says quite calmly.

Grandfather clears his throat, and looks at Dan. "Yes. I thought I could do something that your parents couldn't when I brought you here, but I may have made things worse."

I start to respond, but Dan beats me to it. "Grandfather, it wasn't anyone's fault. They had choices and kept making the easy ones—the wrong ones. The only thing either of them wanted was to live in the fast lane. I guess they just got to the end of the road," he says, then smiles.

Grandfather grunts a slight response and drinks the rest of his coffee.

"Grandfather, your children and grandchildren are our own people. Even you cannot control our destiny, it's in our hands, and we make our own choices." I look directly at him.

And it is true. Dan and I are proof the money and power cannot change who people are—it might only accent our flaws.

I kiss Grandfather on the forehead and tell him that I will be back for dinner—Mr. Goldstein and I have a date with the beach before he goes to his friend's house for a few days.

Mr. Goldstein and I are quite a pair. Both of us walk with a cane now. He has had more practice, but I am not going to let him get the best of me.

"Katerina, do you remember the first time we walked?" he asks as we walk across the sand, leaving Garrett and the limo behind in the parking lot. He keeps an eye on us, just in case...

"Yes. Yes, I do."

Remembering what Mark said about walking in the sand being therapeutic, I reach down and pull off my shoes and carry them in my free hand.

"Yest, I do, too." His English isn't as American as it was when he lived here. "You are strong. I know it has been hard. You were afraid, yes? I know you. You will be okay. Don't ever forget what I tell you." He stops walking to look at me.

"I will remember." I stuff my shoes under my elbow and squeeze his hand. We are pretty hopeless with only one free hand apiece.

We walk along our beach—the place where we came to know each other and to find ourselves.

After my outing with Mr. Goldstein, Garrett and I take him to Karl's house. Garrett takes me back to the beach, then heads home. I have not been alone forever. It kind of feels good to be trusted to be alone. I take a nap, then fix dinner, then go straight to bed. It's a good tired. I'm taking Mr. Goldstein at his word that I will be fine and will get out more than before. Sure, I'll pace myself. But I don't plan to waste a day. The doctors think they got all of the tumor, but maybe there's one cell left that will awaken someday. I am going to stay ahead of the game and get my strength back and live a rich, full life while I can.

~~~

Karen and I are having lunch today.

"Sorry, sorry I'm late," Karen says when I open the door.

"Come in, I wasn't worried. I knew you weren't lost." We leave to walk to the end of the pier for lunch.

After lunch, I'm tired, but say nothing about it as I look along the seemingly endless pier back to the sidewalk. We stop midway and stand at the railing, watching the kids on boogie boards ride to shore. I welcome the rest.

"How are you doing?" she asks without looking at me.

"Fine. And you?"

"The letter came from the Church this morning."

"Really? What letter?" I ask, obviously clueless.

"They denied my request for an annulment." She turns to me and fakes a smile.

"What! Wasn't that a hasty decision?" I ask, forgetting about the time I lost after my surgery.

"It's been a year. They're trying to move cases along, so they don't get a backlog again."
~~~

"Well, still—"

"I haven't told Keith yet."

"Excuse me for saying so, but considering the sex thing with all of those priests, aren't they being a bit judgmental that you married someone who cheated on you and his vows?"

"Two wrongs don't make a right." She defends their decision.

"That's nonsense! Isn't there something about checking your own eyesight before removing a splinter from someone else's eye?" I misquote the Bible, but that isn't the point. "You can't tell me that God would rather that you and Keith stay alone for the rest of your lives, because your spouses left you? I don't think so. I think the Church is wrong."

"I have to sort it out and to figure out how to tell Keith. He isn't Catholic. This is my religion, this is what I believe—what I have always believed."

"I know," I say softly, "it is my religion too. But I can't imagine God withholding happiness for you and Keith. The Church is wrong." I dare to toe right to the edge of the line that a tribunal of nuns and priests have a clue about marriage. Don't get me started on the child-raping scandal cover-up.

"I don't think God would have decided as the tribunal did. Keith and I have a difficult decision to make. The one thing that keeps coming to mind is that no one has treated me like Keith does. He is respectful and loving in the most tender way—the way women hope a man will treat them. I have never met such a thoughtful person." She smiles as she speaks about Keith.

I say no more before I get excommunicated, but in my heart I know that the Church is wrong—maybe not in matters of doctrine, but they are terribly wrong about Karen and Keith.

~~~

Mark leaves on his new album tour. I don't know what Jake is doing. I feel surrounded by couples in love: Karen and Keith, and Dan and Susan. Not that I would consider contact with Joseph, but I miss being in love.

I listen to Ann Zimmerman's song, "Kiss on the Mouth," while I write in my journal for the first time in months. The song seems to fit me—unfortunately. Ann's voice tells of my longing.

~~~

Storm Surge

♪♪ It's winter to spring and summer to fall,
I've seen the years pass and I've seen the stars fall,
I've watched in the flood and I've watched in the drought
But I've watched without you and your kiss on the mouth...
If I had a grand share of all the world's wealth,
Still a pauper I'd be with no kiss on the mouth. ♪♪
©Ann Zimmerman

~~~

I'm tired and a little melancholy tonight. I am sure it will pass. Besides, I need to focus my energy on getting stronger. Mark will be back soon and we can spend time together. I miss him.

My Dearest Maggie, It seems that I should make the most of my wealth by aiding sojourners along life's journey. There is much I want to do and now is the time to begin.

When I finish writing, I'll look for Gwen's business card. As a registered physical therapist, maybe she can recommend a local therapist. Grandfather and I need to gain more strength, even though he will never walk again. I still need to do strengthening exercises. It will be fun to call her and visit for a few minutes, she is so energetic.

~~~

On Monday, I begin half days at work. Gradually, they are full days. Gwen talked to her partners and took a leave of absence to come provide physical therapy to Grandfather and me. Gwen will train Conner to take over Grandfather's treatment when she leaves.

Around the house, with Gwen's skillful therapy, I become able to leave my cane in the umbrella stand. Walking in the garden, I still use it. Gwen is often at my side in addition to two scheduled sessions a day for each of us.

Life seems the same to an onlooker, but I know that it is different. I am different. More determined, perhaps. If McKenzie Enterprises wasn't sure who was in charge before, they know now. The operation is more efficient, and definitely less corrupt.

I learn Grandfather had torn down the apartment building Dana lived in and built a parking garage and luxury condos. I take all the profits from that property and funnel it into the homeless shelters that serve the people Grandfather displaced. We locate the former tenants and find housing for those still homeless.

Zoe becomes my personal assistant more than ever before. She thrives on all of the projects I give her, like finding the displaced tenants. She likes having her own secretary.

After cleaning out the graft in my companies, Sam makes the unions happy when he negotiates benefit packages that are real and direct benefits for the remaining employees. No more shady stuff. Chico has a little army of techy weirdos. He and Race have divided the work. My dear Race manages the household accounting data and keeps our computers and servers running tip-top. Chico freely visits all the companies. No one has dared to complain about Chico, at least, not so that I hear about it.

Jim has a security detail in place, and I think I might have more security gadgets than most federal buildings. Keith retired from the police force, his time in the department completed. He and Jim formed a partnership. They consult on security matters for the McKenzie Enterprise, the estate, and my personal safety.

I still haven't told anyone the shooter was watching me at the beach for weeks before he came to the mansion to shoot me. I haven't put the pieces together, but shooting me at the beach would have been much easier. Something still doesn't make sense about this. They never did discover who shot him. Figures. So that person is still at large.

~~~

The first three months after my return there isn't much time to spend at the beach. To relax, I begin writing a novel. It's a legitimate escape from Miss McKenzie, Kathryn the Great.

Life is good. I *will* it to be that way. No longer am I taking what comes. To Mr. Bradford's amazement, I have developed a keen sense for investing. I invest some in the usual money-generating fashion, but more importantly, I invest in the human factor. The human investments are paying well.

Monica's House for families with AIDS is up and running, following Mother Elizabeth's model. McKenzie Grants for arts
~~~

and sciences in inner-city schools are second to none anywhere. Only when strategically necessary is my name attached to my projects. Unfortunately, far too often the name is needed, but that brings more money from people who are hoping to get a contract bid or something else from me.

Zoe, Garrett, or Sam, and sometimes Grandfather go with me to visit the people in the shelter, so we can assess the needs firsthand. Because of the weakness still in my left leg, operating the clutch tires me, though I do like driving standard transmission vehicles. I usually find someone to drive me to these outings. However, I think any one of them would go even if they didn't have to chauffeur me.

Simply for the thrill of it, I ask Garrett to take me for a ride in Father's Jag once a week. He loves that car. It is easy to get him talking about him and Dad running around town in it when they were at the university.

Without saying anything, I sign the '53 Jaguar title over to Garrett. The day after the new title arrives in his mail, Garrett comes excitedly into my office holding the paper. He puts it on the desk and keeps poking at it with his finger as he talks.

"Miss McKenzie, I, I don't know how this happened," he stutters in a panic.

"Garrett, it's a gift," I answer as I look up from my work, struggling to keep a straight face.

"I assure you, I had no part in this."

"It's a gift," I say again.

"I'll get to the bottom of—" He finally realizes what I said. "Miss McKenzie! I can't accept this." He is awed.

"Father would be pleased. Now, get your car out of my garage. Scoot. Take the day off. Give your wife a ride in your new car."

I pull the keys out of my desk drawer and hand them to him.

"I noticed the keys were gone from the garage. I should a known you were up to no good." Garrett fingers the Jaguar key chain. "Ah, thank you, Missy," he says and hugs me until it hurts.

"You're welcome. Now, go on. Get out of here. I have work to do." I shoo him out of my office.

As he leaves, I smile to myself. I bet Dad is smiling too.

~~~

As the fog continues to clear from my brain, I remember the key in Grandmother's book. I think I found it, just need to see how to get it out of the spine of the book. I wonder how she got it in there?

With the door to the office locked, I remove the book jacket. I can't see anything unusual about the bare spine, until I turn on the desk lamp. I tilt the book and run my finger over it, looking for the area to concentrate my interest. There is a spot, nearly undetectable, where I feel something inside. I don't see any place that looks like the spine was split on the side and repaired. I'm guessing it was slid in from the top when the book was open wide.

I hold the book fully open, lifting the spine opening eye level, with the other end toward the lamp. I'm not sure I see anything, but I tell myself that "possibly" I do. It is smack-dab in the center, so it isn't easier to reach from one end or the other. I try shaking it out of either end. I rifle through the desk drawers, looking for something to poke down the tube-like opening.

I grab a pencil and try to thrust it inside the spine. I can't angle it so the lead tip scrapes along the cloth side. I throw the pencil back into the drawer. Pens aren't of any use. Way back in the center drawer is an old-style letter opener. It seems perfect, but slides right over the spot I've deemed "of interest."

I leave the letter opener in partway and close the book slowly, testing periodically. Finally, I have things just right so the letter opener finds the edge of something, and by the slight "clink" I'd say it was metal on metal. I push harder, and push the tip of the letter opener through the cloth. Damn.

That wasn't the plan, but I decide, what difference does it make if I cut the spine, I can have it repaired. I remove the letter opener and insert the tip through the rip from the outside, making a flap to pry open. There is a small key. Grandmother had meant a physical key, not something philosophical to learn from the book. I feel a bit the village idiot. I don't know how much clearer she could have been. I had the message wrong. She said the key was in the book, well, yes, it was. Goodness! Where did she get that idea?
~~~

Storm Surge

The silver box in Grandfather's upstairs bedroom comes to mind as soon as I see the key. I bet it's a perfect fit. Extra trips up the stairs are something I've avoided. I consider asking Zoe or Eleanor to fetch the box for me, but I think it is best no one knows I have an interest in it. Or in Zoe's case, she doesn't know the box exists. It is slow progress, but not impossible to go upstairs alone. I'll have an excuse ready if anyone comments about me going up now. "Off to take a nap," that should do.

~~~

I'm not winded when I reach the top step at the third floor, but it was a slow labor and I've broken a sweat. That's a good reason not to do this in the middle of the day, next time. I go into my room, then enter Grandfather's old room through the adjoining doorway. I don't think anyone is up here to see me, but if someone is on this floor cleaning, they only saw me go in my room.

My hands jitter with excitement as I lift the silver chest from the shelf. The little chest is heavy. I set it back on the shelf, take my cane into my room, then come back for the silver box. I stay close to the wall so I can lean against it, if I lose my balance. I have to use both hands to carry the chest since I still have residual weakness on my left side.

Breathlessly, I get to my bed and set the chest on it. I locked my door when I came in, now I return to lock the door between the two bedrooms. I don't think anyone will come in, but an ounce of prevention is worth a pound of cure.

I inspect the chest. It needs a good polishing. I fish the key from my pocket, get settled on the bed—pulling my legs up, since I'm not allowed to let them dangle when I sit. I settle the box facing me, kiss the key, and turn the lock. When I lift the lid, papers spring up. They had been packed down tight so the lid would shut. I start removing them, keeping them in their order, in case that was planned. There is a note from Grandmother to me, a letter to her that is very thick, a newspaper clipping, some photos, and bits of paper with notes, numbers, dates— various things, in Grandmother's writing.

Grandmother says she is happy to see that her curious grand-daughter is still curious, or I wouldn't have found the box
~~~

and the key. Happy Birthday, since I must have turned of age to get the trust. *I wish she could see me now.* She hints at the questions again, but writes there are two main questions to be asked about McKenzie Enterprise. She says the letter from Eli Reed will answer most of them and send me in the right direction for the rest.

The letter is ten or twelve pages, written in longhand. The writing is hard to read since the ink is faded. Mr. Reed is writing to Grandmother because he is dying. He has cancer. I look for a date, but find none. He seems pretty certain he won't live, since the cobalt treatment didn't work, so I date the letter in my mind to be prior to the development of chemotherapy.

Mr. Reed starts with information of how Grandfather won the bet to marry her. Simply, Mr. Reed told Grandfather information from a friend about a government contract the friend's company was getting, and when it would be announced. Al [Grandfather] bought stock in the company prior to the announcement of the contract. It seems funny to hear Grandfather referred to as Al rather than Alistair.

I'm three pages into the letter when the writing changes to a neater, more feminine hand. "I am writing for my father, as he is too weak to finish, but he feels he must tell you the rest before he dies."

~~~

There's a knock at my door and Eleanor's voice calling my name, asking if I'm okay.

I hurry to return everything to the box and lock it. I can't possibly return it to the shelf, so I put it under my pillow and fluff both pillows against the headboard. Quickly, I lay down to mess the bed as if I had been resting.

I answer Eleanor that I am getting up now, and would she wait to help me down the stairs. I look back at my pillows, wishing to finish what I started; but I understand that I'm missed if I disappear, after being gone for nearly a year.

Eleanor eases me down the stairs and I join the household activities. Race brings reports and I give him the time to explain them to me, though I don't need the explanation. They all want to "be by me," and I do my best to accommodate their need.
~~~

Storm Surge

After the staff leaves, dinner is finished, and Grandfather has had his share of attention, I inch up the stairs, aware that Stanley is watching to make sure I do okay.

~~~

Once I'm ready for bed, I get the small silver chest again. Mr. Reed's letter is incredible. He gives names, companies, and more specifics than I would have expected. I'll have to read it again, but the big question is what to do with the information.

I put the box in my closet for the night. I've been a pack rat with the things I've found in the two rooms, so I don't think anyone will think anything about it if they see it there.

The key is a different matter. Grandmother was right to hide it well. I pull back the covers and lift the mattress by the hand strap, just enough to be able to slip the key under the box spring, onto the bed frame. It won't be quite as easy to retrieve it. I'll have to lift the mattress, wedge something between it and the frame to hold the mattress and springs up while I get on my knees and get the key out. I'll use a book to hold the mattresses up, maybe the Frost book. Finally, it is good for something.

My sleep is tormented and I wake late. I don't dare break with my morning routine and arouse concern by indulging my interest in the silver box contents. I'll have to save reading the letter until bedtime.

~~~

This time, as I read, I make notes. There are so many questions about all of this. I wonder whether I need to notify the Securities and Exchange Commission about the alleged insider trading Grandfather did decades ago, and probably is unable to recall? This is something to ask Mr. Bradford to advise me regarding, since he knew Grandmother. Maybe she told him about this. Maybe not.

What about the government contract information? I suppose that isn't as important as some of the other information in the letter. The fact that Mr. Reed wrote that Grandfather later rewarded him and his friend
with key positions in his companies is worrisome. Of course, he is dead and the other guy is either dead or old like Grandfather. Jim can get that information.

I guess that's my starting place. I'll give the name to Jim and see what he comes up with, then go from there. I wonder if Grandfather remembers any of this? I wonder if he suspected any residual effect from our investigation last year. Damn, this is still a mess.

Sam briefs me on the investigation details I missed while I was recovering. He kept a file of the letters from the FBI and newspaper clippings, as well as printed anything he found on the internet during that time. I know about the outcome. Some guy got indicted, then committed suicide before he went to trial.

"Great, Sam. I'm glad we have that sorted. If you think of anything else, let me know."

It sounds like it was a superficial investigation resulting in a sacrificial lamb. From what I know now and what I suspect, there is something much more corrupt below this iceberg. Whatever they were, Grandmother had her reasons for hiding this information. I think she hoped I would investigate. I'm not going to let her down.

I ring Chico and arrange for a meeting between the two of us tomorrow at Father's Beach. I ask him to mention it to no one. That beach is used more by L.A. film crews than beach bathers; it's likely it will be vacant.

<div align="center">~~~</div>

CHAPTER 19

The Plot Thickens

Chico is at St. Leo's beach by the time I arrive. This time I leave Garrett at home. I'm not ready for anyone, except Chico, to know what I'm doing.

We sit in the sand. I have a sketch pad and attempt rough sketches of the rock-lined beach while we talk, just in case anyone walks up and sees us.

I brief Chico on the names I learned from the letter, but don't tell where I got the information. I want him to trace those people and see if they are in any way connected to anyone who works anywhere in the McKenzie companies—mine included.

He takes the folded list I palm to him and tucks it in his shirt pocket as he retrieves a pack of smokes. Very smooth. I like his style, even if he does light up.

I continue sketching as we talk. He agrees that they probably think it's pretty safe now, since they skated through the FBI investigation. Maybe they'll relax their guard and get sloppy, or cocky, as he put it. He suggests we look at the major traders of McKenzie company stock, the individual companies, the board of director members, everyone, even the document courier companies. Checking SEC staffers, if warranted, will be a bit more tricky. And we have to look at all "fingerprints" on the government contracts. We'll start with the current contracts and hope to get lucky. Then we can follow the chain backwards and see where it leads us.

"There is another problem, Chico." The way I say the words has Chico's attention more astute. "Remember the guy who shot at me? He spent weeks watching my apartment, missing a lot of opportunities for an easy shot."

Chico says nothing.

"The question is, why wait until I'm at the mansion to take a shot? Had he intended to miss? Was it more of a warning to Grandfather, if he had knowledge of the corrupt activities? The guy who shot the shooter had to be a sniper, not someone off the street with a gun. They never found him, so he must have shot from a safe distance. There would be security cameras on the courthouse entrances. I think this is something else.

"Chico, you can walk away from this, if you want to. I won't think twice about it. You'll still have my trust, and your job is secure. We would say this conversation never happened."

"No, I'm okay to do this. I'll be careful. They won't even know I've been in the system. I can make it look like routine server maintenance, if they do notice."

He needs help, and wants Race onboard. I know we can trust Race, but this could be dangerous. Race has a family. It isn't like I think Chico is expendable, but he's single and has no kids. Me, I'm expendable.

"I trust Race. But he has little kids. Tell him as little as you can about my sniper theory, but make sure he understands that this might be very dangerous. If he has any hesitation, let him back out."

"I will. If there is something else, something that was missed by those piss-ant Feds, we'll get it."

"Be sure to keep the usual reports coming, so Sam—or anyone else—won't suspect we are doing this."

"Of course."

"Thanks. Keep your eyes open. Watch your back. Do you want Jim to assign someone to you, as a 'roommate' or on your staff, or something?"

"Nah. I'll be careful. My grandma lives in the barrio. I can disappear there and no outsider can get to me. My uncles and cousins are tougher than anyone Jim has."

"Sounds like my kind of family."

He takes my tablet and helps me up, since I'm not good at getting up (gracefully) from the ground with my gimp leg. I see a gang tat on his outstretched forearm. Bet he was inducted as a little tyke. Figures. Bet his grandmother made him stay in school too.

"Hey boss, you draw pretty good."

"Buttering up the boss won't get you anywhere that your skills haven't gotten you already." I chuckle. "Seriously, thanks for doing this. Be careful."

We walk back through the tunnel under the highway to our cars.

"I'll keep Race safe. But I'll keep him busy."

"Okay. Chico, let me know as soon as you find things."

"Hey, are you supposed to be driving?"

"I'm good. Just want to keep this between us for now, okay?"

~~~

When I return to the mansion, Zoe gives me a look like she is going to say something about me going out alone. I shake my head to tell her not to ask—and she doesn't. We go to my office and get to work. There are letters she needs me to sign. She updates me on appointment changes. It's mindless activities, which works fine, since I'm still thinking about Chico and the letter, not about working.

I want answers and I want them now. Waiting is going to be the hard part for me. I know it will take months to flesh out the information, so I might as well settle down and accept that I can't have the answers immediately. I'll play my cards close to my chest for now, not to tip any suspicion that I'm a threat. With God as my witness, they'll rue the day when I learn what is going on.

If Grandfather is involved, he will have to take his lumps too. I love the old guy and honestly don't think he remembers much these days. My illness and the cousins' deaths have taken their toll on him. They aren't going to do anything to him now.

~~~

Mark and Jake are headed back to California, and we made arrangements for a dinner date.

We give each other kisses on the cheek and tight hugs. Mark gives me a dozen red roses. I've missed them. I'm glad it worked for Mark to change identities. He seems much happier now that he can be himself. Scourge made more money, but I like the new music better. His fan base will grow. He still gets royalties.

"Wow, guys! The limo treatment, eh?"

"Yes, nothing too good for 'our' girl," Mark says. Jake nods agreement.

"So, where are we headed?"

"Anywhere you like, Kathryn," Mark says.

"I want a big juicy steak," says Jake.

"I thought you were a veg—" I say.

Jake laughs. Those goofs. Still at it, I see.

Mark and I schedule a day for just the two of us. Jake smiles like he's playing matchmaker. Mark and I are happy to accommodate him.

Needless to say, we have a great evening and I'm not near as serious when I get home.

<div align="center">~~~</div>

~ CHAPTER 20 ~

Kathryn's Beach
(Two Years Later)

Quietly entering my room after another of the many humanitarian award banquets on my calendar, I set down the crystal award on the table near the door. It feels good to kick off my shoes.

"Ah, what a grand gala." I drop my wrap on the bed, look in the mirror, and begin to remove my diamond earrings. "Kate, it's never a good sign when you begin talking to yourself. It always preludes trouble, big trouble!" I say aloud.

I smile, as I think of the various decisions over the years that have complicated my life and how ridiculous they seem now. Turning around, my gaze is caught by the gleaming shine of the crystal award. Lifting the cool, heavy award, I study the sparkle of the object, its form, and its weight. It isn't that I don't appreciate the gesture. Certainly, I have earned it with my generous philanthropic works. It is just one more of many "trophies" to add to my undesired collection of awards.

In the beginning, I felt awkward with the recognition. Now, I understand why none of Karen's awards are on display; that's not why we do the things we do. Of course, I understand the need to give awards, the vicarious emotions and excitement the award-givers receive, and need, for a variety of reasons.

Setting the beautiful award on the table, I remove my necklace and place it in its jewelry case, studying its sparkling beauty in the dim light.

"Funny, this necklace is worth more than I would have earned in ten years of social work."

Gently closing the case, I return all of Grandmother's jewels to the hidden safe in my closet. I change into pajamas, then pull the pins from my hair and shake my head to ease the hair out of place, and shake off the formality of the evening. There is something about these events that leaves me fatigued. Sometimes following afternoon society events, I come home, unable to function until I have had a nap.

Tonight, I am refreshed with thoughts of sitting and writing, undisturbed by the world. I crave the quiet moments when I am not required to meet the demands of my social position. I rely less on my diary to release my pent-up emotions and thoughts.

As the days passed, I turned to a new method of release, fiction writing, and found it strangely healing and relaxing. It is freeing in an unexpected way that I never expected. Years of typing reports taught my fingers to fly over the keyboard. I'm slower now with my gimp left hand. I can't keep pace with my thoughts as they unfold into the story of my return to California, now nearly ten years ago.

The interpretation of my memory is questionable. I was careful to make the events in the story pure fiction; they are designed to remind me of something not to be made public. It is the essence of those days that I seek to capture. I'm not worried about the details.

Like a protective mother I have nurtured my manuscript, and my quiet time spent with it. Last night, with a mixture of emotion, I had the distinct sense that the last chapter of the story would be finally written.

With a satisfied sigh, I print the completed manuscript, my first and only work of fiction. The laser printer devours the paper from its generous tray. I lean back in my chair and feel the emptiness I had only a few hours ago melt into a satisfied sense of fulfillment.

Removing the warm, first few printed pages from the tray, I hold them to my chest. I can feel their warmth dissolve my required persona. Lifting the first page, I begin to read. The last page prints and the machine falls silent. It is finished.

While reading, I hadn't noticed the night was gone. Without a hint of egotism, I have an intense sense of satisfaction that I have something that is mine alone. This stack of paper isn't the result of being a quintessential social worker or a McKenzie. It is the product of a human heart, nothing more—nothing less.

I reach for the phone and dial Karen's number. Briefly, I glance at the clock as the phone begins to ring. I grimace. It is only a quarter to six, a bit early to call anyone—even Karen—on a Saturday morning.

"Hello?" Karen's voice reveals that I have awakened her.

I hesitate, then softly say, "Karen, it's Katey."

I hear the sounds of her becoming awake and struggling to sit up in her bed. Quietly, she speaks, "Katey, what's wrong?"

"Oh Karen, nothing is wrong. I, I was wondering if we could meet later today, or maybe tomorrow?" I am embarrassed that I called so early. As a token restitution for the inconvenience, I offer, "I can send a car for you." Damn! That sounded like a rich spoiled brat, a label that I ordinarily avoid like the plague.

"Keith is leaving in a couple of hours. I have a few things to do this morning. We could meet after lunch, if you like."

"Yes, thank you. I have something to share with you," I say.

~~~

As I hang up, Chico calls. He has the final piece of the "conspiracy theory," as we have come to call our project.

He must have called from his car because he is at the door by the time I'm showered and dressed. The minute I reach the bottom of the steps, he takes my arm, then leans toward me and whispers.

"Let's take a drive."

"Okay."

He has obviously found something big. We have been playing cloak-and-dagger with our out-of-the-way meetings for two years. Is this the end of the hunt?

Once we are on the road, he calls me "Miss McKenzie."

This is it. I brace for what he is about to say.

"I found the sniper."

"What! You found the what?" That isn't what I expected.

"It was buried pretty good, but I found the payments."

"Payments?"

"Yes, they paid $50,000 to the guy who shot at you from the gate. Looks like he was to get the other half when he killed you, but he missed."

"Wow. That really isn't much money."

"They paid the second sniper five million to kill him."

"What? That doesn't make sense."

"Just wait. I'll give you the overview, but I have all the details." He pats his pants pocket. "I've everything on everyone."
~~~

I want to say, "everyone?" but got the cue to let him talk and quit interrupting with questions.

He takes a deep breath and checks the rearview mirror for anyone following us up the Coast Highway. Smart of him to go north where there is less traffic. People do take this road, so someone behind us is likely following us because there isn't anywhere else to go but up the road. But I get his point. Occasionally he slows to see if the car behind him will pass, and they always do.

"I don't know how some of this was missed by the FBI, but I suspect there is some CIA involvement in here. Someone in the government is laundering money through your companies. It's going into offshore accounts at about the time 'things' happen in 'certain' countries."

He takes a breath and so do I. What in heaven's name is all this about?

"There's some skimming from the guys in there who blackmailed your grandfather into this arrangement. I can't find what they had on him, but it must be big."

I know what it is—cheating to win his bet with Grandmother.

"Anyway, these guys are bidding certain jobs they are told to bid, they win the contract, take a cut for themselves, launder some for the 'group,' and still supply the goods."

"Oh crap! This scares me."

"It should. This is bad shit. But as long as they think you are satisfied with the FBI investigation, you're probably safe. You can't do anything about this. They'll get you. And next time, they will hire a better shot."

"Thanks, Chico. You did a fantastic job. I've got to think. This is so—oh, wow, I can't believe this. Oh wow!"

"Don't do anything. I was careful. I don't think they noticed I was there. But God—if they ever find out—"

"Okay, we tell no one. I mean no one, not ever. Where's the info?"

"I brought a copy of everything for you. I've got mine stashed 'someplace' safe."

"Good. Don't tell me where you put yours, and I won't tell you where I put mine," I say.

"If anything odd happens to either of us, the other one goes to the media with all of it. Deal? I can make it look like a media feed from Langley. I just have to—"

"Shhh, jeeze, don't tell me. Let's hope they get me, not you."

"They probably aren't ever going to know."

"Probably not. Let's go back to the house now, Chico."

Chico helps me up the steps to the door, then leaves. Inside, I retrieve my cane from the umbrella stand and head upstairs. I'll put the micro drive Chico gave me in the silver chest with the other information. The key goes back on the mattress frame. I still haven't thought of a better place for it.

~~~

When I arrive, Karen opens the door with a cup of coffee in her hand, and holds it toward me with a knowing grin.

I take the contraband drink. Karen turns back to retrieve her cup and lock her house. Within moments, the limousine is on the freeway heading toward the beach, our beach.

I smile, thinking back at the time when I thought Karen was my worst nightmare. Now I recognize how blessed I was to have met her, and become friends.

"So, what is it that has us out and about today?" Karen interrupts my thoughts, knowing that something is up, since I called her early in the morning.

Before I can speak, my face is consumed by a self-conscious smile. I exhale a breathless confession.

"I have written a manuscript, Karen, a novel!"

She tilts her head. "A novel?" She has a excited tone.

"It nearly wrote itself," I confide the ease of the feat. "I know that you love to read. I'd like you to be the first to read it."

"What's it about?"

"A young, well-meaning but misguided social worker who is trying to find her way home again."

"Who is this?" she asks, pointing to the name on the front sheet of the stack of manuscript papers on my lap.

"It's a pen name. I want to see if the story gets published on its own merit—not on the McKenzie name."

After a pause, Karen says, "It sounds interesting. Is the social worker anyone we know?" She has a smirking grin.
~~~

"No, it's fiction—lies, all lies."
"Really? You'll have to read it to me. How about it?"
"I'd love to read to you."
"Good, I'd love it, too," she says.

~~~

After Garrett and our bodyguard checks for intruders, and are content that we are secure, they find the TV remote and begin preparing for the Dodgers game.

Garrett comes from the kitchen and promises to have snacks ready for us before the game starts. The coffee machine is already dripping the rich brew into the pot. It is obvious that Garrett senses—or hopes—that we will be here all day.

I offer Karen coffee and request juice for myself—my permitted drink. We move to the patio. With the ocean sounds in the background, I begin to read aloud.

"*'And you,' he asks, 'what about you?'*"

Karen says nothing as I read. Occasionally, I glance at her for a reaction, but her dark glasses hide the comments of her eyes. The waves break on the nearby beach in a constant rhythm to my words as I read on through the afternoon and into the early evening.

As I lay down the final page, Karen speaks: "Katey, I had forgotten some of the essence of those years."

"It's pure fiction." I hand her the portfolio containing the story. Karen rubs her fingertips over the luxurious leather case.

She opens the cover and tilts the page into the light.

"I never told you, but I was afraid that you were going to die," Karen admits.

"I know," I say softly. "So was I. Thanks for helping me through that. I wouldn't have made it without you."

"Now, look at you."

Karen squints as she studies my face. It's a long moment of silence. Finally, she looks away and says, "After Maggie—" her voice trails off before she finishes her words.

I reach to touch her hand, then put my arm around her shoulder and tilt my head against hers. I don't feel awkward about telling her I love her and knowing she understands. I know I don't have to say a word, and she understands that too.
~~~

"Karen, it's all right. It's not how long we live, it's how wide that really matters."

She looks out at the changing tide. "What did you call your book?" she asks after a moment.

She looks back at me.

I smile widely.

"What? Tell me."

"It's title is, *Kathryn's Beach*."

~~~
~~~

CHAPTER 21

Enigma
(Eighteen Months Later)

Grandfather is very ill and it is clear he is dying. I ask Conner to give us the room. Alone, I hold Grandfather's hand and talk to him. I tell him I love him. I tell him I know about the bet and the blackmail.

He becomes restless. He doesn't open his eyes. He hasn't spoken in weeks.

I kiss his cheek and say, "I forgive you, Grandfather. And I love you very much."

He takes an odd breath. It is his last.

~~~

Alistair Winston McKenzie's funeral is a well-covered media event. There is a huge crowd to send him off. Off to where, I do not know. He knows I love him, and that is all that matters to me.

Karen and I rode in the limo to the funeral. When we drop her at her house, I give her a book, *Kathryn's Beach*. It got published. In the book's spine, I hid the key to the silver chest and all the McKenzie family secrets.

~~~

Dear Reader,
If you enjoyed this book, please tell your friends,
and write a review on GoodReads.com and Amazon.
Thank you, Nadine

~ Acknowledgments ~

My family, aunts and uncles, twenty-seven first cousins, their spouses, children, grandchildren, and great grandchildren who gather for Thanksgiving Dinner at a park in Southern California;

The spirit of our grandfather, Arthur Thomas Stewart, and our grandmother, the love of his life, Minerva Jane Evans Stewart. She was matriarch of our clan, the goddess of wisdom, an example of inner strength, and more importantly the one who taught me to laugh in the face of adversity. Graciously, she left her family a rich legacy;

Special thanks to Terrie Berg, my friend, who started this project when we were snowed in during an ice storm. She called and said she had nothing to read, so I wrote. Terri asked, "Then what happened?" wrote a chapter every night after the kids were in bed and emailed It to her. Without Terrie, there would be no Kathryn. My deepest gratitude is to Terri.

Special thanks to Nidhi Dhawan, M.D., India, for consultation on the medical issues in this book.

Special thanks to Nancy Ross Milner, Ph.D. for fashion design assistance.

Special thanks to Joyce at Design by Joyce for support, advice, and a fantastic website at www.NadineLamanBooks.com.

Special thanks to Ilene Shrimplin Wood for unwavering support and assistance throughout this project.

Thanks for the comments, advice, and commitment:
Elynor Breiding; Tom Brown; Elda Clyma; Judy Craig; Ray Derby; Mary Ann Gabel, Sister Ann Cecile Guame, C.S.J; Father Alvin Herber, C.PP.S.; Asmaa Kadry; Keri Kahle; Karen LaMunyon; Shawn McKee; Beverly Post; Sister Rosemary Rader, O.S.B; Charlotte Stewart Saben; Judge Pauline Schwarm, Retired; Ruth Stewart Selee; Carlene Stewart Smith, and Neil Burton.

~~~
~~~